ALSO BY WILLIAM COOK HAIGWOOD

Journeying the Sixties:
A Counterculture Tarot

The Davenport Trilogy

A Time of Unsearchable Things

Songs of Surveillance:
Stories of Spying, Watching and Eavesdropping

Escape of the Alienated War Babies

An Unexplainable Urge:
Stories of Surprise, Exposure and Remorse

WHEN WE MARRY THE WRONG PERSON

WHEN WE MARRY THE WRONG PERSON

Stories of attraction, commitment, and failure

william cook haigwood

Printed in the United States of America

Published by Cooskie Creek Press

Library of Congress Cataloging-in-Publication Data

ISBN 978-1-7337262-5-2

*For every sad heart
married to the wrong person*

BROTHERLY LOVE

one

Marnie Grayson wanted to marry Benjamin Flaherty. She wanted everything marriage could bring even if she did not really know what all that might be. But at last, as she teetered at the presumed but not assuredly adult age of 27, and with little capacity to evaluate the quality of either her knowledge or experience, Marnie was to become a bride.

It was an attractive role, not the least because it was something she had never before been. She had been a girl, a lady, a woman and even a bitch and a slut. She had been named these and much worse. But never had she been named a wife nor could she even imagine what it might feel like to be named a mother.

A role as bride was the start down a mysterious path and it came with a beautiful costume and a devoted retinue of supporting players that existed for one full and likely unforgettable day only for her. It was more than Marnie could imagine she deserved. In fact, if Marnie let her imagination drift she could not escape the idea, if not the fact, she really did not deserve to marry. Did not deserve Benjamin. Nor had she stopped at any moment since Benjamin embraced her and made his request while pressing into her palm a gold ring bearing a fat, sparkling diamond, had she stopped to ask herself if this marriage was what she wanted or even needed. As with most pivotal moments in her young and distrait life, Marnie was a receiver and not a creator. She depended on others to guide her toward what she could not see and to convince her it was what she most wanted.

"I love you," Benjamin divulged in a soft, intimate close-in-her-ear vibrato.

"I love you, too," answered Marnie as she turned away to stare at the ring in her hand, to hold it up briefly to the dim light shining from outside the car parked in a dark driveway of Marnie's downtown Napa apartment. Benjamin lifted the ring from her palm and set it carefully on the dashboard before tugging at Marnie's dress until it was raised and pushed up over her breasts. He pulled her panties down and quickly was and at last in her, Marnie's shoulders crushed against the passenger door as her new fiancé slammed hard and quick until a sudden spasm hurtled him forward with a loudly expectorated moan.

"I love you," Benjamin panted.

"I'll marry you," answered Marnie.

She thought later her words were an afterthought and lost in the absence of an afterglow. Benjamin already was seated when she spoke, pulling up his pants and wiping his floppy cock with a handkerchief. He was outside the car before Marnie found her panties. He asked if he could walk Marnie to her apartment but that he asked was a timorous and unattractive gesture. Why did he not tell her to get up and go with him? Why did he ask? He certainly had not asked if he could fuck her. He gave her a ring and then took Marnie. Why ask permission now, and at the intersection of her need and his desire when as the presumed knight errant he should really take charge, should shape the ends he proposed by leading her and not following?

His query made Benjamin appear momentarily unattractive and Marnie said "no." She jumped from the car, gave Benjamin an air kiss and ran away with her new ring.

"You must be so excited," said Alita.

Marnie shrugged, as she did when the two friends were in high school and one or the other needed to follow and not to lead. Marnie's failure to answer confirmed how malleably and weakly drawn she had been into her life. She had no capacity to lead and barely enough to follow. The convictions that pushed some of her friends into the corners and crevices of experience, that drove them up steep staircases and through large, heavy doors to meet something that might become a destiny, were still unformed for Marnie.

"You're so lucky," Alita added, which Marnie acknowledged with a nod.

She was lucky. She had been virtually adopted by Benjamin's family, taken as a daughter and under unusual circumstances. She had first dated Benjamin's younger brother, Geoffrey, but when that didn't work out, Benjamin arrived to comfort Marnie in a way that revealed his own attraction to her. The boys' parents were happy to have Marnie back in their lives and, it appeared, happier to have her back than Geoffrey who had taken a path away from his parents, away from their successful wine and food business in the valley, and toward some varying and inexplicably vague destination that had no visible means of support.

Marnie stood at the wobbly threshold of marriage to a man who was the reliable if stolid rock her own father never was. Benjamin was a successful businessman and an endowed heir to a fortune. His parents were wealthy beyond Marnie's imagining and they liked her, were happy to have her in their family whichever brother she married.

And Marnie was grateful and eager to become the other Marnie, the Marnie married and appended to Benjamin and his wealthy and welcoming family. The Marnie with prestige and class and who rose in a decade to heights never imagined by the friends she had known in her youth, aimless sisters swimming in limbos of need and fantasy and desire but without the will or interest to make a run for it. They would be impressed, she thought. They would be stunned by Marnie's success and also envious of her good fortune. And they would all be at her wedding. All would be there to witness her passage into another stratum of prosperity well beyond their own corners and crevices and staircases and big doors of ambition.

In a certain rendering it was the story of a lucky and deserving Cinderella. Except Marnie was pregnant. And she could not name the father.

I t wasn't as if a father were a mystery. Just two men were candidates for Marnie's pregnancy. And they were brothers. One was Benjamin. The other was his sibling Geoffrey, both Flahertys and, in succession, the lovers that had exclusively occupied a full and recent year in Marnie's loopy, undisciplined life.

"The usual," Geoffrey said the third summer day he waited to address Marnie. Marnie remembered the day from the headline on the front page of *The New York Times* that occupied the shelf across from the counter: *Timothy McVeigh Executed for Oklahoma City Bombing.* It was the man who had killed all those federal employees, including dozens of children. She remembered a photo of a first responder standing in rubble as he held the tiny corpse of an infant.

Geoffrey ordered coffee from Marnie at a north town café where she worked as a barista when she wasn't attending business classes at the local junior college. Geoffrey was a repeat customer and, charmingly, a stubborn pursuer. Within a week he asked Marnie out ("but not for coffee," he joked). They had dinner at one of his family's wine country restaurants. He was charming and Marnie thought later and to her credit that she slept with him before knowing the extent of his family's wealth.

She really liked Geoffrey. He was funny, arrogant and playful. He made extraordinary love to her, love that lasted days with its teasing, talking, touching and the inevitable and reliable wallop of exhausting pleasure. He had a sonorous, sexy voice and drove a restored 1973 Corvette, an extravagance that advertised his status as a fortunate son.

He dated her for a week and then introduced her to his parents, wine country royalty who overlooked her vagrant pedigree to embrace her sweetness and daffy innocence. Geraldine and Brant seemed especially pleased that their younger and more volatile son, whom the father, Brant, referred to as the "sheep, perhaps grey if not black," had seemed to settle into loving an attractive and impressively innocent woman. Though what they considered ingenuousness was for Marnie nothing more than undisciplined confusion. She did not know how to choose a lover and so was herself easily chosen.

It had happened that way in high school long after the ghost she tried to recall as a father had finished haunting her mother and departed, leaving the mom of Marnie to fend for herself, eager or so she thought for the affection of someone and unable to find it. Marnie loved the first boy who found her and loved the boy enough to get pregnant. So, God, she could not, would not, do another abortion. It was enough at age sixteen to have her emotionally absent mother make the choice for her, a mother that spent nearly all her time attempting to attract another husband and so desperate she might have given Marnie up in a minute if it meant gaining another date with an eligible male. Marnie's mother was constantly looking for her next man while Marnie spent what she considered too much of her early childhood looking for her mom.

"Surprise, surprise!" shouted Alita as a dozen women in the restaurant exploded in a clamor of applause, all the girls Marnie knew from high school who were now women and who during Marnie's disorienting adolescence forgave her missteps and absolved her of choices.

"She's getting married!" Alita shouted to the cheers of her old friends and a few distant acquaintances. The party was on and Marnie was the main course, the proud and victorious bride, positioned enviously at the juncture of her desultory life with a threshold of stunning wealth. Marnie's mother attended the bridal shower but sat subdued in the glow of her daughter's notable and greater success at finding a prize of a husband.

Though the history of her arrival at this place was for Marnie truly unenviable and the choices ahead nothing she would wish for anyone. In seven months she was going to have a baby and while it wasn't likely she would "show" at next month's wedding, there would be a reckoning. A baby was coming and a baby was, in its pure, new and promising life, a deep and important truth. And who was the father?

"You'll like my family," Geoffrey said when they started dating. "You might not always like me."

"She's the one," he told his parents at another dinner at the Flaherty home on the hill behind their original winery. And they happily concurred. Geoffrey told Marnie he would like to marry her. But
didn't give her a ring.

Though Marnie was careful. She still took her pill. What was
possible? This affectionate family seemed so desirable and yet, by every measure of her own meager life, should be far beyond Marnie's
reach. She would not get pregnant again. Not now. Not until after
marrying Geoffrey.

Which was a good strategy, especially when Marnie discovered
Geoffrey was sleeping with another woman. In fact, she walked in on
them together at Geoffrey's apartment. That was too much, even if
it weren't a problem for Geoffrey. It hurt Marnie deeply. It destroyed
her trust even if it did not end her affection for Geoffrey. Even so, she
told Geoffrey never to call her again.

"You what?!" Alita had asked her incredulously. "Because he fucked
someone else you give up your shot at a life of luxury?"

Marnie hadn't considered this. She did not know herself well
but she thought she knew what was right and what wasn't. She loved
Geoffrey but could not live with a hurt that went to her core. Yes,
she had broken up with Geoffrey. She also stopped taking her pills.
It was a relief to feel free again.

Marnie was not prepared for a call from Geoffrey's older brother, Benjamin. He was furious with Geoffrey for "fucking it all up
once again" and asked if he could meet with Marnie to talk with
her about what happened. He said the family, his parents especially,
were sorry for Geoffrey's bad behavior and, well….

Benjamin ran out of words in time for Marnie to say, yes, she
would like that very much; a chance to meet with Ben and talk about
what happened. She thanked Ben for his interest and concern.

"It's not right, you know," Benjamin said over dinner with Marnie at the same restaurant she first visited with Geoffrey.

"My brother's, well, he has his problems and…"

Marnie interrupted Benjamin.

"If you're going to ask me to go back to Geoffrey, I won't do it,"
Marnie said firmly.

"No, oh no," answered Benjamin before pausing nervously. "I was hoping you might go out with me."

three

Benjamin was all he said he was and at first that was too much for Marnie. He was everything Geoffrey was not: accountable, punctual, responsible and reliable to a fault. Benjamin also was nothing that Geoffrey was: sexy, spontaneous, irreverent, whimsical, and dangerous. Marnie grew quickly comfortable with Benjamin's feckless adoration and when she returned to his parents' home for dinner, Geraldine and Brant warmly welcomed her back.

"It's so good to see you again," Geraldine said. "After the… well…the break-up, we worried about you. You're a beautiful woman and you didn't deserve…well…"

Geraldine had spoken before finishing her thought. Marnie was beautiful. Men had told her as much and the mirror did not lie: a strong profile, high cheeks, large lips and brilliant peacock blue eyes. Long and luxurious black hair she wore full and down and that bounced when she turned, which she frequently did. She saw the strength of her striking looks reflected everywhere. Yet she had no idea how to use them.

Brant nodded in agreement and gave Marnie what felt to her an incipiently parental hug. But she would not think herself as family until Benjamin asked her to marry him. She knew she would not fuck Benjamin until she had a ring. Her quick and sybaritic descent into Geoffrey's subterranean pleasures had nearly ruined her and she would not again make the same mistake. Dinner with Ben's and Geoffrey's parents confirmed on her the renewed status of faux virgin. She was still technically unsullied and therefore remained a good candidate to marry their obviously favored son.

After less than a month of dating and sparring, Benjamin presented Marnie with a ring for which she exchanged her body. She had deftly managed Ben with enough touching and stimulation to leave him feeling happy and relieved, even as he pushed her to remove her panties and spread her legs. She would not do that. Instead she did what she did best, which was figuring out how to live up to the needs and expectations of those most relevant to her and to "fit in" without giving herself entirely away.

"You drive me crazy," Ben whispered to her, even shouted at her in a rising crescendo of desire. If Marnie had learned anything in high school it was how to tease and provoke a man without fully submitting. She had given in once and had learned, she thought, enough to last a lifetime.

Yet more than a month after submitting to Ben in the back seat of his car, she realized she was pregnant. And was it Ben?

"I hear you and Ben might get married," Geoffrey said.

He phoned Marnie the day after Ben proposed.

"I know Ben wants to marry you."

"He's already asked," Marnie answered coolly. "I've accepted."

There was no response from Geoffrey.

"What do you want?" asked Marnie at last.

"To wish you well," Geoffrey said.

His tone was eloquent but modulated by the briefest tremor of sadness.

Marnie thought she heard the sound of regret in his voice, which was momentarily satisfying.

"I was hoping to see you," said Geoffrey. "Maybe we could patch up the past. I mean with you and me in the family and all."

What that would involve, Marnie could not imagine. She struggled with her own difficult feelings about the way she ended her link to Geoffrey. Whatever he might regret, it resulted in something that for Marnie still felt deeply tragic.

"OK," Marnie said sullenly. "When?"

"Saturday? I'll come by. How about four? Maybe I could talk you into dinner."

"We'll see," said Marnie cautiously.

Her hand shook as she ended the call.

"God, you look just stunning!" Alita said as Marnie paraded briefly in a tight, white wedding gown, different from the others in the way it clung to her hips and rolled tightly down her thighs to spread out in a sea of fluffy chiffon before reaching her heels.

"Really shows you off," said Joanie, another high school chum recruited as her second bridesmaid. "Your butt looks great."

Joanie wasn't subtle. At Marnie's bridal shower, Joanie gave her a box of condoms.

"How much is it?" asked Marnie's mother, otherwise taciturn as Marnie and her girlfriends whirled through the selection of her most important dress. It would be expensive. And it would be worn once and never worn again, unless Marnie had a daughter and, even then…the idea of having a daughter was as far as Marnie could go. She felt the dress at her waist, wondering how tight it would feel in a month when she walked down the aisle.

Geoffrey looked and sounded the same.

"She left me," said Geoffrey. "Much like you left me, though it was my turn to be the cuck. An old boyfriend came roaring back and that was that."

Marnie sat in a chair across from the slender couch in her apartment where Geoffrey sat alone. It was the couch on which she had frequently cuddled, smooched with and fucked Geoffrey.

Marnie thought it would be easy to ignore old feelings and to suppress her incomplete desires if she did not touch her old lover. She guarded the distance between them carefully. She waited for his words and bit her lip whenever she felt a need to speak. She listened and that was all. It was a test. She would see Geoffrey for a few minutes and then see him out. She would rise and walk him to the door. Marnie no longer sought her place in the shadows of wealth. It was nearly assured.

four

Marnie awoke with Geoffrey asleep beside her. She slept long and late and tried to recall how a meeting she intended to last minutes turned into an old dance that lasted hours and that produced an odyssey of conquering collisions that smothered her resistance and fed her most vulnerable appetites. How Geoffrey requested a drink and she made one, and another, until he drove her for a meal at a lovely restaurant, teasing her all the way with favored words and memorably tender touches. And then after dinner there was the nightcap.

She poured one last drink for Geoffrey and herself, the one last entrapping drink that engaged her with the unfinished argument, the unexpressed desire, and the touches, the delicious and guilty touches of the lover that knew her body best. It was a provocation and Geoffrey built his charm on the bet that Marnie would, always would, find his words and voice and affectionate bad boy criminality irresistible. Only Geoffrey seemed able to present terms Marnie was helpless to resist. Their brief and torrid intimate history led to the dance—the sweet, arduous, painful and satisfying dance Marnie could not describe or explain.

But here she was again, Geoffrey's willing playmate brought back for an encore. It was barely morning and he snored next to her while she thought she might—must—bolt from the bed in the dark dawn and leave her own room and never return. She would not blame anyone but herself. The sex was so good, so good as it always was with Geoffrey who knew how to build, choreograph, tease, push, hold and speak about desire in ways that held her transfixed, thoroughly aroused, and always willing. Why had she broken up with him?

This was Geoffrey who, as he stirred in her bed, appeared suddenly small and also flaunting like a bad little boy but also as a poisonously addictive attachment she could not abide even if it were for a night all she wanted.

"Get out, get out…" Marnie snarled.

"God, what have I done?" she asked herself out loud.

"You always do just exactly what you want," Geoffrey answered coolly as his eyes opened.

"What we wanted to do…it's what I like about you."

"But you are such a bad man," Marnie heard herself say. "You know I'm engaged to marry Ben."

"And you don't love him," Geoffrey answered with irrepressible confidence. "Isn't that obvious? Let's get real, Marnie. Am I a good man? There are better. If you want obedience and loyalty, Ben is your guy. But I know you. You want a fight. You want a lover who pushes hard against you. You want discipline. You are thrilled to have your body under my control, to have a firm and loving shove against your amorous will. And I do that for you. You may not think you love me. But you need me. And, well, here I am."

"You cheated on me," Marnie shouted. "I did want you. How can I love someone I can't trust?"

Geoffrey considered the question.

"I can't answer that," he said. "I'm unpredictable. And, it would appear, so are you. We have much in common and there's a part of me that belongs exclusively and irrevocably with you. If I'm bad, so are you. Let's be bad together."

"Get out! Get out!" Marnie now screamed. "It's too much. Don't come back ever. Don't every try to see me again. I love Ben. I do. I love Ben very much."

Geoffrey's eyes reflected a wan but certain terror as he slipped out of bed and gathered from the floor his pants and shirt before stepping into the bathroom, leaving Marnie with the bitter aftertaste of an accurate, if damning, assessment of her character.

Marnie felt pressured to serve dinner at her wedding. It was scheduled late on a Saturday and more than a hundred would attend, most friends of Ben and his family who likely expected a meal, and wine, and a full and open bar. But dinner was a difficult subject to broach with her mother who had wearied of the preparations for her daughter's expensive wedding.

"Ben's family is helping, you know that," Marnie reminded her mom. "You aren't in trouble. It's all been arranged."

The real reasons for her mother's petulance had little to do with the wedding's expense. The costs were simply more evidence of extravagant waste on behalf of a thankless daughter who no longer needed—or wanted—her mother's care.

"Just behave yourself," Marnie said to her mother in an angry whisper. "It's my goddamned wedding."

But for Marnie it was also her goddamned pregnancy and nearly two months past the weekend she became both engaged and likely inseminated. She was now in a rush to stand at an altar, any altar, to seal her reckless choice before witnesses, to hide it in the open under an urgent, frightened and sacred promise. Then she would leave on a honeymoon and fade from everyone's attention until a moment in the fall Marnie and Ben would tell everyone she was going to have a baby. Only then would it be safe to disappear behind the cumbrous props associated with an expectant mother.

five

Marnie still worked though Ben told her she did not need to work anymore. She had the early shift at the café and arrived at five in the morning to make coffee, heat rolls and pastries and at last open the doors and the take-out window at 6 a.m. Marnie still worked because if she allowed Ben to become her savior he would also become her jailer.

Marnie was two semesters of study away from holding an associate degree in accounting. It was the life of money merged with her life, the ebb and flow of wealth, big and small, through the structures of acquisition and expenditure. In her mind these were the two fundamental principles of energy and even of life itself. How she was acquired and ultimately expended as a bride and mother was now the central question of her life. And as she struggled against morning sickness brought forward every morning by the oleaginous textures and lardy smells of the café, Marnie confronted the limits of her freedom as a pregnant bride.

"The wedding needs to happen before it rains," Marnie said to Ben. "And your family. All those people who have to fly in. And school will already have started."

"OK, hon," said Ben. "Whatever you say."

Marnie's husband-to-be was accommodating to a fault. He convinced his father to clear the winery's heavily scheduled event calendar to assure the wine caves and garden were available that weekend. Plans for the ceremony continued. It would be non-denominational and officiated by a local superior court judge who was one of Brant's old college friends. The grape harvest and crush would be in full swing and workers would be in the fields.

"It will look like a painting," Ben said happily. "Our wedding will be a work of art."

Why did Marnie worry? Ben loved her and she had sex with him whenever he wanted, sex that was usually stupidly quick and not very pleasurable but its frequency would prove to anyone she was

22

legitimately pregnant by her husband. Though it proved nothing to Marnie who knew in her heart and likely even in her womb that the question of who fathered her baby remained unanswered.

"Eat your breakfast—all of it," her mother had told Marnie the child.

"Are you really hungry?" her mother asked Marnie the young woman.

A woman's appetites were to be managed: all of them, whether for food or for love or for life. It was a lesson taught usually by a mother who had fallen short in the eyes of the world. And Marnie was ashamed by how long it had taken her to grasp, understand and at last reject the self-hatred and denial preached by her mother.

Instead, Marnie accepted the riveting fact of her pregnancy and the daily evidence of its development. She then determined to proceed with the scheduled arrival of her new life, her abiding fear and her untested love at the designated time and place of her wedding. It would be a momentous passage and could not come soon enough.

Every morning Marnie measured her waist and worried she would show. Ten days before the wedding she told her mother and Geraldine she needed another dress, one looser and more forgiving. She had gained weight and wasn't comfortable and while she spoke she thought she saw her mother's eyes roll and, for one brief second, meet Geraldine's in some grimace of common awareness.

"Sure, hon," said Geraldine, always more the friend than Marnie's mom.

"Whatever you want. It's your big day."

Though it wasn't at all. Increasingly, Marnie hated the thought of her wedding day when the eyes of more than a hundred guests would be on her, evaluating and excavating her face, her body, her entire life for clues to the source of the groom's seemingly urgent need to marry. Though it was Marnie who urgently needed a marriage. It was Marnie who raced to the altar.

A week before the wedding Marnie accepted that the role of a mother was preferable to that of a barista, even if it wasn't guaranteed to bring fulfillment or even happiness. She also admitted to herself she did not love Ben. It was a troubling admission because it opened her to the passion she still felt for Geoffrey. And somewhere inside her, perhaps at the locus of her fetus, she could feel the truth that Geoffrey was the father of her child. Though she did not know and, it appeared, would never know. It would be best never to know. Like so many before her, Marnie thought herself someone who desired always to run toward the light and, instead, found herself running headlong into the jaws of a disturbing darkness.

"Are you ready?" Alita asked Marnie the last Sunday before the wedding.

"Six days and counting," said Marnie. "I can't wait."

And she couldn't. She wanted the wedding to come and also to pass quickly. She needed a ritual to frame and at last freeze the voluble terms of her new life. She needed a legitimate passage into her illegitimate motherhood.

six

Marnie sat on her bed like a sad clown. It was Tuesday morning and she was to meet with Geraldine and the caterers to settle the wedding's dinner menu. Instead, she absorbed the televised horror of a burning, collapsing World Trade Center with no understanding why four planes had been hijacked and sent crashing into New York and Washington. Thousands of people were presumed dead in the worst terrorist attack in US history.

And it would only get worse. Shortly after ten, Geraldine called to cancel their caterer appointment and, also, to cancel Marnie's Saturday wedding. All flights across North America were grounded indefinitely, stranding dozens of wedding guests who were scheduled to arrive later in the week. Worse, as Geraldine took a deep breath and spoke through an incipient sob, one of Brant's last living uncles was on the flight from Newark to San Francisco that was hijacked and crashed.

"We can't do it, Hon," Geraldine said. "I don't know when. But not now."

By evening Marnie grasped her tiny place and that of her wedding in the tapestry of a national tragedy. She had no standing and was not getting married. At least one family funeral would precede her marriage, a funeral likely triggered by an invitation to her wedding, which mortified Marnie. It would be weeks and maybe months before she could imagine a conversation that returned to the plans for her wedding. And she would never initiate it out of respect for Brant's loss. Meanwhile, she would grow increasingly pregnant and the terms of her life and that of the life she carried, now spun so fully out of her control, would have to be framed differently.

Marnie had thought she could postpone the truth until after she was married. Now the truth would precede everything. And what was the truth? She had never asked that before. So often she let others describe the truths that, eventually and always on their behalf, she would willingly enact.

"Oh, shit, you'll need a test," Alita divulged.

"What test?" Marnie asked.

"You'll need a paternity test," the attorney told Marnie. "You won't be able to get one until the baby is born. So, yes, you'll have to tell both brothers."

It was an unwelcome truth, and one already previewed when Marnie told Alita she was pregnant and she did not know the father.

The attorney was an older woman named Virginia. She had guided Alita through a bitter divorce and now she explained to Marnie why paternity mattered, as if Marnie did not at least understand that.

"If what you're telling me is true, one is the father which means the other is not. The one who is the father has significant financial obligations. But he might also wish to exercise his rights as a father, even to go as far as seeking some custody of the child, which, of course, would reduce what he would need to pay in support."

Marnie nodded to indicate her grasp of the situation.

"And you don't want to get married?" asked the attorney.

"No," answered Marnie.

"Can you help me with a letter?" Marnie asked. "I can't face either of them now. Ben doesn't understand why I don't return his calls. He's frantic and I can only imagine his mom and dad are really upset."

"Sooner is better," said Virginia. "In this case the truth is your friend. And don't worry. The big problems in life are always insoluble. They can never be fixed. Only outgrown. What you say to these brothers hopefully will grow them. But if it doesn't, we need to be prepared."

"Prepared for what?" asked Marnie.

"Prepared for the worst while we hope for the best," answered Virginia.

"And what's the worst?" asked Marnie.

"That they treat you badly and try to take your baby."

"That can't happen, can it?"

The thought that the fetus she carried could be stolen from her was more than Marnie could fathom.

"No," said Virginia. "No. Unless you're a drug addict or have a horrible accident or murder someone and are caught…no. You need to write your letter and bring it back for me to review. Don't tell them you have an attorney. Just tell them what you told me. You want the baby but you don't want to get married. And you don't know which is the father so they'll need to work with you. We'll see how they respond."

"What do I owe you?" Marnie said as she stood to leave.

"Nothing now, dear," said Virginia. "We'll be fine. And you'll be back."

Marnie tried to elevate herself to a distant height in order to clearly view the dilemma of her growing fetus and the need, now, to act on its behalf. As much as she wished to protect herself from an inevitable and potentially vicious opprobrium, she wanted most to protect the body growing within hers. In this spirit, she began her letter to both brothers with an appeal to a presumed common interest in the welfare of her child.

I am having this baby, wrote Marnie as she opened her letter with its most important and indelible declaration. *And one of you is the father.* Marnie needed both Geoffrey and Ben to acknowledge this likelihood, as she knew Geoffrey would and Ben, at least at first, might not. She expressed her understanding that Ben would feel betrayed and that Geoffrey might wish to run. Could she have melded Geoffrey's intense vitality to Ben's steadfast character, she would have had a husband for the ages. Instead, she was now seeking in at least one of them a crucial accountability for what grew inside her and for their part in its creation. It troubled Marnie to think that what made her most happy was something likely to make both Geoffrey and Ben and their parents very angry. She knew from living with her weary mother that women and mothers, the sources of all experience, were frequently blamed for everything that went wrong.

seven

Men fear women but women also fear women. Her mother was the last person Marnie would tell about her fetus, the mother that during her first pregnancy in high school collapsed in self-abasing shame only to rise up violently in a sudden and condemning whirlwind.

Sixteen-year-old Marnie was a "whore" and "slut" during a fearful evening in which Marnie's mother made her daughter's missed period all about herself, all about her own bad choice to go ahead with the birth of a "stupid and witless" Marnie. She was a mother so enraged by her own bad fortune that Marnie was not only forced to share it, but instructed to accept full responsibility. Marnie's mother later apologized and the daughter forgave her while swearing secretly to never forget.

Marnie would speak to the men and, while she could accept responsibility for her pregnancy, she did not need to excuse anyone else's desire or her own. Somewhere in the pain of this experience was the call of an authentic voice. Marnie at first credited her fetus with such a voice until realizing that without Marnie's words the fetus had no voice at all. It was up to Marnie to speak for the not-yet-child that felt still like something stirring from within a deep, dangerous well.

Ben was the first to phone. And he apologized, which was what Marnie thought she should do.

"I'm sorry," Ben said.

"For what?" asked Marnie.

"Maybe for pressuring you," said Ben. "For asking for more than I deserved."

"You're a kind man, Ben," said Marnie. "I just can't marry you. And now you know why. Please don't blame Geoffrey. He's really not…"

"I don't blame Geoffrey," Ben interrupted. "I've spoken with Geoffrey. We're OK, Marnie. We're worried about you."

"Me?" Marnie asked. "I'm the trouble-maker here. I'm the mother with the baby one of you has fathered. And I don't even know who it is. What does that make me?"

"Geoffrey and I don't know who it is, either," answered Ben. "What does that make us? All of us?"

"Enemies? Rivals?" said Marnie. "I can't have and raise this baby alone. I need some help and one of you…"

"Why not both of us?" said Ben. "What if Geoffrey and I both help you with this baby?"

"But a paternity test…" Marnie opened with her attorney's crucial line of defense. A test would determine the father and hold him personally and fully accountable.

"If Geoffrey and I both want to help you with the baby, why do we need a test?"

"Two fathers….sure…why would two men both want to be the father of the same baby?"

Marnie could not make sense of this.

"Or two uncles…whatever you want to call us, that isn't important. The baby is a Flaherty. Which Flaherty started its life doesn't seem that critical to us. Any of us."

"We'll have to meet with my attorney," Marnie said after a long silence. She did not think of her fetus as a Flaherty.

"You have an attorney?" Ben asked. "Sure. That's good. When?"

Marnie stopped speaking.

The insoluble problem described by Virginia rolled over and beyond her and, in a lacuna between her fears and Ben's words, Marnie felt for a moment as if she had passed through a storm, one she was now above and no longer in.

"We just want to help," said Ben to Virginia as they sat around the conference table in her office. Ben and Geoffrey sat on one side and Virginia and Marnie on the other.

"We don't need to know who the father is," said Ben. Geoffrey winked at Marnie and she turned to ignore him.

"We're Flahertys and so is this baby," Ben continued. "We want to share the responsibility. We want to share with Marnie the life of this child."

"A Flaherty?" asked Marnie. "What do you mean? This baby is mine."

"Yes…of course…" Ben seemed to stumble. "It's just that…" Ben looked over at Geoffrey who was staring hard at Marnie who turned toward Virginia to avoid his gaze.

"It's just that…well…this child has two fathers—godfathers, if you will. Two godfathers and the baby is a member of our family."

"And what does that mean to you?" asked Virginia.

"Well, we'll have custody for one thing. And the child will live with us."

"Will what?" said Marnie.

"Mom's figured it all out," said Ben. "Marnie and the baby can live with us. We have a cottage that will be all hers. We'll provide lodging and board and take care of Marnie and her baby."

"And what would I do while I lived with you?" asked Marnie.

"We have work you would do," said Ben. "Accounting…your specialty and we'll take care of the baby for you."

"We—who's we?" Marnie asked again.

"I don't think you two understand how this works," Virginia interrupted. "Marnie is under the impression we are here to negotiate a support and visitation agreement in which you gentlemen will be equally responsible for providing support and equally engaged with Marnie in parenting. Is that right?"

"Well, yes…" said Ben. "But the child will be a Flaherty and since there are two fathers…which makes us three parents…we'll have the majority of time with the child. In return, we'll guarantee the child's security and cover all its expenses. Marnie will be free to…free to…"

"To what?" Marnie asked

"Make suggestions," said Ben, his voice suddenly strained. "You know, offer your ideas about parenting so we can all consider…"

"I'm the baby's mother," Marnie interrupted. "I'll decide. Do you understand? I'm the child's mother."

Ben looked quizzically at Marnie and then at Virginia.

"She's the mother," said Virginia. "She'll decide. She'll have primary custody."

Marnie stared blankly at Ben and then Geoffrey who seemed to be on the verge of chuckling.

The baby was from her body. Her own body, a body not just her own but one born out of the earth and that thrived among trees and clouds and sky. And so was her baby. Her baby was its own body that no one owned or possessed or that could fit neatly into the legacy prepared for it by Ben and Geoffrey.

"The little bastard could end up inheriting the whole Flaherty estate," Geoffrey grunted. "Isn't that worth something? Marnie, we're doing you a goddamned favor. You give us the baby and you get on with your life."

"I think we're finished," Virginia said while Marnie weighed Ben's insufferable suggestions.

"Well…OK…" Ben announced.

He was flummoxed.

"We have our own attorney and we ,if we need to, we can…"

"Have your attorney phone me," Virginia interrupted coolly as if she were responding to a noisome litigant.

The brothers rose together to leave.

"I told you," Geoffrey said to Marnie who did not look up. "I told you you wouldn't always like me."

"What now?" Marnie asked Virginia after the men had left.

"Plan B," said Virginia. "It sounded too good to be true. No way you were going to give up your child. I wouldn't let you. Hell, the judge wouldn't let you. They owe you support. At least one of them does. And you'll receive a judgment based on incomes. You'll be fine. Your baby will be fine."

Marnie thanked Virginia. She was again alone. Marnie had always been alone. As she left Virginia's office Marnie's greatest sorrow was that she could not marry someone who acknowledged the depth of her feelings and the realizations brought forward by her profoundly physical and psychic transition. She needed someone who grasped the source of both her suffering and the hope now growing in her body. She wished she could marry her attorney and, knowing that to be impossible, Marnie regretted deeply she could not marry herself.

HOME SWEET HOME

one

Noah was a carpenter and Lorraine his lady. Noah met Lorraine in the Petaluma street where he built his fifth home. At the age of 20, Noah Sather was a hard worker having left school at sixteen to ply his chosen trade. Acquaintances who finished high school were surprised Noah had not. But Noah's father, the large, strange man who had taught his son how to swing a hammer and saw a board, ran away from his small family, leaving Noah and his mother without either a forwarding address or an income.

The father was named Mel and it took Noah's mother a week to learn her fleeing husband had emptied their bank account, took an accrued savings of some $10,000 and left not even enough to cover the next month's mortgage payment.

"Your father is a bastard," said Noah's mother. "We are really fucked now."

Noah was an only child abandoned by his only father. Noah was left an angry boy but too frightened at first to know how angry he was. In the summer before what would have been Noah's senior year in high school, he looked for work. A woman friend of his mother was married to a building contractor.

"Reggie's building two homes in the new subdivision across town," she said to Deirdre, Noah's frightened mother. "He could use some help."

Noah applied to the affiliating neighbor's husband for a summer job and got a gopher position doing odd jobs and end-of-the day clean-up at one of the home sites. Within two weeks Noah was doing rough framing and installing sheet rock. Noah was a fast learner and after a month he was added to the crew.

"We'll keep you until school starts," said Fred the neighborly contractor.

"I'm not going back to school," answered Noah firmly. "Keep me on. I can do it."

"Don't you want to graduate?" asked Fred.

"Why?" asked Noah. "I know what I want to do. This is it."

"You won't miss your friends?" asked Fred.

"Don't have many friends," answered Noah.

And he didn't. Noah was tall and slim and silent and hated school. He stood awkwardly in the hallways like a misplaced tree in a desert and watched the socially adept ignore him as they passed by and around. It was a quiet life and he was a silent student. He had always been the invisible one that lurked outside the circle, who sat in the last desk of the last row, in the corner of the lunchroom and at the back of the gym. He could be seen but was usually missed. Now with his father gone and his mother unemployed Noah had a real life ordered by the demands of a real crisis.

"Ok," said Fred. "You can stay on. It pays six dollars an hour. You'll get a share of any profit. You're a good worker. I need the houses finished before Thanksgiving. But there's more work. Believe me. This town has a lot of room to grow."

"I want to be an investor," Noah said to Lorraine when he met her.

Lorraine, insouciant and sexy, had stopped to talk with him one summer afternoon while he sat on the porch of a new home, drank coffee from a thermos and took his break.

Three years had passed since Fred hired Noah who had found his calling and was learning a trade. Fred was waiting for Noah to turn 21 to make him a partner.

Lorraine didn't think of investors as people dressed in scraped, stained overalls and so made a joke at Noah's expense. Noah laughed, too, before explaining why someone who held a hammer and towered over Lorraine like a basketball center and whose sweat stained every crevice of his clothing, might be an aspiring captain of industry. Noah was young. He was just beginning. When the homes were finished and sold he would have a share of the profit. In fact, he would owe a hefty tax that he was proud to say he could pay. Noah offered to explain his life in more detail if Lorraine met him for dinner.

"Can you believe another woman tried to shoot the President today?" Lorraine said as she and Noah sat down to order pizza.

Noah didn't read the news so he was surprised and interested. He shook his head.

"Second time this month," said Lorraine. "How weird is that?"

Noah wasn't paying attention. He looked at Lorraine, her long hair a fluff of light brown curls, her eyelashes large and dark, and her clear eyes probing Noah who himself appeared refreshed, showered, shaved. He was dressed casually in a beige summer turtleneck and crisp, clean jeans.

"And Ford wasn't even elected," Lorraine added. "Probably wonders if he should have taken the job when Nixon offered it."

"You follow politics?" asked Noah.

"Not really," answered Lorraine. "It's just so weird."

The ice broken, Lorraine went on to talk about her family: two parents and two siblings, an older sister and younger brother who all lived a block from the home Noah was building. Her father sold insurance. Her mother stayed home and had raised her and her siblings.

"They're religious people and I've outgrown religion," said Lorraine. "Can't wait to move out."

"When's that?" asked Noah.

"When I get my first dental assistant job…hopefully this fall. I'm two weeks away from being certified."

"I live with my mom," said Noah. "But at the end of this job I'll pay off her mortgage. When that's done I'll move out. She won't need my rent any longer."

"And your dad?" asked Lorraine.

"He's dead," said Noah. "We don't talk too much about him."

Noah was through trying to tell the truth about a father who left his life and never returned.

Their pizza arrived and after dinner Noah took Lorraine on a drive to the top of Sonoma Mountain. Noah parked at an overlook and they talked for another hour about their lives, their friends, their untested dreams and their preferred joys and comforts. Until Lorraine could not resist and slid gently into the hollow of Noah's outstretched arm to lean against his chest. There was a kiss. And another. And laughter and high, delicious tension all the way back to town where Noah deposited Lorraine at her parked car but not before receiving an embrace that caused him to forget the whole world.

two

And I love *you*…"

Lorraine's words answered Noah's first question. It was a fast courtship and he knew no other outcome to expect, so he forced the issue by asking Lorraine to marry him. The second question would arrive from Lorraine's father, who supported a family of five with his one, hustled income.

"Can you take care of my daughter?" Karl asked Noah.

"Yes," said Noah. "Yes I can."

Noah and Lorraine had been dating for three months, both in a hurry not just to have sex but also to move out of the small rooms of their homes that since early childhood had been their only sanctuaries and where, as long as they stayed, they remained children and could never become adults. Which up to a certain point was fine with their parents until Lorraine's mother and father recognized in Noah his essential and tenacious ambition, one usually identified with success.

That Noah had paid off his mother's mortgage was enough for Lorraine's parents to accept and, in fact, encourage the hurried union of their beautiful middle child to a young Noah, still so young they wondered if he even shaved. Noah then asked, and Lorraine accepted.

"What shall we name the children?" Lorraine asked whimsically as they rolled together in Noah's bed.

"Whatever you'd like," said Noah.

He thought he understood the course of his life now. Marriage made it so clear and gave him roles to fill as a husband and also a father. As he built a house, so he would build a family. Rolling around with Lorraine was delicious and lovely. Why wouldn't marriage simply be more of the same?

Noah had already moved out of his mother's home and into a one-bedroom Westside apartment where he and Lorraine rehearsed the compelling sexual passion that was the foundation of their embryonic relationship. Lorraine's parents knew Reginald Corcoran, the local contractor building dozens of homes on the flat valley floor of the town's empty Eastside. They were impressed that the young Noah was a partner with Reggie. They weren't losing a daughter. They were gaining an asset.

Noah understood he was gaining a wife; a young, lovely and fertile woman with enough ambition to appear capable but not too much to challenge his own far-ranging plans. Noah's eyes were on a fundamental and evident prize: wealth drawn from the talent he had for building sound, well-constructed homes and his partnership with an experienced and successful entrepreneur. It was his life and what he rose to address every weekday morning before dawn and what he returned with every evening in the fading sunlight. It was simple work and yet it was not. It required patience, endurance and a commitment to excellence even as he wheeled through a quotidian of repetitive but essential steps. It meant solving problems and not ignoring them or concealing them behind plaster or sheet rock.

"There are no short cuts," Reggie told Noah one afternoon.

"These are quality homes. That's what they pay for. We're fucking artists, Noah. Don't forget it."

A month before the wedding Lorraine, in a weak moment, had a surprising breakdown. She stormed through Noah's apartment after a rough argument developed around what seemed a minor wedding detail.

"I'm fucking sick of my goddamned life," she yelled at last before breaking down in tears. Noah went to her, comforted her until after several minutes they together dissolved into a pool of fearful comfort and agreed not to dig too deeply into the weeds of Lorraine's pain, which was really drawn from her unsuccessful interview with a local dentist.

"It's alright," Noah said, knowing it wasn't.

Their wedding and its marriage were too large and had grown beyond anything they alone could control. Lorraine's extended family was larger than Noah had imagined and spread across the region and country. All were invited to the wedding and many said they would attend. Lorraine was worried and Noah was frightened. But they had no clear words for each other that would admit to worry or fear. Six weeks after the wedding Lorraine learned she was pregnant and, once again a happy couple, or rather a couple determined to be happy, had its explanation for everything.

They lived together in Noah's apartment while he convinced Reggie to sell him one of his new homes at cost. It was a bargain, leaving Reggie with a small and very affordable mortgage. Another fall arrived and Noah moved his new family into their three-bedroom 1600 square foot home with a spacious backyard and a tentative front lawn. By this time Lorraine was six months pregnant and without any immediate hope of a career other than that of a mother to her child and wife to her husband.

At the wedding Noah had looked back at his mother and felt her fading out of his sight and at last left alone in her paid-off Westside home. He knew he would rarely visit her anymore while she, as she always did, gave way to her self-effacing grace, gave way to the future and the baby to come while she ignored what she lost or why. The horrific and inexplicable death of her marriage was a shame without words or facts or meaning. It left her frozen and afraid its dissolution was written in the stars and that she had no other choice but to succumb and finally to die in the grip of a wordless and all-embracing fate. She needed to worry about her son now. He was married and, despite the wedding's lovely words and trappings, she could not control a fear that her son's marriage might not last.

three

I t was a boy.
   The baby arrived late, which was a relief for Lorraine who worried throughout her pregnancy that "everyone" was counting the months to determine if she was a virgin at her wedding, which

she was not and anyway it was not what anyone expected. The baby's birth produced a smaller crowd than the wedding but one that hovered longer and more insistently. Noah's mother was there and, as at the wedding, she appeared to hang back from the dominant presence of Lorraine's extended family.

Noah's father had always been missing. And Noah's response to his father's unexplained absence was understandable.

"I never really knew him," Noah would say to Lorraine when she brought up the subject.

Lorraine loved her father, obstreperous and conservative as he was. He was the dad that, before she knew the world, helped Lorraine to grasp its measure and to feel entitled to a place within it. That was the key. Lorraine assumed she was chosen as a child to grow and live and Noah assumed nothing. His father was gone. Noah had no father.

Though now he thought a life without a father was better than a life without a mother. He didn't know exactly why. But his mother was instrumental in shaping him into a decent husband. She encouraged his ambition and told him to expect a reward that was well deserved. Though Noah wondered at times if he would recognize a reward when it arrived. So he continued to work hard, never acknowledging that all he did well sprung from a deep and saddening wound.

The baby was named Marcus, deliberately chosen because it was not the name of any male in either family. And both Lorraine and Noah agreed their boy child should have his own fresh start.

"He'll stand on his own two feet," Noah was fond of saying.

He loved his new son. He loved Lorraine. If it were possible, Noah worked even harder for his family. During a three-year stretch he pushed Reggie into building a new subdivision in an empty valley north of Petaluma.

"We can do this," he said to Reggie. "I can do this."

"You'll have to," said Reggie. "It's a lot. But if it succeeds, we'll be millionaires."

It did succeed and on Marcus' fifth birthday, Noah flew his family to Disneyland so that Marcus could spend a week in a magic kingdom. Marcus was dazzled but Noah was transformed. Noah now thought himself indefatigable. He was a magician. He could tame seas and build roads through mountains. Certainly some sleight of hand was involved and there was an ethical edge along which all men walked. But Noah knew what he wanted. And he seemed gifted with the knowledge of how to get it.

On the day the first section of Noah's new subdivision was offered for sale, Lorraine asked Noah for a divorce. The passing years that built Noah's wealth had worn out his wife.

"I've done it all," Lorraine said. "I've held a home together. Fucked you on demand. Raised your precious son while you spent all your waking hours of every day away from me. I'm done."

Noah was surprised and shaken, even if he was accustomed to leaving or being left. His limited barometer of emotions could not accommodate Lorraine's acquired and explosive unhappiness. Despite his experience with loss, Lorraine's sudden threat to exit their marriage stirred in Noah a trauma he tried valiantly to hold in. It was the manly thing to do. He thought for a while he was carrying a pain that should belong to someone else.

"I've given you so much," Noah at last said. "Why aren't you happy?"

"Yes, I have so many things," answered Lorraine. "But I don't have you."

Noah thought himself an anchor to Lorraine, without noticing through the years that his wife was learning she did not need an anchor. She wanted wings. So Noah was left without a clue though if he looked there were clues everywhere.

Lorraine agreed to joint custody of Marcus so that Noah's son could still live part-time with his father though Noah had no idea how to parent his young, angry boy. Which mystified Noah who really did think himself a magician, a man with the protean power to move the earth and always find a way to make things work.

Though it was at last clear to Noah that the people in his life were not things. There was, instead, a kind of work he could not grasp or understand. And so, since he knew himself so well, he continued to walk comfortably along the edge which all men walk. It was the legacy of the absent father, which Noah knew as a hard life but one not as hard as life without a mother. Though he did not know why.

The loss of his father left him with the weight of a mother he could no longer carry.

Noah faced the rattling challenge of a failed intimacy. He was a big and gangly man and probably hard to sleep with. He was indirect when he said anything at all. He could not sustain love and also succeed in business. He made his living by pleasing others in ways that left nothing for those he presumably loved. Marcus sensed this and in the days and years that followed became a testy antagonist who challenged all his father had sought forcefully to build. Marcus misbehaved at school. He fussed furiously until given whatever he wanted. He spat at friends and challenged his enemies. By age seven Marcus was an identifiable problem, a child with too many places to be and not comfortable in any of them. Noah quickly ran out of magic and, instead of battling in the name of love, acquiesced too easily to his son's whiny whims. By the time Marcus was ten, Noah had accepted his son's wildness as a strain of his own character.

"At least I'm here for him," Noah said to himself as trouble began to brew.

But when trouble brewed, Marcus—just like Noah's father—ran from him and would not return.

"Marcus is a good boy," Lorraine said to Noah. "You are the failure. You are what drives him into despair and bad behavior."

Noah did not argue. Even as he heard his ex-wife speak resentments he knew were exclusively hers, he also knew what she said was true. He was accustomed to leaving or being left. The wondrous gain of his life was inexplicably driven by perpetual, inevitable loss.

four

Noah married Lorraine during Ronald Reagan's last term as governor. Their divorce was final in the first year of Reagan's presidency. Noah survived by keeping the home. Lorraine might have kicked him to the curb but a savvy attorney told Noah to stay put. When Lorraine at last moved back to live with her parents, the home became Noah's in exchange for a hefty settlement payment to his now ex-wife.

Noah knew what he wanted and also what he did not want. He did not want any further trouble with Lorraine and so discouraged any further contact. It was a trial for his already wounded son who could not grasp why his parents, who both said they loved him dearly, would not speak to each other. Marcus continued to act out and one night Noah received a phone call from Lorraine.

"Your son's in jail," she said curtly. "You might want to do something about it."

"Why me?" asked Noah.

"Because he hung up on me and told me to go to hell," said Lorraine. "You boys are all the same. So fuck you and fuck Marcus. I'm done."

Noah knew Lorraine had withdrawn from parenting, had at last found her elusive job as a dental assistant and now lived alone in an apartment on the town's west side and near the office where she worked. Marcus had hinted his mother had a lover but when asked could not be certain.

"Anyway, it's a woman," said Marcus. "She comes over a lot and spends the night."

Noah went to the police station where Marcus was in custody for assault and petty theft. He and two high school friends had shaken down a geeky student after school, taken his wallet and left him in a public park without his pants. A witness called the police who found Marcus and his friends before they had traveled two blocks. Marcus was still carrying the boy's trousers.

"Small stuff," said the sergeant. "But the parent wants to press charges."

Marcus was released to Noah's custody.

"We'll take care of this," Noah said to his son. "You're going to live with me now. We're going to have rules."

Noah found the name of the victim's parent from the police report.

"Margaret?" Noah asked tentatively when the woman answered.

"Whose calling?" she asked suspiciously.

Noah identified himself as the father of Marcus, her son's antagonist.

"I want to apologize," he said. "I want to make this right."

"How?" the woman asked after a long pause.

"I'm a local contractor. I can offer you services if you need a remodel or some work on your home. I can also pay you."

"Why?" the woman asked again.

"To make things right," Noah repeated, increasingly flummoxed by all the words he was speaking.

"So your boy was in the wrong?" asked the woman.

"Yes," Noah admitted. "We've talked about it. It will never happen again."

"I'd like the boys to meet," the woman said. "I'd like them to patch this up. My son has no hard feelings but he needs an apology."

"Of course," said Noah.

"And I'm running for county supervisor," the woman added. "In lieu of damages I'd happily accept a campaign donation."

"Really?" answered Noah. "It just so happens…"

"I know who you are," said Margaret. "You're one of the county's builders. We need builders. You bring jobs. Let's get our boys together to settle this thing. There may be more we have to discuss."

Noah recognized the opening. He knew who this woman was. She was Margaret Girard, scion of an old Petaluma family and an attorney preparing a political campaign.

"Sounds good," said Noah agreeably. "I'm interested in the election."

A meeting time was set and Noah explained to Marcus that under the new rules governing his life he would need to take responsibility for all his actions. Noah, now an experienced salesman, offered his son a new opportunity.

"A chance to make things right. A chance to put this behind you. A chance to stay out of juvenile hall."

Marcus knew he had no choice and the thought that so much of life was now quickly and suddenly locked down and out of his control was surprisingly and immediately comforting.

Good things frequently emerged from painful consequences and as much as Marcus dreaded meeting Margaret's son again, he was relieved when the boy named Aaron reached to shake his hand with a firm grasp that conveyed a natural confidence in ultimate repair.

"You into heavy metal?" Aaron asked, connecting instantly with

Marcus who had every album made by *Judas Priest*, *Iron Maiden* and *Slayer*. The boys had met in a park and while Margaret and Noah watched, they wandered off together to share their newly invented friendship.

"He's a good boy," Noah said to Margaret. "It's been hard. The divorce was hard for him."

Margaret nodded in a way that spoke more than words.

"Aaron has a father," she responded. "I wish he didn't. But then, if I hadn't married his father I wouldn't have Aaron. And I love that boy dearly."

Noah realized that, much like him, much of Margaret's good life had arrived from the wrong places. Both bore up under the influence of serious wounds. But both were capable and could think of themselves as important factors in the making of the world.

"Tell me about your campaign." Noah said.

It was enough to open one of Margaret's furiously pumping veins as she poured forth for a half-hour the roots of her political activism in her profession as a social worker and her determination to win election as a county supervisor.

"That's persuasive," Noah responded. "I'd like to help."

His offer registered deeply with Margaret who asked if he would meet her for lunch later in the week.

"Of course," he said. "I could show you the new homes we're building east of Ely."

Later driving home, Noah asked Marcus what he thought of Aaron.

"He's cool," said Marcus.

"What about what happened?" asked Noah.

"It was bullshit. I'm sorry. I told him. And it's cool now. No more bullshit. I'm done with bullshit."

five

Noah's second wedding was different from the first. Marcus was there as the youngest best man anyone could remember. Noah, Margaret and the boys gathered in a judge's chambers for twenty minutes while Marcus' dad married Aaron's mom.

"We'll tell everyone later," Margaret had said to Aaron as they all drove to the courthouse. "It's just time, that's all."

Aaron wasn't surprised and Marcus wasn't disappointed. Noah knew the boys well after two years of sharing the reliable lifts and falls of family life. And Margaret was pregnant just as Lorraine had been. Though Noah knew this was different. Margaret grasped Noah's quiet ways, accepted his vigorous devotion to the work at hand and to the growth of wealth. Margaret lost her election for county supervisor but gained enough visibility to be appointed assistant director of county social services. Noah held her hand through a disappointing loss while Marcus and Aaron started high school. Noah, Margaret and the boys all would live together in a new home Noah built for them on a low ridge of Sonoma Mountain.

Margaret had a good salary and Noah had a successful business. They were a good team in many ways of which only a few were known to Noah. He loved Margaret for her charitable character and community regard and thought she loved him for his fervent and reliable strength.

"You're good man," Margaret said to Noah. "You are a good, strong man. I need that now. I need it more than ever."

It's what Noah knew about himself. So he assumed Margaret understood him well.

"I'm lucky you love me," he said to Margaret though Noah did not believe in luck.

Margaret made her way and living in a world of teeming, fraught and disabling human consequences through which families and children were perpetually at risk. Noah built homes and sold them. And while he often heard from Margaret how families might gather, grow, fight or disperse, he never imagined much beyond the four walls he erected to contain them.

"I'm a carpenter," he said one evening in self-defense as Margaret, slightly drunk from two martinis, quizzed Noah about his social conscience.

"I don't have a conscience," he sputtered after a third drink. "I work too hard to think much about what that means. I'm an honest man. I'm trustworthy. That's as far as I can go. I can't speak for others."

The words did not say all that Noah meant but they were enough for Margaret to shift her thinking and then her feelings and at last her life ever so slowly away from her latest husband. She thought a conscience very important. She thought a life without one must be bereft.

The baby arrived seven months after the wedding. It was a girl and a sister to both Marcus and Aaron who high-fived at the prospect of being identical big brothers.

The baby was named Maura and for slightly more than three years she lovingly and unknowingly held for everyone the center of family life. Margaret and Noah rediscovered their team spirit, even if it came at the cost of their intimacy. Though both were surprised to discover they didn't really miss it. They thought themselves close though it was Margaret who realized their common regard depended on them not becoming too close. A life born from her body kindled more love than Margaret ever wanted to share. Noah sensed this and abided it and never asked why.

At some time after Maura's fourth birthday her mother decided to run again for county supervisor. The incumbent was retiring and Margaret could not resist the encouragement of friends and colleagues to announce her candidacy.

"Not for me decide," said Noah. "Yours completely. Whatever you want I've got you covered."

By that he meant he would care for Maura, pay for the campaign from the accumulated wealth of his successful construction business and enlist others who owed him favors. He would pay the boys' college tuition and monitor their restless undergraduate lives at a local university.

The campaign began just as the world crossed a line into another measured century. Noah could not get used to first writing the number 2 when he dated checks that others would deposit before writing their own for Margaret's campaign. Margaret's late meetings after work increased during the spring. An expensive and experienced nanny now resided at the big house on the hill, vaguely supervised by Margaret and Noah who each had a life fuller than parenting allowed. In turn, the nanny named Alberta supervised Maura who it seemed in just one weekend transformed from a toddler into a child and in time to start school in the fall.

Margaret returned late from her evening meetings and then one night did not return at all. Before dawn Noah phoned Margaret's campaign manager who, half asleep, could not say where she was if she were anywhere.

"Not like her," said Noah. "I'm calling the police."

The manager, suddenly attentive, pleaded with Noah not to get the cops involved.

"It's probably nothing. The campaign meetings often run late. She might have ended up on someone's couch. She'll be in touch, Noah. Just hold on."

Noah did not hold on. The sheriff was a friend whose own campaign Noah had supported.

"If you ever need anything, just call me," the new sheriff told Noah after his election.

Noah phoned him.

An all points bulletin found Margaret naked in her car at the end of a cul de sac three blocks from her home. That was as far as it might have gone but for the naked man with her who, half-drunk, decided unwisely to threaten the reporting officer. An arrest was made which produced a damaging police report that recounted in detail the facts of Margaret's backseat tryst with an assistant district attorney. A day later it was a page one story in the local papers and sensational enough to interest the regional press.

"I can explain," Margaret at last said to her husband.

"I'm not the one who needs an explanation," said Noah. "What about all those suckers supporting your campaign?"

In a week there was no campaign. Within days Margaret was no longer a candidate. Within a month she was no longer living with Noah. Within the year she was no longer his wife.

six

Noah was accustomed to looking up at the sky and not toward any horizon. His father had told him not to ask from others what Noah could get for himself. Though it felt to Noah, when he allowed himself to register a feeling, it felt he was always being left or leaving. It stirred up a trauma deep inside that Noah struggled to hold in. And he did hold it in.

The divorce from Margaret was antagonizing and bitter. Her public exposure cost Margaret all her community currency as a candidate, a social worker, and as a woman. She left her job in social services and then left town, landing at last at an agency in a small city north of Sacramento. Once again, Noah kept the house though he drove to Sacramento four times a month to pick up his daughter and to return her. He loved his children and they loved him. He was a kind man and felt deeply through his own losses an invaluable link to his children. Marcus and Aaron remained friends through the divorce, their adulthoods more immediately significant as they graduated together from college and into separate searches for a destiny.

In the year Maura got her period, Noah closed a deal to build several luxury homes in an exclusive development east of Santa Rosa. Maura the teenager decided she needed more weekends with her new friends in her new town and asked to end the regular visits with her father. Even as it cost him more child support, Noah agreed to holidays and summers for visits with Maura. He would let her have what she wanted but he would not let her go.

That summer Noah broke ground on his latest subdivision while the nation was seized by the new century's first and greatest recession. Banks and businesses failed, workers lost their jobs, and home prices collapsed. Noah knew himself and he would not deny death by avoiding life. He sucked up his losses and watched wearily as his net wealth fell by half, leaving him enough to negotiate his debts and still have enough to plan an escape.

"Isn't it kind of early to retire?" Marcus asked his dad as they shared lunch in the kitchen of the big, empty house on Sonoma Mountain.

"Not retiring, son," said Noah. "I know what I'm doing."

"What's up there?" asked Marcus. "Why are you moving to the god damned boonies?"

Noah could not say, would never say, what others might do or why. But he knew himself well. He knew what he needed now and that was a quiet home somewhere far away.

"I need a home in the woods," said Noah. "This ain't the time to hustle, my boy. This is a time to slow way down and to wait. And you're welcome anytime you want to visit."

Marcus knew his father better than Noah knew his son.

"I worry about you," Marcus said.

"Well, don't," Noah said curtly.

It was the end of their conversation.

Noah spent a month driving the back roads of the north coast before finding a five-acre parcel near the ocean mouth of the Mad River in Humboldt County. An old two-bedroom farmhouse anchored the land, which was flat and weedy with few trees but that opened to a stunning view of the ocean and the constant and sonorous sound of breaking waves.

"To call it a farm is stretching it," Noah told Marcus on the phone. "Previous owners had chickens and a cottage business selling fresh eggs. But the land won't grow anything, which is probably why it's so cheap. House is run down but nothing I can't fix all by myself. And there's a river beach that's pretty wide when the tide is out."

The property was a steal, the owners too poor to negotiate since they were weeks from foreclosure. Noah's low-ball offer was immediately accepted. He wished immediately he had offered even less.

"Bad times hurt everyone," said the realtor who sold the property. Yes, thought Noah. One person's bad time is another's good time. That's business. And Noah knew business and had always had his way with it. It was people that gave Noah trouble. The needs of relationship were unfathomable on many levels and he accepted his failure as a lover and a husband.

Noah's new business was home repair and remodeling. He hung his shingle in the local paper and made a point of having his daily breakfast at a popular cookhouse where the local Rotary club met. In two months he had more business than he needed as well as an invitation to join the club. At the club's annual Christmas party Noah met Millie.

"You're a city boy, aren't ya'?" Millie said directly.

"How do you figure?" asked Noah.

"How you talk. How you look around and notice details," Millie answered. "How you look at me. You have experience. You have class."

"Well so do you, young woman," said Noah. "Want to dance?"

Millie was younger than Noah, some six years younger he later

learned. Millie had a grown child who lived near Mount Shasta. She
had been divorced for a decade

She was a secretary for a Eureka law firm and shared a rental
with another woman. It was near the state college in Arcata. She was
small but voluptuous and her voice flowed like a cool, easy brook as
if she were summoning Noah to an unexplored shore.

"Damn, you're fifteen minutes from my house," Noah said to
Millie.

He invited her over for dinner the following Friday. She did not
leave until Monday and was nearly late for work. Millie forgot about
time while Noah forgot everything that happened before he met Millie. He was possessed in some new way he had not yet experienced.
He could not see to the depths of his affection, could not measure it
or contain it as he had previously. He was nearly sixty and felt like a
schoolboy smothered under a powerful crush. He wanted Millie. He
wanted her to come back and never to leave him. He was wildly in
love; his heart on an unexpected expedition into the frontier of an
inexplicable and, for Noah, little understood attraction.

Millie touched him deeply and all he wanted now was to touch
her back, to swim to her shore and bring her to his. Would she come
willingly? Would she come at all? Such uncertainty was a new experience for Noah. He was accustomed to the structures that defined
a marriage and his place in building them reliably into something
politely referenced as love. He knew love as marriage and marriage
as a residence perpetually in need of repair. With Millie, love was a
devouring conflagration with infinite heat and no shape at all.

seven

Noah had never known himself so well. One morning he
skipped breakfast and Rotary and took a walk on the bluffs
north of Trinidad. He watched the endless formations of
briny ocean foam that swam across the sand and into the wind like
puffy cream and then dissolved with the next approaching wave.

The solitude was beautiful and also lonely. It was what Noah
knew best: himself alone to examine his drives, his vulnerabilities,
his weaknesses and his fears.

He would ask Millie to dinner again. He would ask Millie to come over for the night. He would ask Millie to marry him and live with him forever. He would offer Millie all his love and never ask for anything. It was his specialty, to be the quiet servant until a servant was no longer needed.

"No," Millie said directly.

She had dated Noah for two weeks. It was the most fun she'd had in years until Noah asked her to marry him. Millie didn't even have to think about it.

"I'm never marrying again," Millie told Noah. "One bad marriage is enough. I'll date you for the rest of my life, Noah. You are a sweet, kind man and I do think I love you. But I can't give myself to you. I can't let you take me as your wife."

Millie's words confused Noah. He expected what he had always received from a woman. He expected her to accept his protection and provision. Isn't that what women wanted?

"No," said Millie. "I can provide for myself. What I want is a friendship and a regard shared by equals. I don't want to be taken care of. I don't want an obligation. I want trust, yes. I want a kind, sweet lover like you. But I don't want a husband. No, I don't."

Millie's words were for Noah a sweet and intense pain. He loved her more for her truthfulness even as he suffered the rejection of his proposal.

Noah made dinner and served Millie with gratitude. After two glasses of wine they fell again into bed, their sex already friendly and comforting.

A rainy winter slowed Noah's business but pushed him and Millie closer together as they used every common holiday to align their desires with those of the whole world. Thanksgiving brought Marcus north. That he brought his girlfriend was charming and also interesting to Millie who enjoyed hosting them as his father's girlfriend, a place in Noah's life that needed no explanation. Noah shared Christmas dinner with Millie and her son's family and by New Year's Eve Noah and Millie were at last and again alone together.

"So I have an idea," said Noah as he heard the ball drop on the

TV while he rolled away from his sweet, sweaty, naked, ardent and exhausted Millie.

"I want to build you a house."

"Where?" asked Millie.

"Here," said Noah.

He rose from the bed and returned with a sheaf of papers and a blueprint.

"It's a cottage," he told Millie. "Fits like a glove at the west end of the property. Has a view and access to the river. And, of course, access to me."

"And what's the catch?" asked Millie. "You're up to something."

"I'm up to you, darlin'," answered Noah. "No rent. No lease. It's yours as long as you want it. Since we're dating forever it seems like a wise investment that will save you gas and rent. What do you say?"

"I say you sound serious," said Millie. "I won't marry you, Noah. You know that."

Noah knew.

"You won't be my wife, sweetheart. You'll be my neighbor. You'll be my lifelong neighbor. If I make too much noise you can always call the cops."

Millie had to acknowledge her lover's good will and his eagerness to form it into something that would last. What was the value of a ring compared with what Noah was willing to expend to have Millie near him? So used to wrestling with instincts, Millie was stunned by the evidence of something as concrete as it was novel.

"You'd really build a cottage just for me?" Millie asked.

"I love you, Millie," said Noah. "I'll build for you whatever you want. It's what I can do."

When the cottage was finished, Millie held a housewarming. It was a cozy little house that Noah built and from the beginning Millie felt comfortably at home.

Noah and Millie continued to live apart. They shared their beds, their lives, their deepest fears and most dangerous thoughts and concluded always that they would love one another forever. But they kept their own homes in their particular ways and retreated frequently to remember whom each really was when they were not together. So as their love grew so did their neighborly friendship to a point that both could say comfortably and for the first time that they loved someone very dear, someone so close to them they knew another better than they knew themselves.

AS IF FOR
THE FIRST TIME

one

Loretta entered the empty second floor flat on Capitol Hill. She raced up the stairs ahead of her husband.

" We can see the big park across the street," she shouted. Loretta leaned forward to peer through the living room window. "And five minutes from the University."

Her husband Walt climbed the stairs and said he wanted to see the kitchen. He liked to cook and needed space.

"Huge," said Loretta. "And a big window over the sink. A lot of light. You're sure this is only $160 a month?"

"This is Seattle," said Walt. "It's 1972. There's a recession on. We aren't in California anymore."

Loretta's blue eyes brightened in the room's warm light. Walt stood at the back door. A flight of stairs stretched down to a small, grassy yard.

"I think it's perfect," Loretta said.

"Nothing's perfect," Walt responded.

Two years of marriage had inured Loretta to her husband's habitual negativity. He was a scientist, or at least a scientist-in-training. His skepticism fit well inside a college chemistry lab where he labored to earn a PhD. It was a useless and irritating quality where any other kind of living was concerned. Loretta knew this but indulged Walt as he searched every potential pleasure for its inherent disap-

53

pointment. Loretta, however, had no doubt life was rich, loving and full of delicious surprises.

However firm his reserve, Walt also was strong and big and healthy and he cared for Loretta and supported her. And Loretta was sick. She was weak and very small and the victim of an auto-immune illness that had shadowed her since early adolescence, an illness that tired her and weakened her and that might at some time in the indefinite future actually kill her.

"It's damn near perfect," Loretta replied. "Damn near close enough to perfect."

Walt did not argue. He heard his wife when she needed something. He might resent her ebullient and naïve enthusiasm for experiences with the slightest promise of delight, but he knew better than to deny her senses. Her illness had infrequent but alarming symptoms, which might themselves charge and vivify Loretta's commitment to joy wherever she found it.

Two weeks later Loretta ran down the flat's front stairs to post a sign on the mailbox. It read: The Creightons 1228 15th Avenue East.

For Walt and especially Loretta, the move from Berkeley to Seattle had been one of unsettling promise. The promise was Walt's success securing a prized post-graduate placement at the University of Washington, one that paid their way for two years. Unsettling was the absence of any path for Loretta other than that of housewife to Walt.

"You could volunteer," said Walt. "You could find something to do."

Loretta wasn't sure. With a degree in anthropology from Berkeley she was truly an undergraduate fish out of water. She was tired of studying and would take no more classes. She bargained with Walt for a summer trip to Greece for her and her sister. Six weeks. And she promised to return refreshed and ready to support Walt and his inceptive career.

Alone for the first time since his marriage, Walt spent most all his days at the university, a solitary scientist absorbed in research until a young woman lab assistant asked him to join her for coffee. She was the only woman in the department and among Walt's chemistry colleagues found Walt to be the most attractive. Tall herself, the woman named Sandra could see eye to eye with the slightly taller

Walt, which Walt found vitally intriguing. Within a week Sandra was staying with Walt at his flat, eating his home cooked dinners and sleeping with him.

"Hi," the new neighbor said to Walt. "I think we saw your wife yesterday. She was leaving and…"

"Not my wife," said Walt. "A student. She's working with me. My wife's away."

Walt's initial coolness betrayed his guilt though his neighbor had no reason for suspicion.

"I'm Craig," said the new neighbor, a young man close to Walt's age but nowhere near his height. "We're downstairs. We moved in yesterday."

Craig invited Walt for dinner.

"You can meet my wife, Jeanne, and our boy. He's two. His name's Thomas."

Jeanne Harmon and Craig Halstead had arrived in Seattle via a long summer in Alaska. They were stunned to hear from Walt that he and his wife had moved from Berkeley.

"Our home, too," said Jeanne. "At least it was. Do you miss it? We don't."

Walt brought a bottle of wine that was quickly emptied. Craig found another and opened it. Jeanne cooked in the kitchen and served a pesto-suffused cheese pasta preceded by a tossed salad of fresh greens. Thomas sat in his high chair and banged his spoon on the tray. His fluttering brown eyes searched Walt's face for a response. Walt winced each time the spoon fell, metal hitting metal. Thomas' parents, accustomed to the racket, saw Walt's irritation and intervened.

"My wife will be home in a couple of weeks," said Walt. "Loretta…she's on the island of Crete now. What did you guys do in Berkeley?"

Craig had been a high school history teacher and Jeanne was a student at San Francisco State.

"It's my fault," said Jeanne. "I ran away to Alaska with a girlfriend."

"And I followed her," said Craig. "We were on Douglas Island near Juneau. We made a lot of friends but couldn't find work. It was the summer of '69. Friends wanted us to stay but one of them said 'the winters here are no worse than Chicago's' and that was all we needed to get on the first plane going south. We thought we'd give Seattle a try. We left Juneau at the end of August after getting married in front of the Mendenhall Glacier. What a trip."

Jeanne and Craig, still searching for a country life, had rented a farm cottage east of Issaquah while Craig found a part-time teaching job at the city's uptown community college. Then Jeanne got pregnant with Thomas, a pregnancy that introduced the fearful reality they were too far from work, from a hospital, and from the university Jeanne needed to attend to finish her degree in English literature.

"So here we are," said Craig. "Same as you."

It was not the same. Walt and Loretta were at the moment not a family and likely never would have a baby. Walt was screwing a college lab assistant while his wife did whatever she wanted in Greece. Fall would bring a reckoning. Walt would teach as well as pursue research. Loretta would not need to work but she would want an avocation. She would want to do something besides staying home to clean and cook, though it was what Walt's mother had done so it was hard for him to imagine his wife doing anything else.

After Walt left, Jeanne and Craig quarreled. Thomas would not fall asleep and Jeanne, slightly drunk, lost her temper. Loud yelling followed until the child was at last quiet though his angry outbursts rekindled his parents' unmanaged impatience and resentments. More than an hour passed before Jeanne asked first for forgiveness and then for punishment, which Craig knew to be their sex of rough handling, and even a spanking, while Jeanne spoke to herself an elaborate fantasy and, rubbed, licked and fucked vigorously, at last had her orgasm and then fell asleep.

two

There were times when Craig thought his marriage to Jeanne was like an old scar that would not stop bleeding. Their three years of marriage hurt incessantly and certainly as much or more than it conjured joy. The bleeding, though, had produced a bloom in Thomas who now was the common love of their frequently disunited lives, even as the miracle of his toddling emergence failed to hold his parents in graceful tandem. Jeanne at age 25 was still attempting to finish her undergraduate education. Craig was farther along but still only an adjunct instructor at a two-year college. His day job salary covered rent and expenses while Jeanne worked a few evenings as a movie theater usher.

"We're hippies," Jeanne said frequently. "What do you expect?" "I was hoping for more," Craig responded. "I thought we might climb into the middle class."

And then the fight would begin, Jeanne an advocate for the abused proletariat and Craig the champion of free and competitive markets. At least, that's how it invariably concluded, with Craig and Jeanne pushed to extremes they would never otherwise defend were it not for a powerful and core grievance that drove them into prideful, unconstrained conflict. In their midst lived Thomas, an involuntary and inarticulate witness to his parents' periodic upheavals, stormy arguments, and fierce, loud sex that punctuated their family life.

It was after a fight with Jeanne that Craig first encountered Loretta. Charging out his flat for a quieting walk in the park Craig saw the blonde hair of a woman sitting at the window of Walt's upstairs flat. It was not the student he had seen for weeks and that quite suddenly vanished from Walt's life. The woman in the window turned and saw Craig. She waved, her eyes brightened by the light from a table lamp. She smiled warmly. Craig held up his hand and also waved, eliciting a buoyant smile from the woman in the window.

"Walter loves to bake," said Loretta as she served up helpings of a lamb-based stew and poured it into bowls over scoops of fluffy rice. Even as she stood, Craig saw that Loretta was the shortest person in the room, if he did not include his toddler son. However short, Loretta offered a smile that filled the kitchen. Her eyes, twinkling bright and blue, radiated a warmth that filled Craig to brimming with its kindness.

"But I love to cook. And this little stew is a Greek favorite. It's simple but richly flavored. It's something special to come home and find you have wonderful new neighbors. And with such a cute little boy."

Loretta lifted her wine glass and offered a toast to Thomas whose ingenuous smile lit up the dinner table. Jeanne held Thomas in her lap and offered him a scoop of stew, which he refused by arching his back. Jeanne struggled before releasing him to the floor.

"He's willful," said Jeanne.

"He's charming," said Loretta. "I hope he'll spend some time with me."

It was Loretta's idea to invite Jeanne and Craig upstairs for her first weekend home. She engaged everyone with obvious pleasure, her eyes still as bright as Craig remembered from first seeing her in the window. Conversation flowed through multiplying tributaries, pushed along by Loretta's interest in everyone. They talked about Berkeley, about the university, about the park and the neighbor's dogs and the pick-up basketball games in the alley behind their flat. Craig described the mornings he spent with Thomas at the park while Jeanne attended class. After two glasses of wine Jeanne rambled on about her boring night job at the movie theater and offered Walt and Loretta a free admission. Craig spoke about teaching and his hope for a full-time placement. Loretta described her dreamy week on the isle of Crete that Craig sensed was time spent with someone besides her sister. Walt discussed the chemistry of baking and then brought out a batch of brownies for dessert.

It was a convivial evening until Thomas grew fussy and Jeanne took him downstairs to bed just as Walt rose to clear the dishes.

"I'll see you out," Loretta said to Craig.

As they walked together down the front stairs, Craig took Loretta's arm to support her tentative steps. Loretta reached around Craig's waist and held him firmly. When they arrived at the bottom stair she fell against him and lifted her face to give him a slightly lingering kiss on the cheek.

"Maybe you'd let me join you and Thomas at the park," Loretta said.

"That would be nice," said Craig. "Really nice."

Craig left with a sense of something barely under construction. It was the kind of thing he might expect to arrive in a projection or a dream. It was the feeling of a desire to convey something and also the feeling of an intention to be understood. He could not say exactly what it was. But he knew it emanated from Loretta and that it involved a past, a present and a future. The brief kiss had given Craig a taste of Loretta's breath. It could just as well have been her soul.

three

It was Monday morning and after sending Jeanne off to her classes, and hearing Walt start his motorcycle and leave for school, Craig rang Loretta's doorbell. She answered, her hair wet and a towel wrapped around her small, sturdy body.

"We're going to the park," said Craig.

Thomas sat next to him in his stroller.

"I wondered if you'd join us, but I see…"

"Give me ten minutes," said Loretta. "I'll find you."

"We'll be in the playground," said Craig. "We'll…"

"I'll find you," Loretta said again, her eyes sharp and clear as if a new pleasure had been delivered to her doorstep.

Later she arrived at the playground and found Craig sitting on a bench. She sat down next to him, a hand lingering on his knee as she struggled to sit and to steady herself. Craig thought the touch similar to Loretta's kiss on his cheek.

"Beautiful morning, don't you think?" asked Loretta with no expectation of an answer. "I love the summer mornings here. Long, warm days. Do you ever go down to the Public Market? I take the bus and shop there on Wednesdays. Would you and Thomas join me?"

In fifteen minutes Craig and Loretta had their first planned escape together. It was an escape and not an errand. When Craig mentioned checking with Jeanne, Loretta smiled.

"Why bother her about it?" she asked. "We will surprise her with something."

Whatever her meaning, Craig visualized a passage outside his marriage. It was a slender passage; a bus trip downtown and back and in daylight and with Thomas on his lap the whole way. He realized the passage would be the same for Loretta. Our little secret, he thought before also imagining it to be their first secret. And perhaps that's what she meant. It would be an experience Loretta and Craig would give to each other beyond or, perhaps, in place of the habitual loyalties given to their spouses. For an irresistible moment Craig imagined this slender passage as a widening, lengthening path.

"Sure," answered Craig. "Jeanne likes surprises."

Loretta smiled out the window of the bus while Craig held Thomas whose eyes wandered wildly.

"Big adventure for him," Craig said to Loretta. "He'll be tired later."

Loretta turned to look at Craig, her eyes lively with a pleasure drawn from an impenetrable depth.

"So will I," answered Loretta. "We'll all need a rest."

They arrived at the Public Sanitary Market at the foot of Piner Street and walked among the stalls where polished fruits and vegetables made ribbons of brilliant color in their orderly, appealing rows and geoducks glistened as big as hams.

Loretta purchased a pound, her bright eyes clear and brilliant and at work wondering how she might cook them and make their raw toughness into a pleasure: hot and steaming with cream and shallots. Crowds wandered around them like schools of swimming fish and while Craig and Loretta acted busy, they weren't. Loretta bought a cookie for Thomas who sat regally on his father's shoulders and munched happily while spilling crumbs down his father's shirt.

"Here," said Loretta, and pulled Craig and Thomas into a small bistro named Place Pigalle where she ordered small glasses of a fruity wine for her and Craig and a strawberry soda for Thomas.

"We have a lot in common," Loretta told Craig. "Two Bay Area fugitives trying to make a life in Seattle. How is yours going?"

Craig heard Loretta say two fugitives and not four as if to exclude their spouses.

"Reasonably well," said Craig. "It's been a rough landing but I've got this sweet little guy to show for it."

"Rough landing?" Loretta responded. "Mine, too."

Frank words followed as if each had been waiting for years to say something scary and truthful to another who might listen. Their marriages were the source of all their awareness, joys and troubles. Walt proposed to Loretta at a moment when she had few prospects and less resistance and when the symptoms of her illness flared into view in a way that frightened her.

"I'd just graduated from college," she said. "And I had nothing else I could do and nowhere else to go. Walt had a plan. I just didn't realize until we were here it was his plan and not ours."

Craig and Jeanne had no plan.

"I followed her to Alaska," he said. "I had no idea what we were doing. I grew a beard. That was my new identity: rough and wild. But we were city slickers at heart. When we got here we had stopped running. We were in love. But what did that mean? We were scared and decided to prove our love by having a baby. But that hasn't proved anything."

"Still, we love them, don't we?" Loretta asked.

"Of course," said Craig.

Later Craig and Loretta walked together through the market like blessed, undaunted saints while shuffling change to beggars and laughing only at themselves. Thomas drew glances and stares and then the presumptuous kind words of a seller who said to Loretta "your child is so cute and looks so much like you."

"I'll put Thomas down for his nap," said Craig when they entered the downstairs flat.

"May I help you?" asked Loretta.

Thomas was at first fussy in his small bedroom, cuddled between Craig and Loretta who lay together with him until he fell asleep and they arose, still together, to find another room and another bed. There were few words and all of them expected. It would be the experience for both of an old, ancient attraction, perhaps the first each had really known in a way that might be shared with another. There are as many kinds of kisses as there are lovers but for Craig and Loretta there was only one that mattered and it was the kiss that, when their bodies found their chance, caused both to reel and also to cleave.

"Are you OK?" Craig asked as Loretta sprawled beside him, half-naked and still, her skin pink with a flush brightened by an afternoon overcast pouring through the window.

"Never better," she answered.

She smiled. She reached for Craig and pulled him back down to her. He quickly tired and attempted to lift himself but Loretta would not let him go.

Walt and Loretta owned a large, blue Chevrolet van. It was parked in the driveway and used by Walt to get to school during the rainy weather and by Loretta when she needed to run errands. And suddenly there were errands, so many errands, as Loretta left to find Craig after his classes and to drive him into a forested county park east of Issaquah where they climbed into the back and made urgent, thrilling love.

The second and third times Craig was forceful and needy, which Loretta welcomed as he blanketed her body with kisses then took her from behind and expressed in hard thrusts the intemperate resentment he still held for his complicated wife. Loretta did not mind since she was unaccustomed to such ravishing attention. Walt was a subdued, usually silent, lover and Craig's loud and verbal comes were a lovely and endearingly unselfconscious performance.

"God, you thrill me," he shouted at Loretta. "God, god, god…" until Loretta felt the full throttle of his ecstatic tension that she comfortably timed to the release of her own. It was perfect. It was sex in the afternoon in the most absurdly juvenile and yet also thrilling way possible. And it belonged to them in a way nothing else did.

"You know something about me I don't myself," Craig told Loretta as they snuggled under a blanket in the back of the van.

"We're still searching, aren't we?" asked Loretta not expecting an answer. "I think we have something beautiful. I hope it lasts."

They spent the drives home talking about their spouses. They loved them. And both Craig and Loretta loved Thomas. Jeanne was becoming one of Loretta's close friends and Craig enjoyed the times he found them together in the kitchen drinking coffee and making plans. Loretta volunteered to watch Thomas when Craig and Jeanne struggled with their schedules, which meant Craig saw ever more of Loretta. Each weekend the couples had dinner together. Each Monday Craig and Loretta met in the backyard to plan what time they might steal together from the week ahead.

By the end of September their lovemaking had become more than sex as it hovered wildly at the limits of resentments and anguish grown from hard marriages. Loretta endured Walt's furtive, hurried attentions. Craig was a husbandly beast that squandered copious amounts of sexual attention on his repressed wife who, if not frigid, could be firmly and unpredictably demanding. It had been less than a year since Jeanne learned at last to masturbate to orgasm, something that still took the better part of an hour to achieve which was nothing like Loretta who could come sitting on the bus to market, simply by rhythmically squeezing her thighs while Craig stroked the nape of her neck.

Craig and Loretta now had more sex together than they had with their partners. Loretta thought their secret loving both beautiful and funny. She was at one and at home with everything Craig's body drove into her. And Craig never before had experienced such thoughtless, unencumbered delight.

Your inexhaustible appetites so effortlessly contain mine, Craig wrote to Loretta in a secret birthday card. Loretta opened it as they lay naked and swaddled under a blanket on a bed in the full basement beneath the downstairs flat. The fall schedule had both Jeanne and Walt away in the mornings for classes at the university. On Tuesdays and Thursdays Thomas had a play date from ten to noon with a preschool friend down the street. A broken, uncovered window above them framed a busy walk along the side of the house and bathed their warm and primal loving in a white, opaque daylight. Later, they would pick up Thomas and give him lunch. In October they cheered as their formerly hometown Oakland As won a World Series. On Halloween they escaped to buy pumpkins for everyone to carve. Their family errands sustained their marriages with efficiencies and comforts that more than covered for the long, cosseting hours away from home.

It was within these vaguely accountable hours that Craig and Loretta existed as unique partners, sex at the source but also the founding of a much larger feast.

"I love you," Loretta said one especially delicious morning in the basement bed. "I love you, too," Craig answered immediately.

"If we can love anyone, we can certainly love each other," said Loretta.

"It's a free country," Craig responded as they wrapped themselves naked in a giddy, exhausted embrace.

It was not a free country. All their loving was confined to the spaces in the day they selfishly preserved as their own. They did not imagine how they might ever fall asleep together at night and awaken together in the morning. And they loved their spouses and said so often. But Craig and Loretta loved them with a dutiful commitment so different from their urgent attraction for each other. It was as if Walt and Jeanne existed as some other kind of collective comfort that described whatever marriage was, but not in any way that could justify adultery.

During the Christmas holidays Loretta and Walt left to visit their families in the Bay Area. For a week Craig felt frozen, empty and bereft and fought needlessly with Jeanne over a range of bewildering trivialities that included when to open presents and where to take Thomas to see Santa. When Loretta returned with Walt, Craig and Jeanne hosted a dinner downstairs at which the lovers could only signal with their smiles that all was well. It would be another week before the university's classes resumed and Craig and Loretta, returning to the basement bed, renewed their covert vows.

At times they were a storm, two fronts colliding over a plain in a thunderous discharge. At others they were tender and amused, playing for an hour—when they could find one, when Thomas was down for his lengthy afternoon nap—and never tiring of their curious, crafted touches. Light poured through the window, grey and opaque in the winter and, as spring took hold, dark with sharp shadows and warm with the approach of summer. Loretta writhed on the basement's small daybed like a soporific kitten, slipping slowly under Craig to feel his body heat as he felt hers. They could be still, calm and close without movement, at least for a while. Confined within their afflictive yearnings they found moments of vast, blue sky.

A year passed. It was a year of well-managed and resourceful disappearances. The days Jeanne took her turn as primary parent, Craig would budget time to hold office hours at the college. Though there were no such hours. All were spent with Loretta.

Shopping was the best excuse and Jeanne was happy for the trips

Craig and Loretta took with Thomas, which gave her time to work and study. The lovers still understood they loved their spouses and looked after them. Craig now took such pleasure in his life that he had that much more to give to Jeanne. He came to understand her sexual need for submissive punishment and increasingly managed it with subtle, even affectionate, grace. In turn, Jeanne was more patient with their spousal quotidian and much to Craig's delight became a better friend to Loretta.

"I could," said Loretta one morning in the basement. "I could go away with you."

"And how?" asked Craig, as they both realized how crushed they might be under the heavy clouds of a frightening intention.

"We know what we know and who we are," said Loretta. "We hold nothing back. Each morning together is ours alone and the only thing I would want to have if we never again were to live."

"But we do continue living," answered Craig. "As much apart as together."

five

Were adultery still a crime, Craig and Loretta would have been its exemplary and incorrigible offenders. Every contagious moment together affirmed for both that their loving sex was as natural as a sunrise. On Craig's birthday, he received a call at work from Loretta who asked him to meet her for lunch at a downtown hotel. Craig arrived to discover she had taken a room with a view on the seventh floor and ordered the delivery of a cake and champagne. He entered the room to find her naked in bed. He joined her and together they lounged, played and fucked away the afternoon, both returning separately to their homes and spouses and in time for all to attend a birthday dinner prepared by Jeanne.

"We are pretty naughty," Loretta said to Craig after dinner and as he walked her into the backyard and patted her ass as she climbed to the upstairs flat.

"We are the same," said Craig. "Jeanne and Walt—they're the ones who are different."

Loretta turned on the stairs. Her eyes reflected the sparkle of light from a streetlamp.

"Were we each other's sex we might be interchangeable," Loretta said. "As it is, we can't budge. We don't need to."

Craig took Loretta's words to bed with him and as Jeanne honored his birthday with one of her rare efforts to initiate sex, he wondered how the turn of time had brought him to Loretta but in a way that made a marriage impossible. Both had already married, and so young and so quickly. Craig and Jeanne had a baby. Craig felt himself caught in a wildly complex and deepening web that would have frightened him were he not so selfishly grateful.

"When I'm angry with Jeanne, I simply imagine you and a life without her," Craig said to Loretta one afternoon.

There were times Loretta said the same about Walt but these times were rarely synchronized. It was if the two lovers built empty bridges across the distance between them while each waited for the other to take the next step. These useless bridges were comforts as one year passed and another began. And waiting to cross became a luxurious habit that perpetually postponed their unfinished intentions.

On a late fall afternoon Loretta announced at a dinner with Jeanne and Craig she was volunteering at a local Free Clinic.

"Women's reproductive health," she said. "I'm going to assist with services."

She would be working three days a week and, even if the time did not conflict with her mornings with Craig in the basement, it was a surprise that would strain the already tightly strung seams that hid from others their secret time together.

"We'll be fine," Loretta whispered to Craig as she stood with him in the kitchen. "I've needed to get moving on a job track and this is a start," she said. "I want to be free."

Free from what? thought Craig. From Walter? From me?

As it turned out another tyranny ruled Loretta's life. It was her autoimmune illness that was now diagnosed as lupus. And though the implications were potentially severe, Loretta's doctor took an optimistic view.

"This shouldn't interfere with your daily routines," said the doctor in a way that alerted Loretta to the fact she had no daily routines outside the maintenance of her home or beyond the pleasures provided by her invisible time with Craig.

"I need something that counts," she said to Craig who could easily have taken her words the wrong way. But he loved Loretta too much to hear any hint of dismissal.

"Tell me how I can help," he said. "I want for you all that is possible and only what will make you happy."

It was more than what she heard from Walt, who at first worried he might come home some nights to a dark apartment and leftovers.

Life continued but adjustments were needed. Their pleasure with each other existed nearly as another lover in their relationship.

And occasionally they took surprising risks. One morning after Walt left for school and Jeanne took Thomas to the park, Craig climbed the back stairs and slipped naked under Loretta's warm covers just as she stirred. They took together a thrilling rapture from the brash violation of a marriage bed.

"You ought to be with me," Craig said. "We should be married and not to them."

"I dream of waking up with you," said Loretta. "I so want you. I so want you all to myself."

But even as each said what they wanted, they never discussed how it might happen.

One evening Walt worked late at the lab while Loretta gathered a group of women from the clinic who first shared a potluck and then submitted to speculum exams of their vulvas. After the women left, Craig told Jeanne he would take an evening walk and then rushed upstairs where Loretta gave him a flashing view of her cervix in a way that left them crouched over and half-naked in the kitchen until they heard the popping growl of Walt's motorcycle. Craig barely had time to pull up his pants and escape down the front stairs.

At times their urgency was inconvenient. At times it was funny. But it was never a worry. Until one afternoon Loretta saw Jeanne drive away and came downstairs to find Craig. She knew Thomas would be napping. The lovers fell onto the living room sofa and hurried to have what they now drolly referred to as "a quickie." Until the lock on the front door jiggled and the two looked up, their bodies linked, naked and pink, to see Jeanne standing before them.

six

There would be a reconciliation of spirit with nature. The desire shared by Craig and Loretta was immediately exposed but not its truth, not its months of cultivation or its secret verities. Though they both were hot and exposed, neither gave up their freedom to Jeanne.

"I'm so sorry," Loretta said to Jeanne as she grabbed her coat and raced into the kitchen to escape through the back door.

"So what is this?" Jeanne at last asked Craig as he pulled up his pants and moved from the couch to a chair.

"And how long?"

"Not long…" answered Craig.

"Just today," he lied. "It was sudden and unexpected. I'm sure it's my fault but…"

"I'd like to hear from Loretta," said Jeanne. Even if shaken, she was surprisingly calm.

Craig saw his chance.

"I'll get her," he said and raced out the back door before Jeanne could object.

He found Loretta upstairs. In five minutes they had their alibi. It was all so sudden, surprising and unexpected. They hadn't realized how attracted they were to each other. They were so sorry. They could understand how this would hurt Jeanne and they loved Jeanne. They both loved her deeply. They had no time to think it through. They begged her forgiveness.

Jeanne sat in the living room when Craig and Loretta returned. She held the just awakened Thomas on her lap and bounced him on her knee.

"I'm pretty fucking pissed," Jeanne said directly.

"What do you want?" asked Loretta. "It will never happen again."

After telling one lie, another was easy.

A turgid moment passed without words. Jeanne looked out the window and back again at her husband and good friend.

"It will happen again," she said calmly. "And I can't stop it. Just don't leave me out. Don't hide yourselves from me."

And Jeanne began to cry. Loretta jumped to comfort her, throwing her arms around Jeanne's shoulders before speaking directly to Craig.

"We need some time," Loretta said to Craig. "Can you give us some air?"

Craig understood a metamorphosis was underway and that as a lover to two women, two women who were close friends, he could only wait. He slipped on his shoes and left.

"What can you tell me?" Craig asked.

He stood in a phone booth outside a neighborhood tavern six blocks up the hill. After two hours sipping a single beer he at last reached Loretta who had just returned to her flat.

"She doesn't need us to stop," Loretta said. "She just doesn't want to be left out."

"And what does that mean?" asked Craig.

"She wants to be around when we make love," said Loretta.

"Even if she's in the kitchen and we're in the basement."

"And how do you feel about that?" asked Craig.

"I think I'm up for it," she said. "I respect Jeanne. It might be easier for all of us."

"All of us but Walt," said Craig. "How does he fit in?"

"He doesn't, of course," answered Loretta. "He never will."

The first time was the hardest as Craig and Loretta tentatively reckoned with the idea their bodies together were not their own and that Jeanne, present and available, had a vested interest in their intimacy. The next morning Walt left for the lab and Loretta drifted downstairs to have coffee with Jeanne and Craig until, at some familiar brush in the kitchen Loretta collided with Craig and they fell into an embrace.

"Is this it?" asked Jeanne from the living room. "Is this how it starts?"

Loretta nodded, her arms still around Craig.

"Well, don't mind me," said Jeanne.

She was not sarcastic. She meant it.

Craig and Loretta looked at each other and together disappeared down the stairs to the basement. An hour passed and when they returned, Jeanne was waiting.

"I heard you," said Jeanne. "It sounded...lovely."

Loretta smiled.

"You have a sweet husband," she said to Jeanne. "Thank you."

The women appeared to have some understanding not yet shared with Craig.

"What if next time I join you? I'd just watch," asked Jeanne.

"You want to be with us? Be there with us?" asked Craig.

Hearing her need expressed directly at first embarrassed Jeanne. But Loretta nodded yes.

"It's no problem," said Loretta. "I think it might be fun."

Craig said nothing but nodded his acceptance.

It was a tentative beginning but one with lasting effect. Within a week Jeanne not only watched but also engaged, also naked and hot and aroused. Hers was one body among three as she found her place. She was both arbiter and disciplinarian, comfortably attractive to both Craig and Loretta while also a director of their pleasure. Jeanne asked not just for what she needed but also for what she wanted. And often her desire translated into orchestrations of sexual love that Craig and Loretta were happy to perfect and to perform.

Despite the pleasure of performing, Craig and Loretta still needed their own renewal. And so they continued their deception, but a deception now contained within a larger deception. They would still steal time together when Jeanne was gone. They would still ride the bus to the market and still rock Thomas on their laps. They would still drop into the basement when Jeanne was in class. They still believed their connection to be unique and still their very own, even as Jeanne shadowed them, embraced both and at times sought her own time alone with Loretta, which Loretta was happy to give. Where arousal was concerned, where the sensual met the sexual, there was little if nothing that Loretta did not find arousing.

Far outside this knotty, perplexing web was the life of Walt, Loretta's husband whose sexual demands were minimal and pedestrian but whose emotional needs were complex and sometimes severe. He demanded that Loretta provide gourmet meals in the evenings. He held out portions of his pay as an allowance for Loretta that she was to use to buy groceries and supplies with little left over. At some point she bargained with Walt for an allowance that he reluctantly granted, overcoming some innate suspicion she would spend it frivolously or violate his trust. So it was reasonable for Loretta to find in time the autonomy she could not have with money.

Walt appeared every weekend at their common dinners, helped Craig with the yard chores, celebrated with his wife and the family downstairs all their birthdays and their holidays, and drove with them on ski trips and vacations. And Walt had no idea what intense and arousing links existed around him and without him.

"I love you and I also fear you," Loretta said one morning to Craig.

Craig would later understand her words as a prescient worry.

"Do we take all this lovely erotic vitality for granted?" she asked. It was an entitlement without a founder, as if it bore nothing more than the pleasure it gave while together they ignored profound attachments that slithered like vines across their hearts and bodies.

"We now often have all day," said Craig. "It is a convenient devotion we share with each other and also the daily soaps."

He knew, but did not say, they were the makers of perpetually satisfying outcomes even as they tore everyone's trust to shreds.

seven

Craig remembered it later as a sort of lover's quarrel. Walt was called away for a conference that required him to be gone over a Saturday night. Loretta saw her chance to spend a night exclusively with Craig. To fall asleep with him and feel him next to her through sleep and then awaken with him, linger and then feed him a lovely breakfast.

It would be a chance for Loretta and Craig to play house but Jeanne was having none of it.

"Without me?" she declared resentfully.

"Who cares for Thomas?" Craig asked foolishly.

"Oh, I'm the nursemaid? I'm expendable," Jeanne said. "What

about us?"

"That doesn't change," said Loretta. "It's just…"
She could not finish a sentence that did nothing but describe her earnest need to fulfill a fantastic hope; one held so long that Jeanne would never understand.

"Just one night alone together," pleaded Loretta. "Please. It's what you have all the time with Craig and what I never have."

"Fuck you," Jeanne muttered and left for her class.

When she returned, Craig and Loretta were sitting in the upstairs flat having dinner with Thomas

"You keep Thomas," said Jeanne when she came upstairs. "You have a really good time."

And she left

Thomas slept on the couch while Craig and Loretta slept in the bedroom. Though they did not sleep. They were together an entitlement without permission and for one night spent every delicious moment aligned and in love. Thomas found them in the morning, sprawled and enfolded in a quiet, amorous repose. Thomas climbed between them and into their common and enveloping grip of a poignant, if unrecorded history. It was for both Craig and Loretta the perfect moment, one they might have only once while also wishing it might last forever.

Jeanne, however, was deeply hurt, which emerged as resentment and anger despite the best efforts of first Loretta and then Craig. A chill surged into existence that kept everyone apart until Loretta exhibited the serious symptoms of her illness: a butterfly rash across her face, sudden and debilitating fatigue, nausea, and painful, swollen knees. Jeanne was the first to rush upstairs to Loretta, hoping to make amends but, instead, she encountered Walt who had taken a week away from his studies to be the gatekeeper of his wife's serious, if not unexpected, symptoms.

"It's not the first time," Walt told Jeanne wearily. "Her rheumatologist has prescribed some steroids. They've helped before. Meanwhile, she's out of it for now. And she needs rest."

Jeanne asked to see her.

"No," said Walt. "I'll let you know when she's better. A few days. I'm taking her to the clinic tomorrow. After that, she'll need some more rest."

A week passed and at last arrived at the morning Walt returned to school, Craig the first to climb the stairs to Loretta after he heard the rumbling departure of Walt's motorcycle.

"I'm better," said Loretta, now sitting at the kitchen table. "I've been sick," she said. "I've also been pregnant. I'm not anymore."

"You…what did you say?" Craig asked.

"You heard me," said Loretta. "I'm not pregnant anymore."

"Who?" asked Craig.

"I can't say," answered Loretta. "I made certain I would never know. My doctor has had me off the pill for nearly two months. I thought I could manage it. Obviously I didn't. There doesn't seem to be much I can manage right now."

Craig reached to embrace Loretta. She pushed him away.

"No….not now….I can't now, Craig. I don't know what I need or want. Please…tell Jeanne there are no hard feelings. I'm tired. I need to sleep."

Craig walked her to the bedroom and helped her into bed. He lay with her until she fell into a deep, still sleep.

Loretta had snared every possibility left in the shadow of her disease and its uncertain and grave prognosis. Craig left her with his memory of her eyes that radiated for more than a year, so bright, so beautiful and penetrating and yet, at last and finally, utterly elusive. Was this the end? Loretta's love appeared so close to the surface and it was given always, though Craig wondered now if a love so easily shared might also be a love easily and quickly lost.

"It's a big fucking deal," Jeanne said to Craig. "Walt has an offer from a lab. When he finishes at UW this summer he'll go to work for Dupont."

Craig asked where Dupont was.

"Delaware," said Jeanne. "That's what he told me."

"A good job?" asked Craig.

"Yeah…forty-five grand a year to start," Jeanne answered. "He's pretty blown."

It had been more than a week since Craig had seen either Loretta or Walt, a time during which he fell with Jeanne back into the parental and also resentful alliance that was the source of all their common feelings. Without Loretta's presence there was no urge to wrestle with their difficulties, only a need to have them.

The following morning Craig heard Walt's motorcycle start up and leave. He ran up the backstairs and entered an unlocked door. "He's offered to pay for it," said Loretta. "All the schooling I need to become a registered nurse. What can I say? He's my husband."

Craig understood. And why wouldn't he? He could love Loretta more than anyone else in the world. But he could not offer what her husband offered. He could barely support his own fledgling family.

"So you're going to go with him?" Craig asked Loretta.

"It's not to say I have a choice," answered Loretta.

"We always have choices," said Craig.

He knew but could not say that he and Loretta and Jeanne were all partners in Walt's new opportunity and that Loretta, despite her protests, had made her choice.

"When will Walt begin with Dupont?" Craig asked coolly.

"The fall sometime," Loretta answered. "I don't know, Craig."

Craig felt the impact of another encircling breakdown. Like misfiring engines, he and Loretta mishandled a moment that required their devoted complicity.

He reached for her. He kissed her. He held her and felt her involuntary arousal. They fell. They opened. They rolled into the deepest crevice of their cultivated and erotic vitality as if it were an endangered trust. And how surprised and happy they were to discover this, how fatally relieved even in the wake of all their ensuing sorrow.

eight

Craig could not remember when he first suggested to Jeanne they move back to California. He found on a map the small town of Arcata anchored to a large bay on the state's northern coast. It was home to a state university.

"I could get my masters and you could finish your degree," he said to Jeanne.

In some way he could not explain, Craig now competed with Loretta for an opening, an opportunity, for something that would counter a dreaded and inevitable loss with something new on the ground. Unlike Walt, he had no lucrative job offer. Unlike Loretta, he had the freedom to choose his own path out of love.

Craig took a long weekend and drove south to visit the small town north of Eureka and to visit its university campus. He slept inside his Volkswagen and showered in the school gym. He met with a professor who liked him and shared his interest in American history after Reconstruction.

Craig returned to report to Jeanne a host of wondrous positives. He brought college applications and a phone number of the English department chair that, he promised Jeanne, would be happy to speak with her. He also brought a page of rental listings from a local newspaper.

A ten-hour return drive gave Craig the time to plan a sadly wondrous escape from Seattle that thrilled him with its competent generation until, arriving at home he found Loretta in the backyard planting daffodils.

"Was it a good trip?" Loretta asked ruefully.

"It was fine," said Craig. "It was good and also terrible. I can have a new life. So can Jeanne and Thomas. But whether or not we do this, I can't have you."

Loretta stood and fell against his chest. Craig cradled her. He did not care who saw them. He did not worry, even if Walt appeared out of nowhere and, towering over Craig, threatened to kill him.

"I love you, Loretta," Craig said through an embryonic sob.

Next steps were a welcome preoccupation for everyone, except for Walt who needed no preoccupation. He had the promise of an actual and lucrative occupation and that was enough. For Loretta, Craig and Jeanne there were no more trysts in the basement and no more secrets at Walt's expense. No more intimate touches and no more assumptive pleasures that could be written off in the moment since every moment now led inevitably to the end of all their moments together. Passion first froze and then melted slowly into an affiliating and neighborly good will.

Until one afternoon, with Jeanne at school and Walt at the lab, Loretta and Craig walked Thomas to the park to sit and watch him play.

"It's a mess, isn't it?" Loretta said when Thomas left to climb on the monkey bars.

"We all have something new now," said Craig.

"Except Walt," said Loretta. "He's the only one of us with a bird in the hand."

"He's your husband, sweetheart," said Craig. "That bird is in your hand, too.

There was a long, gawky pause.

"Did we each marry the wrong person?" Loretta at last asked.

"Are they the wrong people…or are we?" asked Craig.

A morning in June arrived with a last spring burst of northwest rain while Craig packed a U-Haul truck with luggage and furniture. He and Jeanne had their letters of acceptance from Humboldt State University and had signed a lease for a duplex near the campus. Craig would drive down first with Thomas to set up house and to follow up on leads for a secondary teaching job. Jeanne stayed behind in Seattle to finish her summer studies. At the season's end she would drive down to join Craig and Thomas.

We languished in a fruitless mélange of aimless habits, Craig wrote to Loretta. *We hibernated until everyone was out of sight for the time it took once again to exquisitely die. So real it was to be crushed under heavy clouds of our frightening intentions and to hold nothing back as if we were never again to live.*

He did not mail the letter. Before the end of July Craig was offered a teaching job at a small rural high school—two periods of world history and three of American history.

"It was my BA from Cal," he said to Jeanne on the phone. "Still counts for something, especially in the boonies. But don't hold your breath. I'm not making a city salary, though I can cover the rent."

"OK," said Jeanne. "OK…"

Jeanne's words were tentative and without context.

"And how's Loretta?" Craig asked after an awkward pause.

"Not good," answered Jeanne. "Another bout with symptoms. Walt thinks it's the move that's making her sick."

"I'm sorry," said Craig.

"For what?" asked Jeanne.

"Forget it," snapped Craig and ended the call.

Jeanne arrived in Arcata at the end of August. A few weeks alone with each other were enough and, despite Thomas' excitement to have his parents to himself again, they were not happy to have only each other. Within a month, Jeanne and Craig were fighting. In September, Craig signed a lease for a small studio-sized cottage in the dunes of the shaggy and disorderly coastal village of Somoa. While Jeanne was in class and Thomas in pre-school, Craig moved out. When his phone was installed he first called Jeanne to give her the number and then phoned Loretta, not expecting her phone to ring or for anyone to answer.

"Hello?"

Craig heard her attentive voice.

"Loretta?"

"Yes…" she said. She knew him. "It's you."

"Jeanne and I have separated," Craig blurted.

"I'm sorry," said Loretta.

She sounded sincere and also distant.

"We're moving, too," said Loretta. "We leave in an hour. The flat is empty."

A difficult silence passed between them.

"I'm free," said Craig.

"That's nice," said Loretta. "I hope it works out for you."

Love was Craig's freedom as it was also Loretta's freedom and Jeanne's freedom and, eventually, even Thomas' freedom. But as he heard Loretta's distant voice he knew that to link his freedom to another's would always arouse conflict, as it had with Loretta whose dependency on Walt was itself a freedom.

"Maybe you'd write to me," said Craig. He gave Loretta his address and she wrote it down.

"Thanks," said Loretta.

"I still love you," Craig blurted.

"Me, too," said Loretta. "Listen, I have to go."

"Sure," said Craig. "Goodbye, Loretta."

A week passed as Craig struggled to live in the present and to arrange with Jeanne the terms of their separation. Teaching and studying occupied all the rest of his time until one afternoon he returned to his cottage to find at the door a vase filled with red tulips and blue cornflowers with a note dictated to the florist.

Be gentle in your memories of our pleasure and our pain. Love, L.

In a moment Craig understood why he could no longer love Jeanne, could no longer abide her neurosis-driven pain by offering his own in its place. Craig now owned his love and could offer it freely. He surprised himself by thinking he could be for others, and especially for his son, a source of loving experience and still not sow the seeds of his, or anyone's, destruction. Loose ends still existed and would never be tied. Yet love remained an adventure and for Craig his son Thomas was now at its center. Thomas was the child forced to remain in love with the adults who loved him even as they no longer loved each other.

STOLEN KISSES

one

Thinking made life real for Louis. He did not believe he needed even a body to think. He thought and therefore he was. Some scientist must have said that or something like it. It was a validating reference that helped Louis finish his flight to Puerto Vallarta.

He hated the time it took for a plane to descend and to prepare to land. He filled his mind with equations and platitudes to distract him from a turbulent rumble as the plane veered and turned. He heard the pop of wheels sliding into place and, without looking out his window, felt the whoosh of the approach pull him down and out of the sky.

He grabbed the arms of his seat, recklessly pushing away the fingers of an anonymous fellow passenger. He closed his eyes and grimaced while the plane thumped once, and then again, as it hit the ground. The rest was gravity becoming momentum and meeting resistance. As a scientist Louis understood inertia and, if he had five minutes, could have applied a formula to his experience of the plane's landing. Instead, he released his clinched hands and opened his eyes.

"Welcome, Señor Harvester," said a clerk at the desk of the Hotel Rosita. It had been a half-hour ride from the airport, enough time for Louis to at first regret and then to accept his decision to travel alone to Mexico. His friend Johnny told him to do it.

"Take a trip," said Johnny. "Put this behind you. Just have a good time."

Johnny loved Puerto and told his friend about a disco bar on the Beach of the Dead.

"You'll meet beautiful chicks," said Johnny. "You will score."

Which was easy for Johnny to say since Louis' divorce was not Johnny's. And as good a friend as Johnny was, only Louis grasped what a long and burdensome chain of events, experiences, and regrets were attached to his divorce, all of which he wore with him to Puerto Vallarta.

"*I am alone*," thought Louis as he signed the hotel's guest register.

But he was not alone. He lived every waking moment with the recollection of a long and failed marriage and its haunting history of soaring pleasures and desperate sorrows. He parked his bags in his room and went to the bar to drink his complimentary margarita and then order two more. He sat until evening mulling his life's bad choices while he watched a radiant orange sun fall into the ocean. It was late March and a day past the equinox, which allowed Louis to calculate the location of both the earth and the moon and their relationship to the solar system's monstrous, brilliant and life-making anchor.

Louis watched happy couples arrive for dinner. A solicitous bartender offered to order dinner for Louis but he declined.

"Your wife joining you?" asked the bartender.

"No…I'm divorced," said Louis.

"Sorry, Señor," said the bartender.

"At least we didn't have any children," Louis said and the bartender nodded weakly.

"I'm tired," Louis at last announced and stood to leave.

He ordered dinner from his room and when it arrived on a large tray he tipped the young bellhop with a five-dollar bill.

"No pesos yet," said Louis. "I'm sorry."

The bellhop wasn't disappointed.

Louis ate his tepid chicken taco with rice and crawled into bed. His vacation was underway; his great escape to paradise now a dismal, strange and isolating reckoning.

It was late morning before Louis found his way to the beach, which was just out the wide swinging doors at the back of the hotel. He walked a portion of its length and was at last distracted by the smooth, clear aqua blue of the ocean that lapped tenderly against the soft, fine sand under his feet. He passed hotel after hotel and as he approached the city center Louis encountered clusters of umbrellas and tables set out for guests. He wove among them before arriving at the Malécon, an avenue that ran through the town's historic seaside. It was lined with shops and restaurants and for an hour Louis lost himself among the district's attractions and shiny objects, at last finding a restaurant where the waiter spoke comprehensible English. He ordered toast and huevos rancheros and a cup of strong coffee and sat alone at a small table near the door.

Returning along the beach, Louis found his hotel where he encountered three women arguing with one of the hotel's waiters. The women stood in their swimsuits, long beach towels held tightly against their bodies while they shouted at the stiff and intimidated waiter who shook his head while shouting persistently.

"No…No..no es possible…No…No…"

The disturbance attracted Louis' attention and he stopped to watch, which then attracted a lingering glance from one of the women who suddenly ran toward him.

"Americano?" the woman asked quickly. "You staying here?"

She pointed to the Hotel Rosita's back entrance.

Louis nodded.

"We want to use the beach but the man, he says we can't because we aren't guests. Can you help us?"

"How?" asked Louis.

"We could be your guests," she said. "Your friends."

"Are you?" asked Louis. "What else do you want?"

"Nada," said the woman. "If we are your guests we can sit at the tables. We can spread our towels in the sand."

"And your name?" asked Louis.

"Consuela," said the woman that Louis now fully saw. She was young, likely not yet thirty. Her dark hair was long and her eyes a surprising hazel color that brightened against the smooth copper tone of her complexion.

"You speak good English," said Louis.

"I teach it," said Consuela who looked anxiously toward her two friends who looked anxiously toward her.

"Let's go," said Louis who then walked toward the waiter.

"Son mis invitados," said Louis with a few Spanish words from his guidebook. Relief in his eyes, the waiter turned to leave.

"Gracias," said Consuelo.

"Si, si. Gracias," said the other women.

"Would you join us?" asked Consuela.

Was she just being polite?

Louis was older than them all by at least a decade.

"You think an old guy like me would be fun?" asked Louis.

"You come," she said. "You are our special friend."

As he went in his room to put on a swimsuit and to get a towel, Louis did not care if he were simply the newest gringo to tickle the interest of three Mexican women. They were a sudden and lucky distraction. He would have them for an afternoon. He would buy them drinks and lunch.

He was wealthy by any of their measures and was suddenly favored by the gods. Perhaps they would swim together. Maybe Consuela would stay for dinner. Her English was perfect and what did she say? She was a teacher. Even if he had these women only for the day their time with him would be a compelling bulwark against his otherwise unmanageable grief.

two

Awareness of death is a human problem and, being human, Louis continued to imagine his brewing divorce as something of a dying beast, its fetid remnants of property and possibility scattered in a chilling wake. The cool business of settling accounts was all that was left. There were no children and his ex-wife worked so there was no alimony.

"You are one lucky SOB," Johnny had told him. "You got some savings and all your salary."

"And a big mortgage," snorted Louis.

"Your choice," said Johnny. "You wanted the house."

Louis did not think himself lucky. He was without love. He was without a partner to hear his words and learn his feelings and who could pleasingly return them. He could not curb his appetite for warm touches and reckless hugs. It had been a year. Johnny told Louis he was horny and should go out and get laid. Louis said he was lonely and craved companionship. That was when Johnny told Louis to take a trip.

Louis sat under the umbrella of a beach table with all three young women as their time together became quickly and simply time with Consuela. She spoke perfect English and her friends very little. By late afternoon Louis had splashed with them in the ocean, ordered up food and drinks, and invited Consuela to join him for dinner. She left with her friends and returned to the hotel at seven. She wore an azure cocktail dress. Her long black hair was combed into a flourish that framed her narrow face and highlighted her bright, friendly eyes.

"I wanted a different kind of life," Consuela said. "My parents want me to marry. I say no. No husband now. So I learned English and became a teacher. If I have no husband then I must work."

"How old are you?" asked Louis.

"Thirty next year," said Consuela. "Old maid…"

She laughed.

"Anyone ever ask you?" asked Louis.

"Comprometido…" Consuela announced humbly. "One time. But he was like all men. He wanted babies and for me to stay home while he…well…he would work and I would not. I could not do that. I want children someday but only with the right man who gives me, how you say, *space*. Someone who respects me."

"Do you live by yourself?" asked Louis.

"A roommate," answered Consuela. "Angelina. You met her this afternoon. The tall one."

Louis described his life as a scientist in a meandering monologue that funneled eventually down to his life as a husband and ultimately his current life alone.

"You aren't married anymore?" Consuela asked.

"No," said Louis. "Not married anymore."

The release of these words seemed also to release something in Consuela.

"Let me show you around," said Consuela. "*Playa de los Muertos*, the beach at Mismaloya—they made that Iguana movie there, the old church…I have all weekend…"

Over dessert they made a plan. Consuela would pick Louis up in the morning. She would drive.

The rest of Louis' days in Puerto were organized around Consuela's buoyant attention. When the weekend ended he had visited all the local sights but no longer saw anything but Consuela who on Monday returned to her teaching job at the local secondary school. Louis did not have to ask Consuela to see him after work. She arrived at the hotel each afternoon straight from the school to find him waiting for her at a beach table. They ate dinner and took a long walk along the shore. On his last night at the hotel he kissed Consuela who pulled him fast against her. One kiss but that was all. Louis gave Consuela his address.

"Write me," said Louis. "I'll be back."

"I will write," said Consuela. "I hope so."

I think about the future but live for the moment. I think I am serious about living a good life. But what is a good life? Is it to be married? You must know something. You were married. And now you are not. Why? Do we have children to escape thoughts of our death? Death is certainly a problem for me. Do you think about dying? When I had my Quinceañera I thought I was a big girl. I did not know what that was. Boys and men suddenly appeared, all wanting something. You are the first man who sees me, Louis. You are a friend and it makes me happy to have a good friend.

Louis re-read Consuela's letter. He read it again. He folded it and placed it in his wallet so he could retrieve it and read it whenever he wished.

Louis returned to Puerto at the end of the month. Consuela met him at the hotel and took him to her parents' home for dinner. Louis met Pedro and Juanita, Consuela's mother and father. Pedro owned several local properties and sold real estate. Louis met Consuela's sister Mariella and her two older brothers, Pablo and Ignacio. Per his agreement with Consuela, Louis asked Pedro to walk with him after dinner. During their walk he asked Pedro's permission to marry Consuela. Louis explained his divorce was final and that he loved Consuela.

"Where you live?" Pedro asked in his best English. "Estados Unidos?"

"Si," answered Louis. "San Francisco. You come visit. We visit you. Siempre."

"Bebe?" asked Pedro.

"Oh Si," answered Louis. "Si. Si. Si."

Pedro laughed and nodded.

"OK," said Pedro. "Como se dice…OK?"

After dinner Louis gave an engagement ring to Consuela who, as they agreed in their phone call, accepted it in front of her parents. Pedro called in the brothers and poured shots of Tequila for all the men. Consuela drove Louis back to the hotel and walked with him to his room. She was not a virgin, which might have outraged most of her countrymen but that meant nothing to Louis. They were together. They were at last at the transparent and wordless convergence promised by their first encounter. It had been a chance meeting but one now viewed backwards as the perfection of some wildly improbable fate.

"Te quiero," whispered Consuela."Te quiero tanto."

Her words were beautiful and also fearful. Louis felt the assembling imprint of a comforting companionship and also the terms of an eventual intimacy. He ignored the unsettling rumble of large, disparate chunks of experience colliding at some maundering and newly explosive awareness. They would share and abide this, he thought later. Or they would not. For now he held Consuela more closely and more dearly than his own life.

three

Nothing happened for the first time and to be in love was not new for Louis. But in all her responses, from the most distant to the most intimate, it was apparent to Louis his new wife had never loved anyone as she did him. Love for Louis was a kind of infantile amnesia. The more he considered and beheld Consuela the easier it was to forget he had loved anyone else.

And the more love Consuela offered the more she felt. For her there were no comparisons and when she told her husband she was pregnant she announced it with a tearful, heart-riven pride.

"Voy a tener tu bebé," she said.

"Mine?" asked Louis. "You mean ours."

"I still work," she said. "No hay problema."

Louis had found a job for Consuela teaching Spanish to researchers that worked with migrant laborers in California's central valley.

"No…no problema…" said Louis.

Working was not an issue. Louis did not expect his pregnant wife to work, though she did. Consuela in America earned more each day than she did working a week in Mexico. And she liked the money but not the work. Consuela could teach English to Mexicans better than she could teach Spanish to Americans. She had her own car; her own checkbook and Louis' spacious home in the foothills of Oakland that was now also her home and the nest where she would raise a child. But she missed Puerto. She missed her childhood friends and the core freedoms she surrendered for the mystique of her American life.

On the first day of winter Louis was the proud father of a daughter, a sweet warm baby noisy with verve and audacity. From the moment of birth she screamed for more than an hour as Louis walked with her up and down the halls of the hospital nursery while doctors stitched up Consuela's episiotomy. It had been a difficult birth, but much more for the mother than her daughter who arrived larger than expected and with her fist raised against passage as if to say not now, not until I'm ready. Louis had waited with Consuela at the hospital for nearly 15 hours, reading a day-old newspaper that rehashed Ronald Reagan's election to the presidency and reported the murder of John Lennon.

"We'll name her Antiqua," said Consuela. "My funny aunt on my mother's side."

It didn't matter to Louis. From her first days of life Antiqua was her father's cherished child. When Consuela was able to return to teaching, Louis restructured his work schedule to be home during her classes.

A year passed quickly and then another. Antiqua took her shape as a charming, garrulous and irresistible love.

Louis fell in love with Antiqua. It was a love that grew as his daughter also grew from a struggling baby into a mirthful toddler and, finally, into a willful and charming young girl. She spoke and laughed in two languages and at age four loved her father as the heart and anchor of her life. Or so Louis thought. It was enough. He was no longer alone in this new company he shared with his own fervent flesh and that offered herself ingenuously back to him as an affectionate and affiliating daughter.

Louis grew closer to Antiqua, not aware he drifted farther from Consuela whose discomfort with the big-shouldered demands of her new country pushed her into a deepening melancholy. Consuela quit her teaching job to stay home with Antiqua. She was an excellent mother but at the expense of her intimacy with Louis. One spring she flew to Puerto with Antiqua, a trip that was only the first of several she made to visit her family. Initially Louis was grateful for the time away from Consuela's disillusioned sadness until he would desperately miss Antiqua and resent her absence.

"We are working too hard," said Consuela one night after Antiqua was tucked into bed with her last story and her parents attempted to have sex and could not.

"I think something's changing," said Louis.

Consuela rolled over and did not object.

"Have you thought of going back to work?" asked Louis. "It might be good for you."

Consuela did not answer.

Louis had been here before, or so he thought. After the pain of his first divorce Louis was vigilant for any encroaching sign of another. But to be ahead of any curve required Louis to abandon all hope. He loved his daughter but now wasn't certain Consuela loved him. Louis had promised himself he would never again be surprised, never again be caught by the loss of a love.

What Consuela wanted was within her and also beyond her. Her days living as an American were losing their meaning as she embraced the mothering of Antiqua as the most important work at hand. It explained to both Louis and Consuela why there would not be another job for her. And why she would not look for one.

"I will visit my family again," said Consuela. "It's papa's birthday and Antiqua will love that."

"But you were just there," said Louis. "A month ago…"

"It will be OK," said Consuela. "Just one more visit this year. That's all."

"But you take her with you always," said Louis. "I want her to stay. Go see your parents. Your brothers and sisters. Take your time. But leave Antiqua with me."

"No…" said Consuela. "I want to surprise papa. Last trip. I promise."

It was the last trip. On the day Consuela and Antiqua were due to arrive home, Louis received a letter from Consuela. She was not returning to California or to Louis.

I have no choice, Louis. I have loved you but have you loved me? You were a generous husband but not a caring one. There are problems and you know what they are and yet you would never talk about them. I need another kind of life and, of course, this is my home. It will also be Antiqua's…I am sorry…We need nothing from you. Only to be left alone.

Louis read Consuela's letter as if he were addressing the rewrite of a perpetually sad story. Though it was a new version it still hurt deeply and perhaps more because he was now bereft of two loves, both a wife and a daughter. And while he could fathom Consuela's rejection he could not accept that his daughter also wanted to leave him. How was that even possible? Antiqua loved him and he loved Antiqua. He understood that a person who no longer loves is no longer a person loved and he could let Consuela go. It hurt him to again be another wife's fool. But the disappearance of Antiqua was unacceptable. She was too young to be an agent of loss. Louis was her father and he knew he still lived in his daughter's heart. He had no idea what could be done, only that he would never accept the loss of his Antiqua.

four

I don't recommend it," said the attorney to Louis. "You'll likely not get out of town, much less out of the country. And Mexico punishes kidnappers like any other country, especially when the parent is Mexican and the kidnapper is American. It would cost you a lot and if you make the wrong person angry, it might cost you your life."

88

The love Louis felt for his daughter was violently unrequited. He existed immediately at the threshold of a great and frantic anxiety. So Louis had made a plan and brought it to Mel Winters, a family law attorney he employed during his previous divorce. Louis' plan was to fly to Puerto and visit with Consuela. He would ask to take Antiqua to the park and simply leave with her. It was a foolish and naïve scheme that withered under Mel's questioning.

"And will your daughter be carrying her passport?" asked Mel. "Will she go willingly? And if Consuela says no or insists on joining you?"

Mel told Louis to forget it.

Instead, Mel suggested Louis offer money.

"An amount she can't refuse. And persuade her to return with Antiqua to get it. Then you can take your daughter back and, since she's a US citizen, you'll get some help to keep her here."

"How much?" asked Louis.

"A lot—a hundred thousand dollars? Tell her you're selling the house. Offer a lot of money but something realistic. She knows your finances so don't say something obviously untrue. And don't worry. Once you have your daughter, you'll owe your ex nothing."

It took a week for Louis to at last get Consuela on the phone. At first her parents screened his calls and hung up. Then one night Consuela answered the phone and Louis had her.

"Can't we make a deal?" Louis asked immediately.

Consuela was quiet but she did not hang up.

"What kind of deal?" she asked. "We aren't coming back. I'm not, Louis."

Louis at first described how much he loved Antiqua and how much he wished to help.

"I don't expect you to live with me again," said Louis. "I simply want to work with you to help Antiqua. I want to help her with school. With college. With her future. I want to be the father in her life but only in a way that works for both of you."

Louis worked to sell the sizzle. And in the silence at the other end of the call he knew Consuela was listening.

"Sounds nice, Louis," she said. "You really want to help? What happens next?"

Louis told Consuela he was putting his house on the market. He wanted to split the profit with her. But he needed her to return to sign some papers.

"Papers? What papers? I don't own your house," said Consuela.

"You're still my wife," answered Louis. "At least here. And I need your signature. It's complicated but would you do it?"

There was a long pause.

"I could fly next week," she said. "Where do I go?"

"I'll meet you at the airport and if you brought Antiqua we could make an afternoon of it and…"

Consuela ended the call.

For Louis love now existed at some threshold of anxiety and as he stood outside the Santísima Madre school in Puerto he held tightly to Antiqua's new passport.

"This is it…" said Javier, his companion from the agency. "We walk in like we know what we're doing. Step into her classroom. Your daughter knows you. Tell her to come and you ignore everyone else. I'll be in the hall. We walk outside and get in the cab. We drive to the airport and board the plane."

Despite Mel's pessimism about his client's abduction plan, it was clear Louis had no other choice. So his attorney at last recommended what he described as a "recovery service."

"They'll help you grab her and bring her home," he said. "It's not cheap. Everyone along the way gets paid. But if you get her back into the States you are home free."

So here Louis was, after two months of planning and reconnaissance he stood outside Antigua's school with Javier, a former Green Beret, as his henchman. Louis was moments from grabbing his daughter out of her kindergarten and racing with her to catch a plane. It was the last act of an intricate, carefully assembled scheme. And it was expensive. Louis already had spent $10,000. Antiqua's phony passport alone had cost $500.

Louis and Javier, dressed in suits and ties, entered the school and strolled down an empty hall. Louis peered into Antiqua's classroom and saw her sitting at a table near the window.

"Far from the door," said Javier. "You'll need to move fast."
Louis entered and passed the teacher at her desk. He walked toward Antiqua who saw him, recognized him and reached out to him.

"Papa!" she shouted.

Louis swept her up without breaking stride and walked briskly toward the classroom's rear door.

"We're late!" he shouted without looking back at the teacher who, at first appearing stunned, turned quickly and walked into the hall to see Javier and Louis, with Antiqua in his arms, trotting past her toward the exit.

"A dónde vas?!" the teacher shouted. "Quíen eres?"

Louis did not answer and the teacher screamed.

"Socorro! Socorro!"

Two instructors emerged from their classrooms to see Antiqua's teacher point toward Louis and Javier.

"Secuestrador!" she shouted.

Outside the school Louis followed Javier and carried Antiqua through a courtyard and passed a statue of the Virgin. They crossed a soccer field while behind them a group of teachers drew closer. Louis could see his cab waiting at the curb some twenty yards away. As they reached the street a crowd began to form and the cabdriver refused to open his door. Antiqua's teacher arrived and reached for her, attempting to pry her from Louis' arms.

"You got some cash?" asked Javier. "Start throwing some bills around."

More teachers arrived and suddenly police officers appeared.

"No…!" shouted Antiqua as her teacher pulled at her arms and the crowd crushed against Louis and Javier. "No peudo respirar!"

"El es su padre!" Javier shouted at the approaching officers. "Su Padre!"

Louis could not move any farther, even as he held his daughter firmly.

Later, he would tell Mel what happened.

"It was a tug of war," he said. "I had to let her go."

five

Mel was sympathetic but unhelpful.

"You are playing with fucking fire," he said to Louis as his former client described another scheme to snatch his daughter from Puerto.

"I know what went wrong," said Louis. "Milos explained it to me."

Milos Vlad was the latest recovery specialist to be employed by Louis. Trying to take Antiqua in public was a big mistake, said Milos.

"He said it would be easier and safer to take her from her home," Louis told Mel.

And they wouldn't go to the airport. They would drive to the US Consulate office in Puerto and replace Antiqua's "lost" passport before driving to Mazatlan where a private plane would take them home.

"Easier and safer than what?" Mel snapped. "I can't think of anyplace in the world where the police wouldn't come after you."

"But I'm her father," shouted Louis. "How does a parent steal his own child?"

Mel heard Louis' point. And in Mexico who counted as a criminal depended largely on who was paying.

"How much is it costing this time?" Mel asked.

"Twelve thousand," said Louis. "I took out a second mortgage."

"You really love this child," said Mel. "It's a lot to spend just to piss off her mother."

"I love Antiqua. Yes. And she loves me."
Louis spoke with a conviction that chilled Mel who was happy Louis was no longer his client.

It might be that amnesia is a natural human state and that Louis simply could not long retain the pain of a repetitive experience of loss. He had let his wife go. Why not his daughter? For what he had already spent on a failed abduction, Louis could have flown into Puerto several times in a year and hired a Mexican attorney to negotiate his visits with Antiqua.

But for most of his unremarkable life Louis always had been a visitor. He was an only and lonely child, moved constantly by vagabond parents in search of work so that nearly every September found him the single stranger at a strange new school. His first marriage gave him no evidence of residency, no comfort in the comings and goings of himself and his wife. They both worked and seemed at the end to be convenient, and inevitably inconvenient roommates. Consuela was different until she wasn't and Louis was surprised how little he felt for her when her last letter arrived.

What aroused Louis into a fury was the loss of his daughter. He did not mourn his dying memory of Consuela. But without Antiqua he might himself die. Making love with Consuela had for Louis become ultimately something akin to a duel. But the making and birthing of Antiqua was his opening and salvation. He was the host now of another; the exalted moderator of a child's curious emergence. And Louis, so often the barely tolerated guest, thought he could not live without this child; could have no life at all if his was the only life he could buttress and preserve.

"It's simple," said Milos. "That's why it will work."

Louis and Milos had spent three days in Puerto. Louis stayed in his room at the hotel while Milos cased the neighborhood where Antiqua's family resided. He noticed that early in the morning the grandmother went into the backyard to hang laundry on a clothesline.

"Your daughter follows her," said Milos. "She plays in the yard. Each morning the grandmother goes back into the house and leaves Antiqua in the yard. She's gone for more than two minutes while Antiqua plays. We just have to wait."

The plan was simple. Louis would quickly approach his daughter and scoop her up. Milos would wait in a car around the corner and drive them to the US Consulate where Louis would replace Antiqua's "lost" passport so he could take her home. Milos knew the diplomatic ropes, which was what Louis was paying for.

"Then we drive to Mazatlan and fly to Juarez. We cross the border there. It's crowded and easy. I have connections."

"And if it doesn't work?" asked Louis.

"It will work," said Milos. "Trust me."

Louis did not trust Milos. And the escape did not work.

Everything at first went smoothly with Louis leaping into the yard of Consuela's home just as the grandmother lugged her empty straw laundry basket back into the house. But Antiqua screamed.

"Papa, Papa…!!!!" and the grandmother ran back out to stare directly into Louis' unfocused and defenseless eyes. Louis pushed past the back gate and thought momentarily he was safe, arriving in minutes with Milos at the consulate and Antiqua in his arms. An accommodating secretary heard Louis' rehearsed story: we were visiting, she lost her passport at the beach…she's a US citizen, born in San Francisco…and so it went. The paperwork was easy until the consulate's ambassador called Louis into his office.

"So you're trying to steal your daughter back?" he said in a likely rehearsed avuncular tone.

"She's a US citizen," answered Louis.

"Actually, she has dual citizenship," said the ambassador. "It really doesn't matter where she lives. Mexico or the U.S. Both are her homes."

"But she belongs to me!" shouted Louis, now frantic with the fear another attempt to reclaim his daughter had failed.

"I believe you," said the ambassador. "But tell that to the cops surrounding the consulate."

He led Louis to the window of his second story office and pointed toward a street lined with police cars.

"And we close in an hour," said the ambassador.

"And you'll have to leave."

On his lonely flight home Louis took bitter solace from Antiqua's willingness to leave her mother's home. When Louis entered Consuela's backyard Antiqua ran to him, hugged him, and laughed joyfully. At the consulate she played with the toys he brought while she waited trustingly to go with him. Her love for Louis was an irrevocable truth, as was his love for her.

"You're going to try again?" Mel asked incredulously as Louis described the failures of his second attempt to abduct his daughter.

"What's next?"

As always, Louis had a plan.

"I'm moving to Puerto," said Louis. "I'm taking a month off work and going there to live. This new guy, Ed Gonzalez, is coming with me. He's a counselor. You know him?"

Mel did not.

"Says he does a lot of work with parents in high conflict divorce. Speaks fluent Spanish. We're going to establish visitation and use the courts if we have to. Once we have a schedule and some trust…well, I'll take my chances."

"After what you've tried, good luck with that," said Mel. "I have to say, you sound absolutely crazy to me. But that's love, right?"

"Right," said Louis. "Right you are."

Louis did not tell Mel that Ed Gonzalez was an attorney who frequently represented members of two of the East Bay's more notorious Mexican gangs and that for a fee of $5,000 had agreed to open a negotiation with Consuela and her parents. Ed already had contacted Consuela's father and, after several conversations and the offer of another few thousand dollars, won a meeting with Pedro and Consuela at a restaurant in Puerto.

"He just wants to see her," Ed told Pedro. "He wants to help. He will give you his passport while Antiqua visits with him. He will pay you for your trouble. He wants to make his home in Puerto so he can be near his daughter."

Pedro was suspicious and asked why Louis, after two attempts to steal Antiqua, wanted to live in Mexico.

"Because he's rich," said Ed. "And he can. He wants to be a good father. He wants to help."

Pedro heard these words as they were meant: Louis had money and would share it with Pedro's family for a share of Antiqua's time, for a share of her childhood he would cherish and also otherwise not know.

"Si, si," said Pedro. "También soy padre. Como no."

The first meeting was held in the backroom of a downtown restaurant and was attended by everyone including Consuela's menacing brothers who sat in the background while they stared at Louis to the point he felt fearful.

Louis' story was in order: he was retiring young after a successful career as a researcher, his work in epidemiology so obscure to Consuela and her parents they had no way to understand what he did or what he earned. All they knew was that Louis had money to spend and now he was spending it on them.

"I'm looking for a home to buy," Louis lied. He mentioned a high figure he was willing to pay for a beachfront house. In fact, Louis was nearly broke. He had cashed out the remaining equity in his Oakland home to pay Ed and now rented a studio apartment in west Emeryville.

"He can't take her away from us now," said Consuela as she expressed surprising interest in the idea Antiqua could see her father. "He knows that."

Ed nodded agreeably before negotiating the arrangements, which were simple. Louis would visit at Consuela's home for a few hours a week. Louis would surrender his passport to Consuela before Antiqua could join him in the backyard. Consuela's brothers would chaperone the visits.

"That was pretty slick," Louis said to Ed after they left the restaurant. "They seem almost happy to have me back."

"It's your money they're happy to see," said Ed. "Let's keep them thinking about that. You've literally bought yourself some time. And time is our friend."

"Will they like me?" asked Louis.

"If this works, they'll want to adopt you," said Ed. "Keep looking for property. Take Pedro out with you sometime and let him show you real estate."

"And when do we…you know…" Louis asked quietly.

"When you get an overnight with your daughter," said Ed. "We need 24 hours."

Later in his hotel room Louis sat in a chair and shook with a nervous pleasure born by new fantasies of betrayal.

Louis' first visit with Antiqua was short and fun. Louis entered the familiar home of Consuela's parents and surrendered his passport to Consuela. He was then escorted by Pedro to the backyard where brothers Pablo and Ignacio, muscular and intimidating, sat in lawn chairs playing checkers with Antiqua who turned when she heard Louis' voice.

"Papa!" she shouted.

She was bigger now and surprisingly lanky for a seven-year-old.

Louis watched her heels rise and swim through the air as she ran toward him. He received her in a full and enrapturing hug that lasted nearly a minute. As she backed away, tears could be seen streaming down Louis' cheeks.

"Game of checkers?" she shouted at her father. "I'm good. Muy bueno."

The brothers moved slowly aside to let Louis sit at the checkerboard.

An hour passed quickly, too quickly for Louis to fully notice he had lost one game of checkers and was losing another even as Antiqua talked ceaselessly while they played. She was happy and secure and loved and beautiful and that might have been enough for most visiting parents to appreciate and to find comforting. But Antiqua was for Louis also the most unrequited of loves that now put on ingenuous display all the sweetening features of a beautiful and charming daughter.

"I love you, dear," said Louis as he rose to retrieve his passport and to leave.

"Te quiero tanto!" Antiqua squealed. "You coming back?" she asked.

"Si, Si" said Louis eagerly. "You be good for your mama."

Short visits continued for two weeks while Antiqua grew closer to her father and her vigilant uncles relaxed into restless boredom. One afternoon Louis proposed to Pedro that they take Antiqua together to the beach. They were gone three hours, returning to a relieved Consuela who returned to Louis his passport.

"It was fun," Louis said to Consuela. "Could we do it again?"

Louis waved his passport at her.

"Maybe," said Consuela.

"I think I've found a house," Louis added. "Should be settled in soon."

A week passed before Louis proposed the idea of spending a full day with his daughter in Puerto, ending up at a large public park with dinner at a small restaurant before returning her home. Consuela had taken Louis' passport and consented, his nearly daily arrivals and departures with Antiqua now a reliable routine. At the end of the third week Louis proposed that Antiqua spend the day with him and stay the night at his hotel.

"Last night before moving into the new house," he said to Consuela. He showed her a realtor's photograph of a seaside cottage near Mismaloya.

"You are all welcome anytime. I'll have her home by noon tomorrow."

Consuela clutched Louis' passport and waved with it as Antiqua climbed with her father into a waiting cab that rumbled out of sight.

Consuela waved again, her hand moving frantically as if she

were acquainted promptly with an emerging and inexplicable grief.

seven

On the second day after Antiqua's disappearance, Consuela looked again at Louis' passport and saw it was expired. It was not the passport he had previously given her. She had checked that one thoroughly and if she could climb for even a moment outside her despair, Consuela would blame only herself for the disappearance of her daughter.

It was morning of the second day before the police responded to take a report. Antiqua was with her father who had checked out of his hotel. The police assumed, despite Consuela's frantic and urgent pleas, that the child was safe.

"Así que es una disputa familiar, no?"

"Si…o no..la llevará a los Estados Unidos."

The captain shrugged. America? Who doesn't want to go to America?

"Tal vez la lleve a Disneylandia," said the captain.
He told Consuela he would file a report and check with the consulate. And then he left.

That morning Antiqua sat with Louis in the Panama City airport. Ed had arranged for a private plane to fly them to El Paso where they would slip with other privileged travelers through a porous customs portal. They had left Mexico the same way by boarding a small plane in Puerto. The flights were expensive and Ed took his cut for arranging them. Antiqua, at first exhilarated by a new adventure with her father, was now tired and wanted to go home.

"Soon," said Louis.

He held his daughter on his lap and her birth certificate in his pocket. Louis had realized he had the birth certificate and Consuela did not and with few exceptions in the various and legally fluid ports of call south of the states, the certificate and a wad of bills would be enough to ease a child's passage anywhere.

Antiqua celebrated her 12th birthday while her father counted her fifth year living with him. It had not been easy, especially at first when his daughter realized after several weeks in Oakland she was not going back to Puerto. The cost for Louis to recover Antiqua was an expenditure of both time and money to the point little of either was left to him.

He had sold his home for the resources needed to pay off Ed and a web of expensive accomplices. He had taken time from his gainful employment, so much that when he returned from Mexico his high-salaried job was gone and given to another. Louis found work as an adjunct chemistry instructor at a local junior college but it was part-time and barely covered expenses.

Since Antiqua's arrival he had moved five times, signing single year leases for ever smaller apartments and forcing his daughter each fall to enter a new school. It had been Louis' fate as a child and he felt remorse that it was now Antiqua's though she never complained. Until at the end of sixth grade when Antiqua expected to rise together with a few close friends into their first year at junior high.

"Again?" cried Antiqua. "We are moving again? I can't! I won't!" It was a moment when Louis should have recognized that Antiqua was no longer a little girl. He had anticipated her biology and helped his daughter through her first bra and first period. But he was not at all ready to see Antiqua in this suddenly new and defiant way.

"You'll make new friends," said Louis.

"All my friends are new," said Antiqua. "They are never anything else."

The summer passed quickly, Louis teaching a section of chemistry while Antiqua took a bus to hang out at a mall. One night she was late coming home and Louis phoned the police who found her smoking a joint with friends in a downtown park. Louis picked Antiqua up at the station and grounded her for the rest of the summer. Louis returned from his class one evening, surprised to find the door of their new apartment unlocked. He walked in and called for Antiqua. There was no answer. He went to her room to see the drawers of her dresser pulled out and emptied of her clothes. He went to the closet. Her suitcase was gone.

"Yeah…she said they were her uncles," reported the neighbor who remembered seeing Antiqua leave the building.

"She had her suitcase."

If Louis were to keep his teaching job he could stay only two more days in Puerto. The morning after Antiqua's disappearance he caught the first flight he could book. He sat behind the wheel of a rental car parked a half-block from Consuela's family home. He watched Pedro leave for work and Consuela's two brawny brothers also leave. Looking behind them he saw a third man approach the doorway and enter the street. It was Ed Gonzalez.

Ed shook hands with the brothers and they all separated. Louis scurried down an alley to head off Ed.

"What the fuck?" Louis yelled. "You did this? You fucking stole my daughter?"

"You mean stole her again," Ed said calmly. His hand slipped quickly into a pocket of his loose pants.

Louis backed away.

"You gonna shoot me?" shouted Louis. "Go ahead. What's a life without my girl?"

Ed stood still, quieted by the pathos engendered by a pitiable victim who had once been a client.

"It ain't personal, man. Money talks. So what you got? In this world you either put up or shut up."

Ed pointed toward the house.

"That Pedro. He's got it now. Doesn't look like you got it now. Call me when you do."

Ed smiled wickedly and pushed past a flummoxed and dazed Louis who knew instantly the facts on the ground and how the ground had shifted for both him and the facts.

"Adios," said Ed. "Stay in touch."

It was not that Louis had lost a daughter. It was that his daughter had outgrown Louis. It was her choice to return just as it once had been his choice that she leave. Louis drove back to his hotel and wrote Antiqua a letter on a sheet of complimentary stationary. He told her he loved her. He thanked her for being his sweet daughter.

He would see her again and he did not know when.

She'll be back, he thought to himself. It would hurt to be without her. But he could wait. He would work again. He would save his earnings until he again had enough money. He wasn't finished. He knew what he needed to do. His life was a life of passing days and he would manage each of them one at a time.

IT'S A BOY

one

People make their own luck and Earl Pietro made his by making his own wine. Earl's father was a hops farmer from the county's old days though he had planted two acres of Zinfandel grapes to make enough wine for family holidays. After his father's death in 1987, Earl expanded those two acres to twenty and pulled every last hop plant from the soil to make room for more grapes.

He planted Chardonnay, Cabernet Franc, Merlot, and a treasured, small patch of Pinot Noir that grew near the bank of a big river's tributary that flowed through his land. Every summer coastal fogs drifted up the river in the evenings to cool his temperamental Pinot vines with calming caresses, insuring the slow and complex growth of their subtle, luscious flavors.

"The earth can grow anything," Earl's father said to him before he died. "But you gotta sell whatever grows. Don't waste no time, son. Wine grapes are the future. Grow cheap and sell dear. You can't lose."

Earl abided his father's earnest advice. By the end of the decade the wines of Sonoma and Napa counties were in great demand, the valleys of each suddenly flush with tourists eager to taste, buy and drink what were now the world's most sought after vintages. Earl opened a tasting room and within a year doubled its size. Serried lines of tasters waited in the parking lot for a chance to sip his varietals and, if early enough and fortunate enough, to buy Earl's renowned Pinot Noir, a steal at $47 a bottle.

Earl's sudden fame and even more sudden wealth were a surprise, one his ex-wife of five years missed by a mile. She left Earl during the decade's early recession and when the value of his land barely matched his mortgage debt. All that had changed and Earl, his heart broken by the first and last woman he thought he would ever love, was a devoutly single man.

"Dodged a damned bullet," he told his winemaker one morning during the fall grape crush.

"That woman had me," he said to the few friends who listened.

"But I was cash poor and she was out of love and out of time. Broke my goddamned heart. Never again."

Though what "never" meant was never clear. Earl loved his new life, loved his role as avuncular, knowledgeable host and spent his weekends in his tasting room where he offered corny, ribald wine jokes along with crisp, vineyard gumption. A following grew and Earl was interviewed for an article in a widely circulated wine magazine, growing his following even more until he needed to hire a security company to manage tasting room parking.

Earl flirted with women visitors and barked at the men. He dazzled groups with his wine wisdom and autographed purchased bottles with his signature and the scribbled words "Vino Veritas." It was a shtick and Earl knew and his staff knew and his tasters also knew and loved it. He was a small man but stood tall on a platform behind the wine bar, his shiny, bald head radiant and sunburnt like a globe on fire.

One afternoon he announced it was his fortieth birthday.

"I know," a woman at the bar shouted. "I brought you a present."

Earl saw the woman. She was tall and attractively dressed in a San Remo dress with colorful stitching down the front partially concealed by a rust-colored double-breasted jacket that reached to her knees. Earl guessed her age at around 30.

"How did you know?" Earl asked her as she handed him something heavy and square wrapped in thick paper that bore a floral print.

"And who are you?" he asked.

The woman radiated a confident smile.

"A fan," she said as another woman joined her and lifted a small camera to photograph Earl receiving the gift.

"We love your wines," said the woman taking the photo.

Earl unwrapped his gift. It was a mounted image of Earl receiving a double gold medal at a recent Harvest Fair reception. He held up his surprise birthday present while his tasting room crowd hoisted glasses and cheered.

"And this is from…" announced Earl, hesitating as he looked toward his generous and anonymous guest.

"Ariel," said the woman. "I'm Ariel."

"I guess so far so good," Myrna said to Ariel before biting into a tuna salad sandwich at a Fourth Street café.

"You really think he might marry you? I have to admit that was a stunning photo of him. And he was definitely stunned. But your big plan…has he called?"

"We're having dinner Thursday," said Ariel. "The newspaper sold me a print of Earl's picture. Color 8x10. I work for a county supervisor but I didn't pull rank. Anyone can buy a news photo."

"So a first date," said Myrna. "That's cool, but you don't really expect him to propose. He's one eligible and also very rich bachelor. Take a number, dear. You're at the end of a very long line."

"I'm not at the end anymore," said Ariel.

Men made many plans, thought Ariel. Men rarely questioned their needs while usually acting on their desires. Ariel had her own plan, one that would acquire not just a rich husband but also a father for a child. And after she left him, Earl would support her and her child for the rest of her life.

"We are many mouths, we women," said Ariel. "Men usually want to open one and close another. Women usually hide in their skirts but I'm lifting mine. He will want me. He will see all of me and, while he thinks he has me, I will have him."

"That kind of thing never works," scoffed Myrna.

"Men do it all the time," said Ariel. "Lead women into love and then throw them away. They do it to get what they want because they know what they want. And I know what I want, Myrna. It isn't Earl. It is what Earl represents. It is what Earl owns. He wears his wealth like you wear your big tits: out in front for all to see. It is what he offers to get what he wants. Instincts are at work here. And I don't mind telling you that I'm on offer. If he can meet my price he can fall into me, into my pit, my fissure, my vulva."

two

Ariel's words shocked Myrna with what she later considered their filthy candor. Ariel's desires were a mystery and what Myrna loved about mysteries, especially sexual mysteries, was their vague gossamer and not their disturbing detail. In Myrna's mind it was a womanly art to employ broadly nonspecific terms to describe very intense and idiosyncratic pleasures. Myrna adored romantic novels where a heroine surrendered, succumbed or was swept away. These were words that allowed Myrna, without drawing out loud from a glossary of indecorous verbs and adjectives, to fill in the blanks of a riveting and reliably arousing fantasy. Love was more than instinct. Instinct was the need to piss or shit. Instinct was the hunger before breakfast or the unconscious urge to breathe.

Ariel had no need for a softening narrative that might describe responses supported by instinct. She used the richly cultivated language of her sexuality to describe the terms of her attraction and arousal. She loved to be fucked. She enjoyed deep penetration and said so. She fantasized about big cocks and fingers in her asshole and more than one man at a time in ways that were detailed enough to have been drawn from real experience.

"I know what I want," Ariel told Myrna. "And so I know what a man wants. I don't need to describe it. I can feel it. Just saying to a man what I know he wants is enough to turn him on and bring him home."

Bringing a man "home" was Ariel's way of claiming a conquest. And she told Myrna she was going to bring Earl home.

"Actually, he's going to bring me home," Ariel told Myrna. "To his home that will become ours and then, before he can hope to understand, will be mine."

"Bullshit," Myrna at last blurted. "Why do you think you can fool this guy? He's no dummy. And why would you want a father for your child who is a complete tool, a total idiot? Don't you want to love someone? Don't you want someone capable and good to love you?"

Ariel did not. If Myrna could see into Ariel's mind she would share her friend's indelible image of a long river that flowed through channels, rapids and rocky shoals. The river's mouth formed the flat and frightening geography of Ariel's youth: a long bay that threatened always to carry her out to sea until one year she discovered the river's source and it's lovely climb deep into the comforting valleys and uplifting hills of her origin. It was her last year as a child when hair grew everywhere and gave her new self-generated smells that were like an earthy, grounding perfume and that informed her first self-inflicted and revealing amusements.

"Earl is a kind man," said Ariel. "Why wouldn't I want a kind man as the father of my child?"

"You talk like he's already married you," said Myrna. "Like you can know the future."

"I know the future," said Ariel. "There are no surprises where a kind man is concerned. A kind, rich man is not a secret, even if he tries to hide in plain sight."

"And why should he like you?" Myrna asked. "Why should he love you?"

"I'm a flower," answered Ariel. "I'm its calyx and its sepals. And he is an attentive and busy bee who must make a life for itself. Really, Myrna, it's all so very natural. I could be any flower. But I'm not. I'm Ariel."

Ariel knew politics though she wasn't herself a politician. She worked for a harried woman supervisor whose county district included Earl's winery and was evenly divided between liberal Democrats crowded into the district's one urban corner at the edge of a large city and a sea of rural Republican farmers and ranchers spread widely and separately into the north and west. The supervisor won her second term by less than 500 votes and struggled to make all her constituents happy, though she was a Democrat and made no secret of her sympathies for her party and its youthful and attractive new president.

"I like your boss," said Earl at his first dinner with Ariel. "I hate that Arkansas traveler who got elected president. Hadn't been for Ross Perot, he'd be history."

"What don't you like about Clinton?" asked Ariel.

She wasn't intimidated. Earl had picked her up for dinner. And wearing her flattest flats while he wore his highest heel cowboy boots, Ariel at five feet nine still towered over the five foot six Earl.

"He's a liberal," said Earl. "And I'm not. I've worked hard to make my way. Hard work is what makes this country great."

"You mean like the farm workers who pick your grapes?" asked Ariel. "How much do you pay them?"

Earl stared hard at Ariel.

"I'm just asking," said Ariel. "Do you think any of them will own a winery some day?"

Earl did not have to struggle for his answer.

"Daddy always told me to take care of the people that work for us. Anyone picking my grapes has health insurance, an eight-hour day, and a good, living wage."

"Fair enough," said Ariel. "As far as Clinton goes, we can agree to disagree. Maybe if we spend some time together I can influence your point of view."

Earl liked the suggestion of more time together.

"Or I can influence yours," answered Earl.

"I don't doubt you have much you can teach," Ariel responded coyly.

Ariel's politics were only the first visible edge of a naughtiness intended to attract Earl's interest though she suggested at once her willingness to behave.

"We'll have to see," she added in a way that expressed a deeper interest. "You're a smart, attractive man. I imagine you can be persuasive."

Earl visualized another date with Ariel. She appeared alert, wise and perceptive. And she was a political enemy, no less, one willing to spar and wrestle with him. Earl had been out of love too long to know what it would look like to fall in love again. He watched himself enjoying himself enjoying Ariel. He liked what he saw and wanted more.

Ariel welcomed Earl's kiss as they stood outside her condo. But since it was their first date, she sent him home. Any other ambitious woman might have taken Earl inside but Ariel did not. Ariel sought a man devoted to her and who without argument would overlook all of Ariel's many failings and let her live her naughty life. Such a man would be like a father she imagined and never had: an indulgent patriarch that would come to live largely for only one reason. And that would be to make Ariel loved, comfortable, delighted and pregnant.

three

His winemaker thought Earl had lost his mind. But he would not say that or ever question his boss's decision to marry Ariel though he had listened to years of Earl's jeremiads about his first wife who said she loved him and then betrayed him and walked away. Earl was always thankful she left before his struggling winery at last grew its first unique and successful vintages. The winemaker named George knew he had something to do with Earl's success and so, when Earl talked about marrying again, George at first worried that all his good work might be lost to a woman who knew how to manipulate the terms of success and survival.

"She's a dear," Earl said to George. "She knows something about me I don't know. And she loves me."

"And how do you know that?" asked George.

"She says it," answered Earl.

It was not an answer that impressed George who could see that Earl was not so much drawn to Ariel's love for him as he was to the pleasure of loving Ariel. The difference was significant. Earl was tired of looking for love. He enjoyed the admiration of the crowds that filled his tasting room and the affectionate notoriety his presence inspired. But he wanted something more and also less. Some kind of love that was smaller than the crowds and also larger than his aching, lonely heart. He was ripe picking for a clever woman.

George knew this and asked Earl what he liked about Ariel.

"She's a strong woman," said Earl after a shallow pause. "We don't always agree about things. Especially politics. And she's… well…she's loyal."

George wished to ask Earl how he knew she was loyal but was aware he had no standing to raise the question. He wanted to suggest that Earl have his attorney draw up a pre-nuptial agreement that would protect his assets. But he could not.

"Love is strange," George said instead. "It can make you plenty happy and it can also make you sad."

Earl smiled.

"You think I'm fucking up, don't you?" he said directly to George.

George blushed and turned away.

"Don't you worry," said Earl. "You make wines and leave it to me to make love."

What George did not know was that Earl wanted children. Earl wanted an heir that he imagined would be nurtured from infancy into a brilliant, trustworthy and dutiful custodian of a father's wealth and legacy. And Ariel wanted the same thing. She told Earl she wished to be a mother, a caring and loving presence in all the lives of a grown and integral family.

"We'll be old and withered and our children will take care of us," Ariel said one evening after a long dinner with Earl at his favorite wine country bistro. It was all Earl needed to hear and the permission he wanted to list like a rudderless boat toward Ariel's vision of a family and to embrace her and to fuck her and to fertilize her.

By the date of the wedding Ariel was already pregnant. She had been good, she thought. She dated Earl through a cool spring and into a summer of lassitude and quiet, warm evenings. She fed and cultivated his thoughts and worries in much the way Earl cultivated his grapes: gently, patiently and with an eye toward a fall harvest.

She teased him with political jokes and arguments that ran only to the very edge of his endurance, an edge deeply interesting to Ariel as she measured the steps needed to bring Earl home.

"No, I don't hate Clinton," said Earl one evening as they sat in his Seville in front of Ariel's apartment building on West Third Street.

"He's a good ole' boy, I suppose. And he won some southern states. I just can't get behind a welfare agenda. Americans need to work. And they don't work enough."

"I see a lot of people who work too much," responded Ariel. "They work in the streets, in shops, in bistros, in the fields, and they barely make enough to survive. How many hours is someone supposed to work?"

Ariel knew that after investing a lot of money, the biggest effort involved in making wine was watching and waiting.

Earl knew this, too, and didn't argue. Ariel rewarded him with her first passionate kisses and touches she alone controlled. When Earl surprised her with an engagement ring, she invited him inside.

Ariel thought it a good omen that the day of her and Earl's wedding coincided with the harvest of his prized Pinot grapes. She had Earl more than halfway home. She was both a bride and a mother-to-be and well along with a plan that could not fail. Earl was thrilled to become a father, so happy he waved off his financial advisor's suggestion he keep his property separate from Ariel.

"My dear wife and the mother of my child," Earl said dismissively. "She wants to make a family. And this is a family winery."

The wedding was quick and only a few guests were invited. One was Ariel's supervisor boss who saw a chance to reach across the political aisle. A judge officiated and a private reception was held in the old, big house behind the winery where Earl thought he and Ariel would live for the rest of their lives. Ariel, who even in flat white shoes towered over Earl as they stood to be married, could not wait to take her place. She would work until later in her pregnancy, when she would take a leave from the county. Though if all went well, Ariel expected she would never have to work again.

"You fucking did it," said Myrna to Ariel as they stood together in the first floor bathroom. Myrna wore a grunge-style floral dress, a green and yellow turkey feathered boa wrapped around her neck.

"I didn't do anything," said Ariel. "Earl has done everything. It just happens to be everything I want."

Ariel knew how power was brokered and understood the best place to hold it was in another person's belly.

four

The winery's fall harvest pulled everyone on deck. For three punishing weeks in October, Earl and his crew hovered over his Pinot vines, testing sugar levels and watching for rain. A bad storm could wipe Earl out, dilute grape sugars and create a mildew that would doom his fruit. One year he spent $10,000 to cover the vines in plastic and still they spoiled, leaving him with barely 20 percent of his crop.

Earl's busy days and nights were a relief to Ariel. Already she was exhausted from the lingering morning sickness of her first trimester and could barely manage sex with her impetuous husband who believed Ariel loved him more than life itself. It was Ariel's interim role to imprint on Earl the deepening perception of an ever-deepening love. But with her body reacting to its own invasion by another, Ariel was surprised to find herself awakening to mornings of nausea and weakness and a fearful trembling. Was she still attractive?

She had no energy.

And Earl needed her, asking her one morning to manage the tasting room until the Pinot was harvested and in its barrels. And while Ariel entered her life with Earl thinking she was making a family, she soon learned she was actually joining one. The harvest brought Earl's many relatives closer: cousins, a brother, and an uncle and who Earl said were all investors in the Pietro winery.

"So they own some of it?" asked Ariel weakly one evening over dinner.

"They own most of it," answered Earl. "They seeded this business with their savings. And I haven't let them down. They've made their money back five fold."

These were all new terms that Ariel never anticipated but in her haste to win Earl had never bothered to learn.

"So he's not the sole owner?" Myrna asked Ariel as one afternoon she helped her friend close the tasting room.

"He's still rich," said Ariel. "And I'm six months along. I'm thinking by Christmas we'll have a baby and then we'll see. Stopped working last week. Have an extended maternity leave into next spring."

"You mean you might stay with him?" asked Myrna. "He seems nice, but he's so short. Does that bother you?"

Much bothered Ariel but their height difference wasn't a problem anymore.

"I don't want a husband," Ariel said firmly. "I want a baby. You know that."

Myrna nodded.

"It's always seemed weird to me you want a baby and not a husband," said Myrna. "Most women want the husband first and then the baby."

Ariel was far beyond Myrna's ingenuous and also artless view of a woman's life. For Ariel marriage was a myth that had far outlived its ritual, one that had lost most of its power and all its relevance. Her mother had done nothing to protect Ariel from her father's abuse, a power and desire she described defensively as his "instinct."

"Men are just like that," she told Ariel.

If men were like that, then Ariel did not want one.

But she wanted a baby. That was instinct. Her instinct. And Ariel's marriage was intended to be the opened gate and, at last, the gift of something sacred. Once she accepted it, the gate would close.

It was a crisis. It was not what she expected to happen. Ariel was losing the baby. No, she was losing her grip. She was told the baby could survive but there were problems ahead. When a pregnant woman's water breaks at 26 weeks, it's a crisis. Ariel lay in a hospital bed on the top floor of the UCSF Medical Center hospital, her fetus still within her and still alive. But for how long?

"We'd like to get to thirty weeks to have a decent chance," said her consulting obstetrician. Dr. Lovejoy's was the kind and avuncular voice in Ariel's hospital room while scurrying nurses remained quiet as if withdrawn and prepared for the worst.

"And how do we do that?" asked Earl. He had followed the ambulance from the winery where Ariel lost her footing on a stairway in the cellar and fell down two flights of stairs to the cement floor. Earl met her at the county hospital and, when the attending obstetrician threw up his hands, followed the ambulance to San Francisco.

"Rest…and pray there is no infection," said Dr. Lovejoy.

"Watch and wait. If we see the head there is a surgery we can try to keep him in there. One thing at a time. And what we need is time."

Ariel stirred fitfully, exhausted from a daylong ordeal and under the influence of painkillers for the scrapes, bruises and broken ankle suffered in her fall. Earl reached to hold her hand and she pushed him away. It was Earl who had sent her to the top of the cellar to retrieve an unlabeled bottle drawn from an old vintage her husband wanted to open to celebrate the end of the harvest.

She grieved for her baby, even before she grieved for herself and the turn of events that had converted her independence and presumed control of Earl into a nightmare of sudden dependency. If she could not move, how could she prevail?

"We'll get through this," Earl whispered as he tried again to comfort Ariel who had not wished to get through anything but the end of her pregnancy and the triumph she imagined for her motherhood. It was a triumph that, as Ariel considered it, would free her from Earl and give her back the only life she truly wanted: that of a mother without the father, a father that would stay away even as he paid for everything, a father banished as her mother should have banished Ariel's father while Ariel raised a beautiful, loving and happy child all by herself.

It was instinct, of course, though Ariel now was helpless to execute any plan and weighed groggily the new terms of her bargain. If the baby died would she try again? She was tired of Earl and could not imagine another effort to get pregnant. If the baby lived could Ariel manage its care? And what kind of baby would it be? A troubling, sick or significantly disabled baby that would absorb all of her or, worse, bind her forever to Earl?

"I'll be downstairs," said Earl. "I can nap on the couch."

Ariel did not answer. Earl left and sleep did not come. Ariel seethed through her medications, even as she was groggy and destitute among the ravages of a suddenly fraught and endangered pregnancy.

five

It was an infection that set the course of Ariel's pregnancy. Just as the doctor had feared, a rogue bacterium entered into the proceedings associated with Ariel's endangered childbirth. And once a nurse's thermometer registered Ariel's incipient fever, there was only one chance: to give birth to a human utterly unprepared to live outside the womb but one that also could not stay within, that also would not survive the womb's sudden and rapidly engulfing septicity. It was the worst choice imaginable and it was left at last for Ariel to make.

"We can do this," said Earl, words that meant nothing to Ariel who knew Earl had nothing in mind.

"What would you do?" Ariel asked with what sounded to an attending nurse like peevishness.

Earl was not a woman, much less a mother. He stared at Ariel with his vacant eyes. He had no idea.

"We'll spare no expense," Earl erupted, as if there were some way to buy his threatened family out of danger. Ariel knew there wasn't. It was her choice and one between either the certain or the probable failure of her pregnancy. To keep her baby inside definitely would kill it. To deliver her baby now would expose it to a profound and likely failure. It would enter its life unprotected and too early to assure its survival. And even if it did survive, what quality of life could Ariel imagine for a fetus born nearly three months before it was naturally due?

Ariel tried to sleep while Earl spent an hour with her doctor. When Earl returned to Ariel his eyes were red with unrelieved sorrow. He had visited the hospital's Intensive Care Nursery and viewed a number of prematurely born babies, some as small as a rat and their apparent life evident only in the sonic beeps of an attached monitor.

"He'll get the best care available," Earl said to Ariel.

He was shaken but if Earl were shaken, Ariel was crushed. Not only did she now depend on Earl for more than his money, she faced also the reality of a potentially lingering and likely life-long dependency. In this way the burdened dead were no different from the burdened living and a life Ariel once thought likely freeing and full with joy now appeared to her as an obligatory specter.

And Earl's love for his all but doomed child was so full and un-requitedly real that it chilled Ariel. To take any comfort from Earl's deep if clumsy caring would break the pact Ariel had made with herself; that no man—no single man—ever would come between her and her baby. Ariel alone would decide, which would not have been so hard had the choice been simply about the conditions of her child's certain existence, not a choice between whether her child certainly or just nearly died. If Ariel knew an incantation, she would weave a spell though she knew that her hospital room was no place for magic.

Within twenty minutes of Ariel's assent to delivery, Dr. Lovejoy lifted the fetus through a Caesarian incision cut deeply across her abdomen. Thoroughly sedated, Ariel recalled a moment when a shriveled, naked and bony figure rose over her and then quickly disappeared from view. She heard sighs and words she could not understand. And then she fell asleep or so she was told when Dr. Lovejoy sat down by her hospital bed and she opened her eyes and weakly stirred.

"We have a baby," said the doctor. "Good work."

"So it's good news?" asked Ariel.

"So far so good," said the doctor. "The little guy wants to stay. Vitals are strong. He's breathing on his own. What's his name?"

Thinking there were still months before his birth, Ariel had not yet imagined a name.

"Adam," said Ariel. "His name is Adam. Will you bring him to me?"

"We need to go to him," said the doctor.

Two quiet nurses lifted Ariel into a wheelchair and pushed her out of her room and through several halls toward a dark alcove sealed by two large doors that swung wide as Ariel's chair approached. In a vast chamber aligned with what appeared to be several glass-enclosed bassinets, Ariel saw Earl standing at the foot of one, his face drawn down into the glow created by a panel of perpetually flashing lights.

He turned to see Ariel, his eyes red, wet and weary.

"He's breathing," Earl said to Ariel. "He's…he's so small."

Dr. Lovejoy said Adam weighed two pounds six ounces at birth and might lose an ounce or two before gaining weight. The baby was being fed intravenously and getting help with his breathing from an artificial surfactant applied to his lungs. Otherwise breathing would not be possible without the application of dangerously high levels of air pressure.

"Babies don't get their surfactant until a couple of weeks before full term," said the doctor. "We have a drug now to help with that."

"Sounds risky," said Ariel.

"Not as risky as it used to be," said Dr. Lovejoy. "But we're not out of the woods. Adam's got a lot of growing to do."

"When can we take him home?" asked Earl.

The doctor first looked at the scrawny, tiny infant naked before him, tubes and wires spread out from its every limb and orifice. Then the doctor looked away.

"I can't tell you," he responded. "A month? Six weeks? We don't know what will happen until it happens. We're hoping for the best. So far, he's physically healthy as long as we support him. We just can't say yet what his early birth will mean for his growth and development until he's on his own."

Earl held a hand to his face to suppress a convulsive sob. His obvious love for the baby was beyond anything Ariel might have imagined possible and so much greater than the love Ariel had for Earl. For a moment it seemed to Ariel it might be possible to leverage Earl's love for the baby as a support for her own independence. But it wasn't so simple. The baby needed extensive and expensive care and, regardless of where she was or how she lived, Ariel would always need Earl to be involved.

The expense of care frightened Ariel as she imagined living alone with a severely disabled baby that might, over time, become a severely disabled child. For a moment Ariel wished to jump from the wheelchair and run. But if she left Earl without the baby she would leave with nothing. Earl and the baby had become a multitude that outnumbered her in ways that would leave her lonely, bereft and, most worrisomely, broke. Ariel's new life was not born out of her womb, nor out of her soul, nor out of the creative plots hatched in her spinning scheming brain. It now arrived out of a darkness she never before had considered the core of all possible creation.

six

Adam was six months old. He was small. He was quiet. He was always well dressed and had just begun to crawl. He voiced sounds but usually just cried for what he wanted, which was mostly to be held and soothed. There were times when Ariel thought being held was all that Adam needed or would ever need.

Adam's nursery was the largest bedroom in Earl's home and it was filled to brimming with every toy, device and furnishing that might stimulate the attention, growth and, most importantly, engagement of a new baby. And Adam was a new baby even if he still looked too much like an old, withered man.

"He's growing," Earl crowed. "He's still growing."

Ariel listened and said nothing. There was so much about Adam that could not be said anymore. He had been sick. His heartbeat was irregular. A neonatologist visited twice a week to assess how Adam grew and gained.

"Progress is slow," said the doctor. "But the little guy is a fighter."

The last comment was meant to be supportive but it only de-

115

pressed Ariel who had not expected to have a baby that would have to fight for its survival.

And was this a fight Adam could win? Ariel already had asked and that the doctor refused to answer was enough to convince her the fight might already be over.

"What are you afraid of?" Myrna asked Ariel as they sat on a hill in the vineyard and shared sips from a bottle of Chardonnay.

"That he'll die," said Ariel, pushing hard against an urge to cry. "Or that he'll never really arrive. That he'll always be small, helpless and incapable of living."

"And Earl?" asked Myrna. "What does Earl think?"

"He doesn't think," said Ariel. "He just loves this baby as if he'd had it himself. He talks endlessly and hopefully. 'My son' he says all the time. 'My son will run this place someday.' Really. It's impossible. If we didn't live in the same house I wouldn't know we're even on the same planet."

"Sounds like Earl has a lot of hope," said Myrna. "And you don't?"

Ariel did not know what she had anymore. She was married to Earl but had not slept with him since returning from the hospital. And Earl did not seem to care. He lived for the baby in exuberant ways Ariel quickly realized she could not.

"I hate this baby," Ariel sputtered. "Why did I have it?"

The words were too hot, even for Ariel's dear friend Myrna.

"God, Ariel," said Myrna. "It's a baby. It's your baby. Why can't you love your baby?"

It was a small question but one that had an answer too large for Ariel to fully entertain. To love her baby she would have to love Earl and she did not. To love her baby and also Earl she would have to love herself and all the choices she had made along the way.

There was no way for Ariel to peel back time though she imagined scraping away her current life as she might old paint on a weathered wall. She had expected to care for her child, of course, but to care for a child that would bloom and flourish in the glow of a mother's joy and completely out of the range of a feckless, unattached father. Instead, it was Earl who had attached fully to Adam and become the damaged child's unrequited champion.

"How's the little guy doin'?" George asked Ariel when in the spring he visited the winery's tasting room.

"Hard to say," said Ariel who liked George. He was young, strong and gentle and today looked particularly attractive.

"The last Pinot goes into the bottles today," said George. "Want to watch?"

Afternoons at the winery were a perpetual bore and Ariel jumped at the chance to spend an afternoon with a man who was not Earl.

"Having a hard time with the baby?" George asked Ariel as they stood to watch wine bottles roll on sliders to be filled through a steel spigot from old wooden barrels.

"It is hard," said Ariel. "It's the hardest thing I've ever done. And Earl is no help."

George nodded discreetly. Later, he sat with Ariel alone in the cellar and poured glasses of wine that they lifted in a toast.

"What do you think you want?" George asked Ariel.

"Right now, I think I want you," Ariel said directly. For the first time in weeks she was more than slightly drunk.

George smiled knowingly.

"You're one beautiful woman," said George.

"I think I've always wanted you," said Ariel.

She took George's hand and placed it on her large, brimful breast.

"What about Earl?" asked George.

"What about him?" asked Ariel sarcastically. "He's not important."

"But he's your husband," said George. "He's the father of your child."

"I don't need a husband," said Ariel. "I need a lover."

George forgot Ariel was the wife of his boss just as Ariel also forgot. They were suddenly together and alone and closer friends than most and now the wine spoke for both of them. And it was the best. George was the strong, surprising and welcome affirmation Ariel for so long had desperately needed.

"*I'm still desirable,*" she said to herself as she returned to the tasting room, happily and thoroughly mussed. Instinct was still alive in her.

She imagined herself at last free from her child's foolish and doting father and, in a ripe and wild fantasy, able to elude all entanglements. In a week she would return to her job with the county. She would leave the winery every morning and not return until late. Earl had hired a full time nurse for Adam. Ariel would buy some time. It cost her nothing.

seven

Hope going back to your county job works out for you," Earl said to Ariel over breakfast. "You seem excited."

"I'm sorry to leave now," said Ariel. "Adam…he's…well he's…"

She could not find the words and Earl did not help her.

"He's on his way," said Earl. "Adam is going to be fine. I wish you believed that the way I do."

Earl was a fool. Ariel tried to remain attentive to her husband's futile hopefulness but could not see how Adam ever would become anything but a forever developmentally delayed invalid.

"It's a lot to ask," she said.

"We're his parents," said Earl. "What is it that's too much to ask?"

Ariel did not respond.

As she walked to her car, George waved from the cellar and ran toward her.

"I'll be in town today," he said. "Can I see you? It's important."

Ariel looked furtively back toward the house.

"Phone me at 11," she said to George.

Then she climbed into the car and left.

Her boss was happy to see Ariel, which made Ariel happier than she'd been in months.

"And how's the baby?" asked the supervisor.

"Not what we'd hoped for," answered Ariel. "The early birth has created lots of problems."

"I'm sorry," said Ariel's boss. "Do you need some help? I can contact county services and…"

"We're fine," said Ariel. "We have all the help we need."

Ariel dove fully into her work, driving out to a rural corner of her supervisor's district to mediate a land use dispute between two ranchers over access to a county road easement. She finished in time to meet George for lunch.

"Earl wants me to leave," said George. "He says he's taking the winery in another direction. But I think he knows about us."

"Shit," said Ariel. "How? He's as dumb as a post."

"He'd like us all to think that," said George.

"When will I see you again?" Ariel asked George.

"Give me a week. I have a lead on a winemaker assistant's job in Napa. I'll call you."

Ariel kissed George goodbye.

"Where's my boy?" Ariel shouted up the stairs as she entered Earl's home.

She ran to the nursery and found Adam, his small body concealed in the arms of the nurse. He opened his large hazel eyes and stared absently at Ariel.

"There's my boy," said Ariel. "My dear boy. Mama has missed you all day."

Earl entered and approached just as Ariel lifted Adam from the nurse's arms and sat with him in the rocker.

"Welcome home," said Earl, notably cool to Ariel's sudden and surprising burst of attention. He stood nearby and watched Ariel as the nurse handed her a bottle of warm formula. Adam attached to the bottle's nipple and sucked vigorously.

"Good appetite today," said the nurse.

"Yes," said Ariel. "He's growing. I know. He's going to be a big boy. Oh, you little darling! Mama loves you so much."

Ariel buried her nose in her son's small bare chest. Adam released a high-pitched squeal of sensational delight.

"Well, this is new..." Earl announced quietly.

"What's happened to you?" Earl asked Ariel.

"Nothing…" Ariel announced, stifling what seemed like a sob.

"I've found myself. I've been here the whole time. This little guy. My son. My dear son. I'm the luckiest mother in the world."

"Really?" Earl asked again.

He shook his head and left the nursery.

Earl had been badly married once and it was natural that the experience would feed his suspicions about Ariel and grow in him a familiar awareness that something in his new marriage might be seriously wrong. In the panic of Adam's risky birth, Earl resisted the incubation of his fear though while he at first assumed nothing, neither did he rule anything out.

"I know about George," Earl told Ariel that evening after Adam went to sleep. Earl was the great godfather of the wine family who knew what everyone was doing.

Ariel knew what Earl knew but she denied it anyway. Earl had paid especially close attention to Ariel and now Ariel realized she had not cared enough about Earl to pay close attention to him.

She was seized again by an instinct to survive and again she cried.

"It's all my fault," she said. "I've been so afraid. But why would you think I'd have anything to do with George?"

Ariel spoke her fears in a way she hoped would arouse Earl's instinct to soothe and protect. Ariel knew him to be a loving father and appealed frankly to her husband's vow to hold her close.

"It hasn't been easy, Ariel," Earl lamented. "These last months since Adam's birth have been awful. I saw you and George leave the cellar together last week. It seemed pretty obvious how you felt about each other. I've let George go. I thought tonight I might ask if you wished to leave."

Earl's words did not surprise Ariel who for months had imagined herself gone, though to think now of leaving defied every instinct to survive, and every instinct she now recognized in the small hungry eyes of her infant son.

"George? Really? He offered to show me the Pinot bottling. That was it. I barely know George. Why would I want him?"

Ariel worked hard to conceal her surging desperation.

"I'm the mother to your son, Earl. I love him and I love you."

Earl wondered if he could believe Ariel. It was instinct that drove both his doubt and his urge not to doubt. One way or the other, the truth would emerge. For now, the instinct they all shared to survive—father, mother and son—felt like the tentative tendril of a larger and more enduring possibility and, where Adam was concerned, also the only thing that mattered.

"I have some news," Earl said. He had prepared for this evening with Ariel, an evening he had now intimated might be their last together.

"I have put all my remaining ownership of the winery into a trust to support Adam's care," he said directly.

"And since the winery is not community property, I don't need your consent. I've agreed to be paid by the winery as its general manager. Adam is my chosen heir and I've created a trust that will sustain him and become his legacy when, as an adult, he takes over this winery. In sum, all of this now belongs to Adam."

In a moment, Ariel realized that what Earl had created, he had given to others. And what he created was no longer in any remote way available to her.

In that terrifying moment Ariel realized she had no assets and that, in fact, she never had assets. Earl's wealth was real, but it would never belong to anyone but their son Adam. In a moment Ariel understood that what she thought she had acquired in marriage was never hers and that her husband, who she assumed she controlled with her guile and charm, had seen through her and beyond her. In fact, he could ask her to leave and she would have no choice but to go.

"Think it over," Earl said quietly. "You are this boy's mother and there is a place for you here, if you want it. You'll have everything you need, even if it isn't always what you want."

Ariel turned away to look once more on the squirming small body of the baby that was hers and perhaps the only thing left that was hers. It's precious, tenuous life now flashed at her like a beacon.

"Yes," she said finally. "I'm his mother…you're right…We'll take good care of him. Won't we?"

Earl nodded.

"You'll take good care of him," Earl said. "His life depends on it."

Unsaid was the truth that the shape and quality of Ariel's own life also depended on it. Without Adam there would be nothing for Ariel, nothing at all.

LOVE BACKWARDS

one

No one wants him to die," said the voice at the other end of Isaac's call. "Though he seems to want to die. Professor Marin needs to eat something…and he won't."

It was the first Isaac heard about his father in months, a man he spent much of his adult life ignoring. No news was always good news where Meredith Marin was concerned. Meredith had been a terrible father to Isaac, a man from which Isaac could not live far enough. Now his father was in a crisis and Meredith's best and likely only friend was calling on Isaac to respond.

"What's the problem now?" asked Isaac, his irritation evident. He did not tell the caller named Raymond that he did not care if his father died.

"He's not trying to be a problem," said Raymond. "Your father was found by the police when he stopped showing up for his classes. He's sick, Isaac. And we don't know why."

"He won't tell you?" asked Isaac.

"He won't speak," said Raymond.

"Where's Sarah?" asked Isaac.

"He left her," answered Raymond.

"Why?" asked Isaac. "She's supposedly the love of his god-damned life."

"You don't believe that," said Raymond. "I don't think any-one but your father ever believed that. Now…and at last…he has stopped believing."

"When did he leave her?" asked Isaac.

"More than a month ago. He rented an apartment and told Sarah he'd come back for his things. He never did."

Isaac asked Raymond what he wanted.

"What can you do?" Raymond responded. "I've tried everything."

"Shit. Where is he?" asked Isaac.

"Oakland," answered Raymond.

He gave Isaac an address.

"A studio in a four-story building across from the lake. He actually has a view. But he keeps the blinds closed."

The fact was momentarily irrelevant until Isaac at last arrived at the Grand Avenue address to see his father sunk and unnaturally still in a double bed within a deeply darkened room, his sad eyes barely visible as they opened to view the arrival of an elusive son.

Raymond had contacted the professor's physician who agreed to meet Raymond and Isaac at the professor's apartment.

We need to move him," said the doctor. "He's unresponsive. He hasn't eaten for a while. Maybe a week. Probably more. Though he's been drinking a lot of bourbon. He disappeared from the college and told his students to take two weeks off. Someone on the faculty finally noticed and began asking questions. He's sixty-one years old but he looks like he's eighty. He needs 24-hour care or he'll die."

Isaac signed some papers and then Raymond asked Isaac to meet him that evening for dinner.

It was summer by the bay so the evening fog was thick and wet and cold. When Isaac arrived at the restaurant he and Raymond agreed to eat inside.

"Because he was never there," Isaac answered. "He never loved me. He left my mother and me when I was 10 years old. He married this crazy bitch because why, because she looked just like my mom? And where was he? He called but never came by. He wrote to me but rarely asked me to visit. And Sarah, she was no help. She wanted nothing to do with me. No children. Just my dad. And the one time I was invited to visit she drank all weekend like a goddamned fish and yelled at me for dropping a breakfast plate. I thought then I didn't need this old fuck and his new girlfriend and I was right."

Raymond was quiet until Isaac finished his rant.

"It must have been hard," he told Isaac. "You were just a kid and you couldn't be expected to understand what was going on. I worked with your dad at the college. I know he's a complex and troubled man. And it would have been better for everyone if he'd shared more with you. And he didn't. But there is a story, Isaac. It's one you don't know and it might help if you did."

Dinner arrived and Raymond poured Isaac another glass of wine.

"What would you say to the idea that, instead of marrying Sarah because she looked like your mother he married your mother because she looked like Sarah?"

"What?" asked Isaac. "My dad knew Sarah before my mom?"

"That's part of the story," said Raymond. "And your father wrote it down. I have it. It's in journals and letters and a manuscript he tried to write one year. He thought it would be a book. But he could never face it, I guess. And he couldn't write. You know that. Ever tried to read his textbook on cultural anthropology? The reviews were awful. Needless to say, it did not get him tenure at the college."

"So what are you saying?" asked Isaac. "That my dad had his reasons for being such an asshole?"

"Your father was a more deeply troubled and complex man than even he might have been able to know," answered Raymond. "Let me just say that the terms of a first love are sometimes the terms of love forever. At least they were for Meredith."

Raymond opened his briefcase and extracted two spiral notebooks and a typed manuscript, its apparent hundreds of pages held together by a thick, blue rubber band.

"Maybe these will help you understand. Maybe not. It's a true story, Isaac. The promise of each new day was for your father a chance to reclaim and relive the perfection of love. When he first fell in love he was too young to claim it. Later when love returned he was too old to have it. He wanted love in the monuments he tried to restore. He lost love again when he encountered only its ruins."

"What are you talking about?" Isaac asked impatiently.

"Just read these and after you do, ask me any questions."

"How did you come to possess all this?" asked Isaac.

"Like I said, Meredith hoped to turn it into a story," answered

Raymond. "And I've been his friend for quite awhile."

"Why should I read it?" Isaac asked.

"It might help you," said Raymond. "It might give your anger a rest. You don't need to carry so much. It can't be all that useful."

Isaac flared and Raymond held up his hand to silence him.

"How's the real estate business?" Raymond asked after a long, awkward pause.

"Been better," said Isaac.

"And Maura?"

"She's good. We…we're doing OK…lost a baby last year."

Isaac reported the news as if it were a baseball score.

Raymond slouched against the back of his chair and looked far beyond the window of the restaurant as if searching for any warm light.

"You never told Meredith?" asked Raymond.

"I don't tell that fucker anything," Isaac snapped.

"Do me a favor," Raymond said with the tone of a demand. "Read these."

He thumped the stack of papers and journals with his knuckles as if to awaken them. Then he stood and left.

two

Sarah thought his name long for a first name. Meredith sounded like a last name. His last name had fewer syllables than the first. Where did it come from?

"An uncle…or somebody…" Meredith told Sarah.

Meredith said he and Sarah lived two blocks apart. He asked Sarah to walk home from school with him. He had to ask her and did not understand why. She looked up and down the hall before answering. She said she would. And they did and there were few words to match their thousands of steps through the rising foothills of north Berkeley. She liked to ski in the winter and her parents and sisters were leaving in a week for a resort outside Truckee.

"Beautiful white snow…we never get any here," she told Meredith. "Do you ski?" she asked.

Meredith did not. He would not. His parents never would consider it. It was an expense and the secret of his parents' survival, as

Meredith later learned, was to avoid all expenses. In such a way his mother could avoid work and his father could avoid ambition. Their dance of life was not a dance of love, though it was a dance that moved them almost annually from one house to another. And in this house and in this year Meredith was 15 and old enough to fall in love and not know or care why.

During the fourth week they walked home together, Sarah pulled Meredith into the forest of a small hillside park and kissed him on the lips. Its arousing surprise pushed Meredith into the first felt conception of his bounded life's potential for ecstasy. He wanted more and pushed Sarah hard for it. For Sarah such a kiss was the thoughtful and heartfelt summary of all her desire. For Meredith it became merely the opening of a door to some future and inevitable consummation.

More kisses and touches fomented a struggle that would define their first years in love. And they were in love. They said it in the languages they studied in high school, *je t'aime* from Sarah and *te quiero* from Meredith. They loved saying their love words in another language and every night on the phone repeated them to each other as a sturdy and circadian declaration of their determinedly merged lives.

Until one summer night in their junior year their walk home fell into disarray and their evening phone call weighed heavy with some seemingly inscrutable resistance.

"My parents think we spend too much time together," Sarah told Meredith. "They want me to date other boys."

"Do you want to?" asked Meredith, suddenly anxious and vigilant.

"I don't know what I want," said Sarah. "Je t'aime. I have to go. Marge and I are sleeping on the sun porch tonight. It's so hot."

Meredith did not sleep and at midnight he crawled out his downstairs bedroom window to slip in darkness through the neighborhood and arrive in moments to stand beside a sleeping Sarah, her hair in rollers as she snored on her pillow. He shook her gently.

She was embarrassed and told him to leave.

"Come back tomorrow night," she whispered so as not to wake her sister.

And the next night she was there on the porch again and he was with her and for nights thereafter they occupied a lovely and licensing darkness. They wandered away and found their secret places in the small parks and footpaths of their silent, sylvan neighborhood. They touched each other in all possibly responsive ways.

"I can't screw you," Sarah said one night as she writhed under Meredith's familiar touch.

"I won't ask you," said Meredith compliantly. "Te quiero."

The terms of such a love were the terms of a deepening and maturing trust. Until one night Meredith's suspicious parents together watched him crawl through his window and followed him to Sarah's house where they recognized a frightening and potentially expensive threat to their security. Meredith was grabbed by his husky father and driven home and beaten. A problematic love was now for Meredith an illicit love that, despite its rewarding and poetic enchantment, could not survive. Later as an adult Isaac had found a notebook full of messages Meredith had written to himself.

Though we tried. Though we still wanted each other's nubile disorder and I did not think I would live without you, the "you" hidden in the folds of your flannel and chenille where I found your smell and burrowed constantly for its scent. It was a forbidden knowledge that was not simply our bodies but the awareness that the present was more than a brief space between a then and a therefore. It was a chasm at least partly of our own making that swallowed us whole and, in lurching, tectonic shifts, threw us back into history. We were Eloise and Abelard. We were Pyramus and Thisbe. We were Tony and Maria. You told me love's idea and I described its desire, at least until my parents arrived suddenly to introduce the sexual and moral trauma that would begin our mutual scarification.

Still, we tried. We lasted another year, honing our secrets in the notes and letters that became our first permanent record. We died when our young President died on that dark day in Dallas. Like him, we were led to slaughter by the collapse of hope and the arrival of others to take his place, not knowing others also could arrive to take ours.

"So, OK, I'm surprised," Isaac told Raymond over the phone. "I don't know why he kept this such a secret. Big fucking deal. First love….but Sarah? Really? This is a total mind fuck."

"Maybe for you," Raymond responded. "But you can see, can't you…your dad is describing himself at age 15. What were you like at 15? When did you first fall in love?"

"I was a crazy kid at 15," said Isaac. "A crazy kid with a mean father," said Isaac, his resentment evident to Raymond.

"Much like the father of your father when he was 15," responded Raymond. "Must run in the family. How far have you gotten?"

"Twenty pages or so," said Isaac. "It's awful but I can't stop reading. Sarah…damn, trying to feature her as a young and innocent virgin…no…"

"You have a long way to go," said Raymond. "Stay with it. I'll try to answer your questions."

What Raymond wanted to say was that when Meredith first fell in love with Sarah, they were a boy-man and girl-woman as much tied to the poles of their genders as they were in love with each other, though like most boy-men Meredith tried to bear burdens he could barely lift. And the heaviest, of course, had no weight.

three

When Sarah left Berkeley to attend a women's college in the distant, expensive East, Meredith remained at home though lucky—or so thought his parents—to be accepted to Cal. This allowed him to live at home and to walk the two blocks east from his old high school to attend classes on the university campus. And the price was right: college was free to California residents and a $200 Rotary Club scholarship covered Meredith's fees and books.

After earning his degree in history, Meredith was recommended for graduate school and just in time as his salary as a graduate teaching assistant allowed him at last to leave his parents' home and to share an apartment with two roommates. At semester breaks and during the summer he stopped by Sarah's house. One day he knocked on the door.

"She's in New York for the summer," said Sarah's mother. "I'll tell her you called. If you give me your address I'll pass it on."

Meredith knew that his awful teenage break-up with Sarah was the marker her mother used to push him away. Her smart, lovely daughter was too precious to fold back into contact with a failed and adolescent love. Sarah's family was wealthy and Meredith's was not. Sarah's mother had found her successful husband in college and it was understood, though not spoken, that Sarah's expensive education was intended to produce a similar result.

When Michelle found Meredith he was teaching a weekly section on 19th century European literature. At first she sat nearby and, after the first time he acknowledged her with a smile, waited near the door and blocked his exit. She had questions. He had answers. And he was chosen, or so it seemed. Meredith asked Michelle to have dinner with him. They ate at a bistro on Telegraph Avenue and ended the evening in Meredith's apartment where they soon moved to his bedroom and, at last, into his bed. Michelle was a virgin.

"Yes," she said boldly as Meredith walked her quickly back to her dorm to beat the midnight curfew.

"I picked you. You're a dear. I wasn't wrong. I hope you call me again."

Meredith did. He was not in love but the sex was fun and Michelle, five years younger, managed it all with an unusually assertive tenderness. Within a month they were inseparable partners though forced to part for the summer as Michelle flew home to Michigan and Meredith waited sullenly for some news of Sarah. Occasionally he took a bus to the old neighborhood and watched Sarah's family home for any sign of her. It was the home that appeared frequently in his dreams, much more than his own.

The next time he saw Sarah he wasn't dreaming. She walked outside to check the mail. He surprised her. And she was surprised though she searched through the mail before searching his eyes.

"What are you looking for?" asked Meredith.

"A letter," she answered curtly.

"Who from?" asked Meredith.

"My boyfriend," answered Sarah.

In your family no one spoke. In my family no one listened. Beauty attracted me, but without intention that beauty raged in your dark places, which I found so easily, those places that could not exist without transgression. Now those places belonged to another who drew you down into his underworld of drives and drama. You were devoted despite being perplexed.

So Michelle waited like a rock, like a shape without motion and we were co-mingled like a gravel of unremarkable stones and indifferent masses. And Michelle was pregnant though we lost it, even as our sex was a reliable liturgy of simplicities that so fully satisfied her. We were together long enough to watch our bodies age. Our bodies weakened but our feelings annealed and hard under soft skin and at last resistant to all appeals. And we married, even as I broke Michelle's trust. It was the only way to learn how deeply you had broken mine.

I met you for drinks just before the wedding. Your betrothed's rich family in Connecticut would host you. Tyler. His name was Tyler. Then post-doctorates for you both. He would be at Yale. You ordered one drink, then another. And another. And you would have ordered more but I had no more cash. Good-bye and an air kiss and a strangely familiar but unfriendly hug. Later that summer I married Michelle.

"So he didn't love my mom?" Isaac asked Raymond as they drank coffee at a Starbuck's near Isaac's office.

"You can't say that," said Raymond. "He stayed married to Michelle for more than twenty years."

"He lived with us for barely ten," said Isaac. "When that woman wrote my dad to say she'd left her second husband and wanted to see him, well…he jumped. What was that all about?"

"Sometimes people have a hard time distinguishing love from the idea of love," answered Raymond. "Especially while chasing a lost youth."

"But it was my dad who lost it," said Isaac. "That's not my fault. That's not my mom's fault."

"That's nobody's fault," said Raymond. "Old voices are sometimes heard like earnest ghosts, old voices formed like a shadow in a room. They can be everywhere and all the time."

"People need to take responsibility for what happens," Isaac pronounced.

"You told me you and your wife just lost a baby," said Raymond. "That has to be really hard. But whose fault is that? Who's to blame for you wanting to have a child you could raise and love and watch grow only to suffer its sudden death? Would you try again?"

Isaac struggled for control. Raymond's question was impertinent and even cruel. But it was the question Isaac still asked himself a thousand times a day. He had no words and turned away.

"Joy is always under construction," said Raymond. "You can't rope people to plans like you can a dog to a fence. Binary knots connect all partners and also make all enemies. Meredith loved you.

He loved Michelle. Yes, he also loved Sarah. He loved more than he could manage and he loved people who could never reasonably be expected to love each other."

"Yeah…" Isaac said weakly, still fielding the tensions aroused by Raymond's question.

"I hated Sarah. I hated her guts."

four

When Meredith celebrated his 37th birthday, Michelle surprised him with a special dinner and a 10-year-old Isaac gave his father a watch he still wore. Meredith knew he would return his wife's considerate favor when in a month they observed the 11th anniversary of their 1974 marriage. It was their Watergate wedding, occurring on the same day in August when President Nixon resigned. There would be the usual jokes, though considerably muted with the beginning of President Reagan's second term.

"We might have been better off if Nixon had stayed," Michelle said often, the conservative dominance of national politics one of her most aggravating anathemas.

"Sarah…really, it's you?" Meredith spoke firmly and pushed the earpiece harder against his ear.

"Long time, yeah?" she said. "I'm back home. Staying with mom while I get established."

"Established?" asked Meredith. "Last I heard you were on a tenure track…"

"Not anymore," said Sarah. "A lot has happened. A long story. Say, would you meet me for a drink?"

Meredith would have met Sarah anytime and anywhere. He was an associate anthropology professor struggling to earn tenure at a modest state college in Hayward. His life was less than he hoped for and Sarah's voice was angelic and an intervention in the desultory progress of his drifting career.

"You look good, Meredith," Sarah said warmly. "It's comforting to see you again. I feel at home."

So much had changed and so much had not. What Meredith

saw in Sarah was more than what was on view. Had she been anyone else, any other old girlfriend, Meredith might have run away and burned all the evidence. But not Sarah to whom Meredith was unreasonably and unconditionally attracted. He was helplessly loyal to his first true love and its constantly hectoring attraction.

Meredith saw love seen backwards, perhaps a risky love but never a dead love. He ignored Sarah's subtly disheveled appearance, her noticeable weight gain and the missing honey yellow hair Meredith recalled that was now bleached blonde until it was a nearly uniform shade of dirty white, and Sarah's loud, acquired laugh that grew louder as another drink arrived and then another.

Though in her words she was the same thoughtful and enveloping woman he had loved, the same Athena of his youth who spoke to him in verifiable truths and whose love once, and still, lifted him higher and farther than he'd ever been.

"I'm looking for work," Sarah said bluntly. "Preferably not college teaching. I've learned photography and I need something that will let me do more of it on my own clock."

Meredith used his links with a few college artists to find an opening. On his recommendation Sarah was able to use her art history doctorate to acquire the position of assistant curator for a private East Bay museum that specialized in regional history and art.

Sarah continued for months to dance toward Meredith and also dance away until Meredith, mad with grievous annoyance and perturbing desire, left Michelle and Isaac to live in a small rental cottage behind a house in the Hayward hills. Sarah met him there, finally fucked him and joined him in what was intended to be a celebration of their true and unspoken desire. It had to be true to cost Meredith so much. At times one would sink while the other swam. But Meredith and Sarah performed all their strokes together, locked now like Paolo and Francesca in a predestined, inevitable and balefully fortified embrace.

Truth was scattered like a sibyl's leaves. How did we make out of our apparent closeness such a deep and unbearable divide? I found you nurturing your neuroses so cool and so smart that they were largely unrecognized even as I lived with them always. Now you bear my scrutiny as I bore yours. It is a scrutiny without investigation. No discoveries await, only reckonings and regrets. Is it the price of true love or simply the price of truth? Your voice is like sonorous snow, its words covered and cold.

Your fall was clear if slow: from academic tributes into adjunct teaching and through your quick divorce from Tyler who was gay and never really wanted you and who pushed you toward Dr. Mulligan who gave you only a difficult miscarriage and also your rebound rush into the arms of Mr. Freed who convinced you to leave the academy and to support art…his art. And so after two and a half marriages begun and ended through a decade you at last searched for me. I told you this and you were instantly pale, your eyes wide like those of a small mammal suddenly surprised in a trap.

Who were we in our lives that formed a microcosm of experience before any was felt or described? A baby held Michelle and me spellbound until the first year he wove his own and lasting spell around each of us. And then he was a child and then nearly a man and then you found me. You found me and like dreamy drunks we let a winter's sudden encounter absorb our wills.

"I guess I'd be angrier if this made any sense," Isaac said to Raymond. "I guess I'd also be more understanding. But who's to say? I seem to remember Sarah better than my father. Maybe that's my problem. I blame her for everything. I do. This is the woman my father left my mother for? This is what he threw his family away for? He moved into his little bachelor shack in the hills and Sarah followed and the place just stank. I remember visiting once before they married. *I'm marrying your father,* she said to me. *I should have married him first.* First! As if whether it came at the beginning or the end, my father's love was a coincidence. The place was filthy and, as usual, she was drunk. Meanwhile my mother is working like two parents to hold me and us together. What the fuck was he thinking?"

"Sarah had no children and maybe she wished she did," said Raymond.

"And I understand that from where you watched and lived, well, it makes no sense. Your father was a slave to love, and not just to love, but to a certain kind of love. A common mistake is to assume love makes sense when it is not remotely possible to grasp what a miracle it is that love, or even life, exists in a black, dark and empty universe. That anything works to anyone's expectations is truly a marvel. The seeds of this drama were sown for your father at the same age you were when he left you."

For Raymond there were an infinite number of ways to talk about love. He hoped that Isaac might grasp just a few beyond the singularity of his own broken bonds with his father. Perhaps Isaac might see more deeply into the breakdowns that encircled him amid the misfiring engines of his father's love.

five

Raymond remembered asking Meredith if he really needed a best man at his wedding.

"When did you get divorced?" asked Raymond.

Michelle had filed the papers months before. And Meredith agreed to all her terms.

"It's final," said Meredith. "At last all of this is over. It's the end of the Nineties and time to get married."

"It's actually 1997," Raymond told his colleague and friend. "And Bill Clinton has barely begun his second term. And this is your second marriage and Sarah's…how many? And what about your son?"

Meredith said his son would not attend.

"OK," said Raymond. "I'll do it. And it's at city hall?"

Meredith nodded.

Raymond taught art history at Hayward State. He met Meredith at a faculty reception.

"For an anthropology instructor you spend a lot of time in the art department," Raymond said to Meredith.

Meredith explained his interest in anthropology included the human impulse to make art. Besides, he was a drinking buddy of Marv Chavez, an instructor and pop artist whose friends included Wayne Theibaud and Roy Lichtenstein.

"He's put Cal State Hayward on the map," said Meredith.

"So has Theodore Roszak," responded Raymond. "History rules."

Meredith laughed and Raymond did not. Raymond's good friend had problems and one of them was his bride Sarah.

"She's an artist and a historian," said Meredith. "Doing photography now. And I love her. I always have."

"Has she always loved you?" asked Raymond.

Meredith did not answer.

It was a new year and nearly a new millennium, which Meredith and Sarah thought propitious for the purchase of an Alameda condominium, equidistant between Hayward and San Francisco where Sarah increasingly spent more of her time.

"Buy now!" the realtor ranted. "Prices are going through the roof. In five years this place will be worth twice what you're paying for it."

Sarah had drawn on her family's trust to study photography at the Art Institute and, with an art doctorate already in hand, advanced quickly. Two art galleries began showing her early photomontages of found objects and when a few prints sold the galleries picked up her unusual figure studies that placed nude models in odd juxtaposition within landscapes that included laundromats, dive bars and public bathrooms. Through a network of cultivated art world links she extended her work into a topical and prevailing conversation that reached all the way to New York. One important month the was written up in the pages of a well-read edition of Art Forum.

"It's just for a couple of weeks," Sarah told Meredith. "I'm on some kind of verge and I either do it now or not at all."

It was not so much that Sarah needed to travel east to promote a touring show of her recent photographs. It was that she seemed particularly interested in a New York gallery owner named Mel Montagu who had organized the exhibition. Five years of marriage to Sarah had passed quickly and Meredith, still a professor without tenure at Hayward State, needed now to stand by while his first love, his bride and now his artful and too often distant wife, basked in a suddenly bright and resplendent limelight.

"I'll miss you," said Meredith as he stood at the departure gate and reached to kiss on the lips a wife who, instead of her mouth, offered her cheek.

In our first year together I learned through your cautious range how to manage a perpetual penance for my transitory transgressions and to buttress your modesty and guard your strait gate. We sang our stories into abiding histories of delectable danger though we were never really at risk, not like Gary and Susan who fucked and then worried. One night I parted your legs and, through a strong, deep kiss massaged your vulva, reaching through its bristle with stammering tenderness. For a moment I felt your complete and conscious presence. Later, you fell down,

"This is all getting a little weird," Isaac said to Raymond as they shared a table at a café on Telegraph Avenue.

"So she cheated on him. That's a surprise? After the way he treated me and my mom I'm supposed to feel sorry?"

"No," Raymond interrupted. "He knows what he's done. He has no idea you've read anything he's written. How can I say it any more clearly? Meredith's story is not about you."

"Well, it sure as hell should have been," Isaac shouted.

"Why?" asked Raymond. "Because your story is about him? What is your story?"

Isaac was silent.

"I was deprived of his love," said Isaac.

"And as a result, he was deprived of yours," said Raymond. "And it's all too late…all of it. Too late for him to show his love and too late for you to receive it."

Isaac confronted Raymond's thought but it was one he had no strength to resist. In a fading moment his life seemed a first scintilla of experience before any was felt or described.

six

At age 61, Meredith continued to struggle with whatever Sarah said, in her art or otherwise. He read her comments in an article in Aperture. She was not always truthful even as he continued to hold the expectation she would be. Her time away from his was her own. He accepted that now and also that such time might include others.

"It's enough that I love you," Sarah told him after a week spent in Chicago. "Why must I love only you? I love myself certainly as much as I love you."

"I've lost track," Meredith responded. "I've lost track of who we love. Though I have vivid memories of those I've loved and who no longer love me."

It was the last night they slept together. Thereafter, when Sarah returned from one of her many photo trips or gallery shows, she slept on the condo's living room sofa. She would have moved out, but it was 2009 and the national economy had collapsed along with the fragile value of their condo and the once promising sale of her photographs. She told Meredith she needed to travel to make sales. Meredith knew she traveled now to make friends and to make love.

Meredith also knew he would never have tenure, even as he completed his twentieth academic year at a college so seemingly without identity that it had just recently changed its name from Hayward State College to California State University East Bay. It was an unwieldy name that left Meredith wondering what identity ever could be attributed to such an amorphous geography as an "east bay." And who was he? He did not need tenure to retire within a year and receive his full pension. But tenure was more than an honorarium, it was a herald and, while he believed he likely did not deserve it, he resented others—instructors with half his wit and barely a shred of his experience—who received it.

"You're more successful than I," Meredith told Sarah one evening. "I have to say that you leaving the academy to achieve recognition as an artist, well…it absolutely confounds and discourages me."

"We do what we can," said Sarah. "You tried and I tried."

"But I thought we were a team," said Meredith. "I thought we reunited to know our one, true love."

"True love?" asked Sarah, sipping a second Margarita. "What is ever true about love?"

And with those words Meredith felt Sarah slyly withdraw, as if falling back again into the first nocturnal shadows of their passion, the first dark nights of love that hid all of its shape and definition or how it might actually ever appear. For Sarah "love" drove her leaps from one possibility to another and motivated a still fervent ambition.

For Meredith love was buried deep in a past that waited to be dug up and resurrected in a way that would hold its place forever. Sarah's artistic renown moved her past Meredith in a way that confirmed his life had been lived in the shadow of a perfected love for a still unperfected woman. There was no way to freeze love. It was as mercurial as anything embraced and worn down by time.

You revived a consuming interest in your own body as if seized by an urgent, new puberty. And while only an echo of the first, it was your new memory of the younger woman, her narcissism, her sexual imagination, her obsession with mirrors and clothing. It was late to grow into your place in the world. Still, I hear your voice shout at me, which I asked for as if seeking the company of earnest ghosts.

"Have you ever considered visiting your father?" Raymond asked.

He had tried for three days to reach Isaac by phone. At last, Isaac answered.

"I've been busy," said Isaac. "My mom needed me to help her move. She sold the house in Berkeley and bought a house in Mendocino. Has a boyfriend again."

Isaac mumbled the last sentence.

"Is that a good thing?" asked Raymond.

"For her," answered Isaac. "What's happening with Meredith?"

Isaac still referred to his father by his first name.

"He's not good," said Raymond. "Still in the hospital and his vitals are not stable. Doctor says they're doing all they can but still can't turn a corner. Doctor says he's never seen anything like it, as if your dad's body is rejecting all medical efforts as it might an infection. He had a small stroke while living alone. But now it's having a large impact. His heart…well, it's very weak. You might say it's broken."

"I should see him," Isaac said after a brooding silence. It was one thing to wish a father dead but another to actually lose him. A living father still held the potential of a refuge, even as Isaac wanted none and yet also needed it.

"He would like that," said Raymond.

Isaac was silent for several minutes.

"How is it possible to love someone who didn't love me?" Isaac finally blurted. "I could, I guess. I do. But what's the use?"

"It's not that your father didn't love you," Raymond said calmly. "He didn't know how."

seven

Meredith died in the presence of his son.

Isaac, who long wished his father dead, now should have been fulfilled. Instead, Isaac stood to watch his own hands search his father's chest for a pulse, to try to find some source he might massage back into existence. But Meredith was gone.

"I'm not finished," Isaac blurted. "Wait…I don't know what to do with this."

Raymond saw Isaac's distress. There was so much, too much, that he still needed to understand and to feel.

"You have time," Raymond assured him. "Your father has no more time. Your father knew when he would die. We don't know when we will die."

Sarah approved Meredith's cremation and authorized a service at the college that, it surprised no one, she did not attend. Several faculty members, including Marv the famous artist and his colleagues, organized an observance and reception. And Michelle attended, standing discreetly at the back of the hall and leaving quickly before drinks and food were served.

Raymond delivered a eulogy. He began by quoting some last words written by Meredith in his journal.

Like Arjuna's soldiers already dead before battle our carefully reconstructed re-membrances fall all around and bleed mortally into the vanishing recesses of this time and its experience. Our joined lives were once a sovereign assurance hiding the anxious notion that nothing is assured. I was dependent on a star's distant incandescence to prove my presence. Devoted as I was to the precision of an orbit, I can now think myself free.

Meredith's words were wide enough in meaning to reach farther. Raymond used them to talk about his scholarly friend who was kind, feckless and trustworthy and whose long tenure at the college was at last rewarded with an honorary designation as a professor emeritus. Later, Raymond and Isaac would scatter Meredith's ashes on a slender, wooded trail behind the vintage Merry-go-round in Tilden Park.

"It was his childhood escape," said Raymond. "We walked it together often and he would tell me his stories of love and life."

Though Raymond later spoke another eulogy and only to himself.

Meredith never cracked the code, never understood what ducks he needed and how to stand them in a row. Love was his life and it had been suppressed, even more than any potential he might have shown for success. He understood. He would, by his own description, be an "adequate" instructor, not charismatic but certainly well read, not connecting with students but certainly friendly, not a colleague to deans and vice-presidents but well thought of by the office staff to which he was obsequiously grateful for any small printing job or favor, especially when he needed late changes to a quiz or an exam.

Meredith was an agent without agency. He had one life purpose and it belonged to Sarah. His love was undefined and not carefully researched, not in the way he conducted his scholarship with its innumerable citations and footnotes to substantiate its arguments. Meredith had no argument where Sarah was concerned. Critical thinking was not involved, though for Sarah—a modern woman becoming ever more contemporary—all her attachments were thoughtful ones through which she argued and grew herself into a prominent existence. This was Sarah's destiny, as much as Sarah was Meredith's even as all his love was absorbed and employed by her. All his affection was applied on her behalf and channeled into the deeply creative adventure that Sarah saw as her destiny.

Isaac also spoke later and only to himself.

The voice of my father is in his writing about love and it is so different from the one shouted across a room or delivered in a lecture or spoken to me in either affec-tion or anger. He found in his life only the placeholders between the time he was with us and the largely imagined time he could again be with Sarah. And why? What held him? What was it that held him? What of himself could he not manage or control that sought compulsively the singular touch of the girl/woman he first loved? Why could he not see her as anything other than what she first was long before time and inertia wore her down just as they did him and me and mom? They found in each other only their opposite and corrupted interiors that, so old and for so long, could never again merge one with the other.

Michelle drove north and said to herself out loud what she would never tell anyone else.

I have a new lover and am over my old sorrows. Meredith has no more sorrows so I suppose he's lucky in that way. I've been eleven years without a partner and now I'm with someone who cares and shows he cares. It confuses Isaac who is left with the legacy of Meredith in ways I'm not. I often wondered how a really brilliant man could succumb to the riveting and unrelieved feeling of a first love to the point he would surrender a happy and successful marriage of nearly twenty years. It's harder on Isaac. He's related to Meredith and I am not. Isaac is left with the legacy of Meredith in a way I never will be. Meredith was too much of my time but he's gone now. For Isaac his father is a viral infection without relief.

Sarah gazed out the window of a jet winging toward New York and tried to sort out her thoughts.

No point in showing up for the dead. Meredith doesn't care anymore. I don't either. In the few honest conversations we could stand to have with each other, he and I acknowledged that we were such disappointments to our families that it was a comfort to be together. We were both such self-absorbed and incorrigible failures we could live in abiding comfort with each other without judgment. It was a mis-erable way to feel but it avoided all disappointments. My liaisons and affairs were hurtful but not really troubling. They were my unique failures just as Meredith's obsessive love was his. He was a disappointment to his wife and son and I was a disappointment to him and he to me. I loved Meredith for the time he was really with me. It was such a relief to live with someone as miserable, as disappointing, as easily prone to failure, as myself. It is the only way true love exists: in the delicate balance of equal strengths, though most of us find love in the common weightlessness of equal weaknesses. For that I am grateful to Meredith. At least I had love, however despairing and flawed. I gained weight and he lost weight. I'm a full-figured old woman and he died a gaunt shadow. My mistake was that when I married Meredith I did not tell him I was only visiting. Everyone wants a lover to lift them up. Few really wish to, or expect to do all the lifting.

Meredith had no words anymore but if he could speak he might have said that love wasn't measured by the barometric pressure of any single moment. Love existed over time and true love, like the weather, occupied every place and all the time. Though love felt in the moment was as precious as love in the distance and perhaps more precious because it existed beyond history. The history was a photo album. The moment was the love. And there was no way to predict how a moment of love might grow its reality into the expression of a lifetime. Meredith would have sold his soul for the illusive return of a moment of true love. Who would not? But it was gone, even as every illusive reconstruction teased him into the belief that he, like love, would last forever.

one

There were no schools of love for either Andrea or Gilly. No schools for two girls who learned to love during recesses and after the last bell and who found nothing at home that might teach them how to come together. Though they did.

But not without first going with others when they first left school and at last left home. The school of love is sometimes the school of hard knocks though a willing and affectionate teacher can arrive from time to time. But as Andrea knew, and Gilly learned, even if a dear love arrives at a timely and important moment, there is no assurance she will stay. Love teaches lessons that burn with fear and pain if love ever is to arrive again.

It was what Andrea thought on the morning she moved with her son Chase into Gilly's large home in the hills of the Carmel Valley. Though Andrea was not Chase's mother. Another woman gave birth to Chase. Her name was Lupen and she was dead. Andrea met Lupen in school and fell in love with her and though they could not marry, Andrea and Lupen wanted to have a baby. A clinic in Santa Cruz agreed to inseminate Lupen and when an avuncular physician named Dr. Hightower confirmed the conception, Andrea and Lupen celebrated with an urgent embrace that held them together through one night and another and another.

"We are forever," Andrea whispered as she caressed Lupen's strong arms and pressed hard against her sinewy buttocks while they lay restless in their east Salinas cottage.

"We are such a strong love…giving birth to more love."

Andrea knew that moment lifted Lupen, who glowed with arousal and held tightly to her lover's embracing hands at the base of her belly.

"I'm going to get big," said Lupen. "Big and lazy and grumpy."

"Grumpy?" asked Andrea.

"I can't get high," said Lupen.

"You can't, anyway," answered Andrea. "That was our deal. No more drugs."

"I know," said Lupen. "But I can still be grumpy."

There were no schools of love where Andrea and Lupen could learn how best to bridge a vast canyon that separated one's heartfelt faith from another's hard won and painful addiction to every known and available derivative of methamphetamine.

"You can't," Andrea sighed as she pulled her hands away from Lupen. "Please tell me you won't."

Lupen promised and was better than her word. The pregnancy proceeded, Lupen getting three months off from her job as a waitress at the wharf while Andrea continued working as the valued manager of a winery tasting room on Monterey's Cannery Row. The baby was born and it was a boy they agreed to name Chase after an attentive and attractive counselor from Lupen's days as a homeless addict.

"He's all our love," said an exhausted Lupen as she held the newborn to her breast.

"All of it," agreed Andrea.

The birth of Chase occurred within an optimal, if narrow, zone of comfort. A week after Chase arrived, the attending doctor phoned Lupen with a disturbing request.

"Can we get you back in here for some tests?" he asked directly.

"What's wrong?" asked Lupen. "Is Chase OK?"

"He's fine. It's you we're concerned about."

It often begins with a lump.

Doctor, I have a lump.

Where? the doctor asks. The breast?

"How did you know?" asked Lupen. "I thought it was a cyst."

"It's not," said the doctor, a woman in a white coat who held an x-ray up to the light as she spoke with Lupen and Andrea.

"How's the baby?" asked the doctor.

"Fine," interjected Andrea while Lupen tapped her fingers anxiously against the examination room table.

"This little guy is our joy," said Andrea as she rocked in her arms the swaddled, sleeping infant Chase.

"Come here and see this," the doctor said to Lupen.

The x-ray was a photograph comprising only light and shadow. Bright white light outlined the familiar slope of Lupen's breast. Within the outline the doctor pointed to a dark, fuzzy blip.

"This is it," she said. "It's been there awhile. Looks like cancer."

Lupen went suddenly pale.

"Well, is it?" asked Andrea anxiously.

"We need a biopsy," said the doctor. "ASAP."

A surgery confirmed the worst and Lupen, the proud mother of Chase, was handed instantly a crucible that for several months held her and Andrea's full attention while they struggled to find hope in an increasingly hopeless prognosis. It was hard for Lupen to accept that a mastectomy was essential and she would need to stop nursing Chase. She allowed precious weeks to pass before consenting, only to learn the cancer was well beyond her breast and fruitfully anchored in her lymph nodes.

Andrea organized a six-month celebration for Chase during which Lupen sat weakly at the kitchen table of their two-bedroom Santa Maria Street rental.

"Mommy's going to make it," Andrea said as she bounced Chase on her lap.

Lupen laughed before slipping back in her chair to fall asleep. Two more surgeries were scheduled but only one occurred. Two days after Chase's first birthday, Lupen died in bed, Chase beside her as he shook a rattle and laughed while Lupen reached for him, her arm stretched as if to offer a fading, distant wave.

Andrea was a Soroptimist. She might have described herself as a lapsed member of the women's business club Andrea's employer insisted she join.

"Business is business," said her boss Maria, the owner of the

Carmel Valley winery whose tasting room Andrea had managed for several years. And Andrea's membership was good for business. The club held a benefit tasting at the winery each year that impressed Maria. Andrea remained an active member until she met Lupen and had a baby with her. One morning Andrea wondered how as a lesbian with a child she could continue to pose as a straight lady of business. She notably avoided discussing her personal life with members and thought of them to be generally conservative and boring. Without telling Maria, Andrea stopped attending club meetings.

"Hi, Andrea. It's Gilly," said the voice at the other end of the call. "The club misses you."

Gilly invited Andrea for lunch to discuss what the club might do to draw her back into the fold. Andrea had told her boss her sister died and she was left to care for her nephew. The lie bought some time for Andrea to determine how she would cover childcare, pay rent on her cottage and keep working. Gilly had been one of Andrea's few Soroptimist friends, a successful family law attorney who recently divorced her husband. The break-up was painful and over a couple of coffees Gilly had shared with Andrea the bitter, teary details of her failed marriage.

Now Gilly was reaching out and Andrea did not resist. It was not hard for Andrea to draw Gilly into her orbit of need. She held nothing back and told Gilly the whole story of her life with Lupen, the birth of Chase, and the breaking of all their hearts that left Andrea to bear alone all their pain.

"I don't have enough for next month's rent," Andrea confessed as tears filled her eyes.

"You guys can live with me," said Gilly.

It was more than Andrea expected but no less than what she needed. That Gilly offered a home was beyond an opening. It was a divine intervention.

"How can I ever thank you?" answered Andrea after a lengthy, confounded pause.

"Accept it," said Gilly. "That's all."

"You have room for us?" asked Andrea.

"Room?" laughed Gilly. "You can have your own floor."

And then Gilly was quiet while Andrea weighed instantly all the baggage of her complicated life of loss and gain. Gilly heard her stifled sobs of gratitude.

"It's nothing," said Gilly. "We're sisters."

2

And they were sisters of a sort. Sisters in a business sorority that struggled to maintain its membership but also sisters who were outcasts, Andrea thrown from love by the death of her baby's mother and Gilly rejected by a rich and philandering spouse with wealth to burn. They were women with hard stories and legitimate grievances and for weeks these constructed the syntax of their affiliating connection.

Gilly's large home in the hills of Carmel Valley did indeed provide an entire floor for Andrea and Lupen's son, a space comprising two bedrooms, a living room and a full bath.

"The house was built for guests," said Gilly. "Lester has a big family. They gave him the money so they could have a place to stay when they visited. And now that they don't come anymore they are waiting for me to fail. I got the house in the divorce and the old bastard was happy to give it to me. He hated it, though. He hated their visits. He bought a house on a hill in the Carmel Highlands with an ocean view. It's too small for his family and they're pissed. They love to leave their boring life in Texas and come to California. Not so easy now. So they're waiting. No one thinks I can make the payments. A family law attorney that does pro bono work for impoverished moms…what do you think?"

"What's the rent?" asked Andrea.

"Whatever you can pay," answered Gilly. "I took the house in the settlement and Lester owes me. I took the house instead of ten years of full alimony. He pays me a little, enough to cover some bills. If I marry again, I lose his checks. But I love this house and never want to leave. It will work. I'm good at what I do. It's just that I work for my money and Lester has never worked. Trust funds are a mixed blessing. He was rich and will always be rich. But that's all he is. There is nothing else to him but the need to gratify any immediate impulse. And he can do that, and that makes it impossible for him to grow into any wondrous, painful experience that might convert him to an empathy for anything beyond himself."

So Andrea realized she owed her good fortune as much to the whims of a rich, piggy man as she did to the heartfelt sisterhood that was forming with Gilly. Lupen's death had broken Andrea and now Gilly's loss rescued her. Andrea needed a lifeline while Gilly simply needed a tenant and perhaps a friend. It was at first an awkward match and for weeks reverberated with gawky encounters and exchanges until one evening Gilly helped Andrea put Chase to bed and in a way that was sweet and collegial and therefore began to feed the hunger each had for a warmer and deeper fondness.

"You're good for me," said Gilly as she left the bedroom Andrea had converted into a nursery.

"You're good," responded Andrea. "You are a good woman and I'm so grateful."

The women embraced in a suddenly hard and heartfelt hug, both wiping away tears as they separated.

"See you in the morning," said Gilly.

"I'll make breakfast," said Andrea.

Andrea Minalla was far from her origins and the occasionally violent insecurities of a childhood with rough brothers, an always angry mother and a mean and abusive uncle. Her grandfather Guillermo slipped across the border during the previous century's big war and worked in the vineyards of the valley while raising sons, one of which followed in the business and became a field foreman and eventually a trusted cellar supervisor. His name also was Guillermo and he was Andrea's father until one night during a particularly frantic harvest he climbed to the top of a fermentation tank to adjust a valve and, trapped between a shallow roof and the tank, suffocated in a cloud of carbon dioxide gas released by the tank's furiously fermenting grapes.

A generous legal settlement for the winery's negligence allowed Andrea to graduate from a Catholic high school and to study business and accounting at a local junior college. Her aptitude was immediately apparent and rewarded. Her family history in wine appealed to Maria, the owner of a regional winery that specialized in soft reds and bright, acid-rich whites. She hired Andrea out of school and after two years as an accountant promoted her to tasting room manager.

It was during a tasting that Andrea met Lupen, a wild woman

who arrived with a group of other women determined to get enough free tastes to make them happily drunk. Lupen knew nothing about wine but enjoyed listening to Andrea explain what made grapes into wine and why that was important. Self-conscious about her large breasts and wide hips, Andrea avoided men and shunned any who expressed an interest in her. And many did. And so did Lupen.

"Would you ever get a drink with me?" Lupen asked over the tasting bar. "I bet you hear that a lot."

Andrea had never heard those words spoken directly to her. Never permitted herself to hear them. Embarrassed, she laughed and left the tasting bar.

As a Soroptimist, Andrea was assigned to raise funds for an agency that supported women overcoming drug and alcohol addiction. She visited the agency to observe its work and was introduced to a client. It was Lupen.

Within a month they were dating, Lupen the more experienced and assertive and Andrea the quiet "unButch" of an at first passionate relationship that opened all her pores and that gave her the first ground on which to build a new and loving life. Within weeks the two women were lovers, enveloped in a volatile and creative fulfillment that rose high above the conditions of daily existence.

Lupen gave up her drugs and Andrea gave all her love to Lupen. So much love that another was needed to represent and absorb it. The insemination of Lupen was easy to arrange and out popped Chase, a boy with two moms who would learn love as only women could teach it. It was all set out clearly before her and Andrea had only to accept it until Lupen became sick and died.

three

It took months for Andrea to right the ship of her life, even with Gilly's kind and patient assistance. Chase began his second year knowing something was wrong and that someone important to him was missing. And as much as Andrea tried to be Lupen and as hard as Gilly tried to support Andrea, neither woman could fully interpret or assuage the incoherent fears of a budding toddler still struggling with a sudden and calamitous abandonment.

Chase's second year of life was rougher and more terrible than even the usually terrible twos as he searched hopelessly and helplessly for the body that bore him and that was the source of all his vital tastes, kisses and smells.

"Did you try the bottle?" Gilly asked again.

"I've tried everything," Andrea said, exasperated. It was two in the morning and Chase had been screaming for more than an hour.

"He seems angry," said Gilly.

"He's frightened," said Andrea.

Whatever he was, Chase was inconsolable and his night terrors were now a routine that awoke Gilly and also embarrassed Andrea who took responsibility in a way that wasn't necessary but that she thought required. Chase was her child now, even if Chase behaved as if he had no mother.

"He's fine during the day," Andrea said pliantly to her host and benefactor. "At least the that's what the sitter says."

Andrea kept her job at the tasting room by employing a part-time nanny named Liza and racing home for an hour in the mornings and afternoons to manage meals and to comfort Chase as he settled down for naps.

But nights were becoming horrific as Lupen's toddler worked through a gripping grief he could neither describe nor understand. And Andrea worried that Gilly would tire of the noise and disruption and ask her to leave.

"Are you frightened?" Gilly asked Andrea.

"I don't know how you can put up with this much longer," said Andrea. "It must be hard on you."

Gilly moved closer to Andrea as she stood over Chase's crib and reached to rub softly the baby's back. Chase squirmed violently until his agonized cries diminished and he at last stopped thrashing.

"This is life," said Gilly. "God, don't worry about me. We're sisters, hon. We're in this together. And I wouldn't want it any other way. I love your boy. I love you."

Andrea felt Gilly's arms suddenly around her. It was a quick, earnest and self-conscious hug and over as fast as it was offered.

Gilly had loved her fifth grade teacher and so much she advertised it with letters and stares and rambunctious stalking. However much she tried, Miss Seligman could not lose Gilly at recess, during class, or before or after school.

"You are my favorite forever," Gilly told Miss Seligman, a twenty-two year old woman starting her second year as an elementary teacher and who recognized her student's attention as a guileless and also obsessive crush. Miss Seligman tried at first to gently distract her adoring pupil with special assignments and honorary chores like taking roll or supervising recess. Though these recognitions only bound Gilly closer to her mentor and grew even more affection than Gilly could fully grasp or contain.

A friend told Gilly she was gay to love a woman so much. And Gilly, not understanding what that fully meant, then told everyone she was gay. It was a confession as badly received as it was misunderstood and that left Gilly isolated and afraid. By eighth grade a confident, menstruating Gilly conformed to a fully appropriate and acceptable heterosexual existence. She dated boys but by tenth grade learned that fucking them was no fun at all, though she found the handling of penises and erections fascinating and reveled in getting boys off, even sucking them until just before they came. Her fantasies began to dwell on the use of a penis to arouse another woman. And there were many she thought attractive though her experience with Miss Seligman was an indelible reminder that the real love of a real woman was fraught with real danger.

Gilly graduated high school with honors, went to college and studied law and met and married Lester Greenspan who said he loved Gilly who then said she loved Lester. An awkward, alcohol-fueled wedding was a rehearsal for the unsettling eight years of their marriage that produced little intimacy and no children as Lester's parents and siblings dominated their garbled relationship with their own assertive and sloppy interventions.

Now Lester was gone and Gilly did not miss him or his family. She instead was fixated on Andrea's large breasts and a cautiously repressed desire to suck their nipples. Gilly the adult was now the sad but wiser ex-spouse who could split herself easily and not threaten Andrea with sexual fantasies that grew inevitably out of their accelerating intimacy. It was enough for Gilly to help her new friend through the suffering and death of her partner and the crisis it created for her only child. If she did nothing else, Gilly would still fulfill her determined slavery to love.

A night at last arrived when Chase rested in Gilly's arms and fell asleep and, when set in his small bed, did not awaken. The evening's silence left Gilly and Andrea alone together without a crisis or the words to manage one. Instead, they talked about their lives and love and the qualities of Andrea's attraction to Lupen and, inevitably, Gilly's attraction to Andrea.

"I suppose I've been waiting too long to tell you how I feel," said Gilly.

"Not too long," said Andrea. "I've been here the whole time. And now I'm here for you."

The words were easy and enough. Gilly and Andrea agreed to combine their strengths to manage every obvious weakness. They would stretch a canvass of attraction over the tragedy, hurt, desire and disruption that formed the circumstances before them. Passion ruled and, without the discipline of love's qualifying rigors, set its supreme and dislocating traps.

four

A new century was barely three years old and Christmas was coming. Chase, too, was three years old and could easily and affectionately say the names of his two mothers. His threes had settled him down as they often do for most every child. And his new mothers were deeply in love with each other and also and commonly attached to him.

He was in a family but not one either of his mothers could boast about or describe to anyone but their close friends. Theirs was not a love for public consumption and it was not because their friends did not know the deepening links between Andrea and Gilly. If the associating world comprised just their friends there would be no problem. But there were neighbors and bosses and clients who never would understand how two women could together create a nuclear family and, in fact, hated for any number of unexplored reasons the very idea of it.

Andrea told her tasting room boss she had found a rental and day care for her son. Gilly told her law partners she was renting a room in her house to a single mom. Andrea and Gilly together told the same story to their club sisters, earning a standing cheer for a networking success presumably groomed and made possible by joining the Salinas Soroptimists.

The spacious home on La Rancheria off the Laureles Grade above Highway 68 was a long way from Andrea's east Salinas cottage. It was a distance that lifted her dizzily from the miasma of working poverty into the high hills of consoling wealth. Though neither the wealth nor the house belonged to her. All Andrea really owned was the magnetic attraction that held Gilly tightly to her. And she had held it for a year.

"I wish we could get married," said Gilly one evening as she caressed Andrea's breasts while they lay in bed.

"I love you so much."

As much as Andrea took pleasure and comfort from Gilly's effusive affection, as much as she also enjoyed and cherished their deepening entanglement, Andrea also knew that if Gilly stopped loving her there would be nothing to protect her or Chase. That Gilly wished she could get married gave Andrea comfort but no security.

"We can't, can we?" asked Andrea. "You're the lawyer."

"Not yet," said Gilly. "But we could draw up an agreement. We could name each other guardians and beneficiaries for the other."

"So if something happened…?" Andrea asked vaguely.

"Nothing's going to happen," answered Gilly. "I love you. And you love me."

There were no schools of love and without one Andrea could not understand what was true and what was not. Gilly's love felt real and for nearly a year had sustained them in ways that settled into a mutual and satisfying quotidian of companionship, chores and sex. The sex, especially, was easy and good and better than any Andrea had ever before known. Gilly could make love all day or behave like a shy little girl or get into what she called her "doggy-style" mood and want really hard sex.

Importantly, Gilly initiated their sex in all ways that thrilled and satisfied Andrea but left her often as the passive receiver. All she had to do was open herself, which so far was easy with Gilly. But what if

Gilly stopped chasing her? What if Gilly's passion faded as it often did for women in relationship? What would Andrea do? The curriculum of a school of love might teach how to anchor love through storms of anger, fear or withdrawal. Gilly wanted to marry her and that gave Andrea hope, even if marriage weren't legally possible. That is, until it was.

Gilly started mornings at her office by skimming several newspapers. An attorney-at-law needed always to know what laws were being made and what were being broken. She read on the second Friday of February that the mayor of San Francisco had the day before authorized city hall to perform and recognize the marriages of same sex couples. She stared at a front-page photo of two women exchanging vows in front of a robed, woman judge. She saw another photo of a line forming outside San Francisco city hall, men coupled to men and women to women, all waiting to get married.

That night Gilly asked Andrea to marry her. Andrea laughed before Gilly showed her a small box that contained a set of wedding rings.

"Tomorrow is Valentine's Day," said Gilly. "I got the last available room at the Sheraton for the weekend. We can have the honeymoon first and get married Monday. I've hired Liza to watch Chase until we return."

Andrea read the news account of Thursday's weddings in The City and tuned in the broadcast reports of Friday's raucous and celebratory parade of brides and brides and grooms and grooms as they mounted the steps inside City Hall to meet quickly with officials who issued marriage licenses and then to stand before judges and volunteer ministers who quickly married them.

"Who do we tell?" asked Andrea as she and Gilly drank a cocktail in the Sheraton Lounge. "I mean, even if this is legal, can we get away with it?"

"We can tell our close friends," said Gilly. "No one else needs to know."

"What if someone takes our picture? What if we make the newspapers?"

Gilly sat quietly and gathered her thoughts.

"I don't care about anyone but you, darlin'," said Gilly.

Her words silenced Andrea who fell into her own place within Gilly's shadow, the woman who was her sponsor and salvation, who was the other parent to Lupen's child and the founder of a wondrous feast.

After making love all weekend and ordering enough room service to keep them fortified, the two women left the Sheraton at dawn on Monday and took their places in the line forming outside San Francisco City Hall.

"Gay Nation!" shouted the couple at the top of the city hall stairs. The doors opened at 9 a.m. and by noon, Gilly and Andrea were married.

"I've never been married before," Andrea said meekly as Gilly drove them home. A turbulent winter ocean sloshed against the coastal bluffs outside her window.

"It's easy," said Gilly. "I've done it once and made enough mistakes for both of us."

"Mistakes?" asked Andrea. "What mistakes?"

"Marrying the wrong person was the first," said Gilly. "The second was staying married, meaning I kept making the same mistake again and again. Day after day and year after year."

"That's not us, right?" asked Andrea.

"No, not us," answered Gilly. "We're perfect."

They were brave women who had formalized their love by crossing together into a new frontier of commitment. It was a beautiful story they thought they could always tell themselves, a story that was reliably happy as long as it never had to end.

five

Without lessons in love, Gilly and Andrea struggled at times to play house. They had their collisions over old habits and new expectations, Gilly sometimes overbearing with a need for schedules and lists while Andrea met the day first before deciding how to use it. On workdays Gilly often was out the door before Andrea and Chase were dressed. And when Gilly returned in the evening, a day's dirty dishes usually filled the sink.

Their first big fight was over the time dinner would be served.

But it was over more than that. What was dinner to be? Who chose it and shopped for it? And when? Gilly wanted to post a schedule. And Andrea couldn't understand why.

"When do we have dinner?" Andrea asked, mocking Gilly.

"When we're fucking hungry. That's when. I can't tell Chase when he should eat."

Those schooled in love might see a fight as the way to open a door to a better understanding and more cooperation. Gilly saw only the disturbing failure of her spouse to meet her needs while Andrea retreated into a fear that Gilly would never accept or understand hers.

"I'm laid back," said Andrea. "No big thing."

But for Gilly it was a big thing and one of many not yet spoken that emphasized the two women's differing needs and styles, their diverse interests, their opposing fantasies and, at the core, their contradictory methods of communicating. And while the women eventually clawed their ways back to a mutual regard, with each fight they traveled longer distances to find it. Only the sex remained wild and wondrous even if in its aggressive passion it concealed the incipient roots of a vague but harmful dissonance.

The emerging tension was felt most by Chase who almost precisely on his fourth birthday began again to act out the rumblings of a submerged tension. Newly clamorous voices rattled the walls of his cavernous home and he could not know when. But whenever he heard them he was helplessly compelled to add his own. He too had grievances and now to his wailing grief he added words to describe them.

"Mommies no good," he shouted. "Mommies must go way and go to bed. Mommy Gilly please go way and die."

What death meant to a four-year-old was never discussed but Andrea and Gilly both heard Chase wish it on Gilly and stopped their fighting.

"We can't do this anymore," said Andrea to Gilly. "It's hurting him."

"What if he had a brother or sister?" asked Gilly.

"What?" asked Andrea as if not believing what she heard. She waited for Gilly to answer but Gilly said nothing.

"And how?"

"We could have a baby," Gilly at last blurted. "We're married."

"We could have a baby anyway. But who?" Andrea asked. That she did not ask why encouraged Gilly to continue.

"I could support you," said Gilly. "I earn enough. You could quit your job and stay home."

"Then it's me," said Andrea. She asked no questions and waited for Gilly to respond but again Gilly said nothing.

"So how?" asked Andrea.

"You've done this," said Gilly. "You tell me. All I know is that I love you and I love Chase and we're married and I want to have a baby with you."

That night they made deep love, their touches oscillating between two extremes of hope that formed a vital circuit of response. They awoke in each other's arms, Chase climbing into bed to join them. Gilly left for work while Andrea phoned the Santa Cruz clinic and asked to speak with Dr. Hightower.

It was May before Dr. Hightower could confirm Andrea's pregnancy. But it was good news and even though neither Andrea nor Gilly had any idea how they would manage to keep their marriage a secret, not to mention their pregnancy, they were optimistic conspirators.

"It's no one else's business," said Gilly defiantly. "Easy for you to say," said Andrea. "What do we say when I swell up like a balloon?"

"You'll have left work by then," said Gilly.

"And the club?" asked Andrea.

"Our friends will know," said Gilly. "Maybe then we can tell everyone. It doesn't matter, though. I love you, hon. We're going to have a baby."

The following morning Gilly took a call at work from a local news reporter.

"You Gilly Greenspan?" asked a sharp woman's voice.

"Not Greenspan anymore," said Gilly. "Who's asking?"

The voice identified itself and asked if Gilly were the woman who married Andrea Minalla at San Francisco City Hall in February.

"Who wants to know?" Gilly asked. "And how do you know we're married?"

"Public records," said the reporter. "We're doing a story on same sex locals who got married. Tell me, what was like to…"

Gilly hung up the phone and did not answer it again.

"Will there be a story?" Andrea asked after hearing from Gilly.

"Not about us," said Gilly. "I said nothing. Don't worry."

Andrea had no time to worry. On Sunday the Herald published a page one story on local same sex couples that were married in San Francisco. The feature led with a photograph of two men who owned a home in Pacific Grove. Several couples were photographed and spoke warmly about their marriages. A separate column listed the names of same sex residents who were married in the City. In a moment Andrea found her name and Gilly's listed together.

"Shit!" shouted Andrea. "What now?"

"I guess we tell everyone," said Gilly. "Don't be afraid."

"Everyone already knows," said Andrea. "Damn. Maria. My family. My brothers. My mom."

"I love you," said Gilly. "We don't need to apologize."

"No, of course not," said Andrea. "We need to hide."

Gilly thought she was right but Andrea knew she was wrong. On Monday Gilly's law partners held a meeting to discuss how to handle her marriage to Andrea. The firm had several wealthy, conservative clients and Gilly was asked to lower her profile by taking some time off.

Andrea was met with a cool stare from Maria when she arrived for work on Tuesday.

"Not God's plan," said Maria to Andrea. "You should know better."

On Wednesday Andrea's brother Roberto pushed past tasters at the bar to confront his sister.

"You marry a woman?" he shouted. "You break your mother's heart. We never want to see you again. Go to hell!"

Visitors scattered and left the tasting room. Roberto spat at Andrea before Maria phoned security. By noon Andrea had submitted her resignation and left.

Thursday morning Gilly and Andrea sat together at the breakfast table. There was nowhere either had to be. Liza was dismissed and Chase, thrilled to have his mothers to himself, drifted blithely through the halls of his large, muted home.

A school of love might have instructed Gilly and Andrea in the economics of marriage and how to share and account for their now common property. Three weeks after the story appeared in the paper, Gilly received a certified letter from Lester's divorce attorney stating that since Gilly was now remarried, Lester would cease paying alimony.

"It's in our agreement," Gilly told Andrea. "And it isn't much. We're fine. I have plenty in the bank. Don't worry."

Marriage had done nothing to loosen Gilly's control of her assets. Andrea, who had nearly nothing, wanted to know what her spouse was worth.

"Enough," said Gilly and that was all she would say. "Even if something happens to me, you're taken care of."

"You sound like a man, sometimes," said Andrea. "I'm not some dumb housewife."

Gilly tried to express sympathy but seemed determined to conceal her finances. And then August arrived when a ruling of the state Supreme Court dissolved their marriage and four thousand others. The San Francisco same sex weddings were determined to be illegal. The two women were left where they began, but worse: the world knew about them, not the whole world but their small world. And that was enough since places they were now pariahs outnumbered the places they were welcome.

The court decision saved Gilly's job since she was no longer legally married to another woman. But it left Andrea in limbo. She was barely four months pregnant and without a job and Gilly was no longer her wife. What Andrea needed now was a husband and a woman husband would be fine but without any legal access to her household wealth Andrea was left virtually bereft.

Fall became winter while Andrea stayed home and Gilly worked. Andrea cooked, cleaned and played house while her tummy grew. Gilly labored into the late hours to hold onto her job at the law firm.

Andrea answered the phone one morning to hear Maria's voice. "Someone's trying to reach you," she said. "Keeps calling." "Who?" asked Andrea.

"Don't know," answered Maria curtly. "She wouldn't say."

Maria gave her a phone number.

"Things OK?" Maria asked.

"Fine," said Andrea. "But I'm not married anymore."

"Yeah," said Maria. "Too bad, I guess. Gotta go."

And she hung up the phone.

Andrea did not recognize the number, it's prefix an area code for a vast region of the state north of San Francisco. There was no name and Maria had referred only to "a woman." Andrea struggled for a half-hour to recall without success any tendril of her life that reached into the state's far northwest.

"This is Andrea Minalla," she said to the woman that answered her call, a voice that sounded aloof and also anxious, suspicious and yearning.

"Damn. At last…" said the woman. "I've been looking for you for four years. I'm Lupen's older sister."

"She has a sister?" asked Andrea. "She never told me about…"

"No, I bet she didn't," said the woman. "She wanted nothing to do with us. We loved her but she couldn't get that. She was stoned so much and mom hated it. And dad, well, he wasn't good with this stuff. He freaked out and then Lupen freaked out and…"

"Whoa!" shouted Andrea. "What's your name?"

The woman's name was Erin and she apologized for her outburst.

"Lupen hitched a ride outta here five years ago and we never saw her again," she said.

"And where is here?" asked Andrea.

"Boonville," said Erin. "Mendocino County. Where Lupen grew up."

"And me?" asked Andrea. "Why me?"

"Took forever," said Erin. "Sorry for the surprise. Public records led me to an arrest report in Monterey and I began asking around. Found out Lupen was enrolled in a drug program. A counselor wouldn't say much but said she'd left and had a baby. Your name came up as a friend. A woman named Andrea who worked at a winery. I've been calling every damned…"

"What do you want from me?" Andrea asked suspiciously.

"Sorry for going on," said Erin. "I just want to find my sister.

And if she has a baby, well, I'm her aunt and maybe I can help, maybe there's something…"

Her voice trailed off.

"I don't have any good news," said Andrea. "I'm sorry."

"What can you tell me?" asked Erin, quieted by Andrea's assertive gravity.

Andrea succumbed to the flood of a hundred different thoughts and as many feelings.

"There's a baby," said Andrea. "His name is Chase and he's well cared for."

"Oh God," said Erin. "Oh dear God."

"And Lupen…Lupen is dead."

It was Erin's turn to succumb and for at least a minute Andrea heard only the sound of deep, heavy breathing and then nothing.

"Would you meet with me?" asked Erin.

Andrea knew her news was not a surprise.

"When? Where?" asked Andrea.

"I can come to you," said Erin.

"Let's meet in the city," said Andrea. "It's safer."

"Safer for you?" asked Erin.

"Safer for all concerned," answered Andrea.

Whatever concerns Andrea might have had were assuaged by Erin's disheveling sobs when she learned how her sister had died.

"Was she in pain? Was she alone?" asked Erin as they sat in a small café on Union Street.

Andrea shook her head.

"We both were with her, " she said. "Me and Chase. Would you like to see some pictures of him?"

It was early afternoon and the café was empty, a location close to the bridge and an easier destination for Erin who had left at dawn to drive down from from the north. Andrea arrived early so she could appear prepared and in control. There might be issues.

And there weren't. Erin was dressed in a grey wool suit, her bright brown eyes heavily mascaraed in an apparent effort to appear strong and responsible.

"He's…he's darling," said Erin who saw much of Lupen in Chase's face. The photographs shuffled through a chronology that started with a few snaps of a naked baby and then moved forward to the child's earliest months and years at last landing on a photo of Chase playing, his arm around a pre-school buddy.

"Can I see him?" asked Erin.

"Is that what you want?" Andrea responded. "Is that all you want? Lupen worried, you know. She worried her family would come looking for her. The family wouldn't want her but would want to take her baby. I need to tell you that I'm Chase's legal parent. And as long as I'm alive that will never happen."

"No, of course not," said Erin. "There isn't much left of Lupen's family. Our parents are dead. I'm married and have two boys of my own. We'd love Chase like our own, of course. But take him? Why would we ever take your boy?"

Andrea could not think of a reason and found her body responding to Erin's ingenuous grief. When Erin reached across the table to touch her hand it was all Andrea could bear.

"It's been a hard time," Andrea blurted through a stream of hidden tears.

"Come see us," said Erin, flashing immediately the terms of a well settled and country hospitality.

"Jasper…that's my husband…Jasper and I live in the Anderson Valley. We have some acreage. Jasper is a foreman at a vineyard. You could stay in the cottage…My boys would love to meet a cousin."

"First, I need to have my own baby," said Andrea after pulling herself together.

"Thanks. That's nice."

Andrea gave Erin a few of Chase's pictures to keep. Then she stood and walked out of the café and into the fading light of a low sun and its trailing, persistent chill.

seven

In January a healthy and darling girl named Marnie Anne was born a month early to Andrea, named after relatives on both sides of the Gilly-Andrea family. It was not enough, though, to draw the interest or regard of either Gilly's or Andrea's associates and relations who, even with the political dissolution of their marriage, would not acknowledge that either Andrea or Gilly still existed.

162

Andrea stayed home to mother her baby and Gilly continued with her law work while weeks turned into months and Gilly commenced as she always did to structure chores and over plan while Andrea did no planning at all.

"We need a schedule," Gilly said emphatically.

"Why?" asked Andrea. "You still won't tell me how we pay for things. You still won't share with me the fundamentals of our daily survival."

"It's not your concern," said Gilly firmly.

"Then why should I care?" asked Andrea. "Why should I fucking care about anything?"

Without consensus the challenges only grew. By Marnie's fifth month it was apparent to both Andrea and Gilly that Chase was reacting badly to his new sibling. One evening he tried to tip Marnie out of her crib and send her crashing to the floor. Andrea saw it just in time and caught her baby and did not tell Gilly who would not understand why Chase was banned from the nursery. If Gilly had secrets, so did Andrea and unspoken secrets eventually pushed Andrea and Gilly wordlessly apart. A month passed without any sex and without sex there appeared also to be no more common bond or uncommonly wonderful love.

Gilly offered to give Andrea a weekly stipend of $500.

"Yours. All yours to do with what you want," said Gilly.

The money briefly mollified Andrea until the second week when, without the bearings of a known income or the facts of a budget, she realized she had no way to know the actual value of her allowance or the true value of anything. Meanwhile Gilly's work hours grew longer and later until one night Gilly did not come home, slipping in before dawn though Andrea was waiting for her.

"Yeah…" Gilly at last admitted. "I'm in love again. It's not a big deal. I still love you. It's just…well…she sees me."

It was clear to Andrea that Gilly could afford to make room for a new love in a way Andrea could not.

"I don't want to break up," Gilly moaned tearfully.

Andrea heard her and agreed to stay while she also counted the weeks ahead to a date when her saved money from Gilly would be enough to give her choices. Both women felt the onset of a wearying despair. And the despair a school of love might have taught how to manage instead consumed everyone. Andrea realized she could not bear her current life and Gilly knew, but did not say, she could no longer bear Andrea.

On a hot spring morning Andrea phoned Erin and asked if she could visit with the children.

"Of course, hon," said Erin with a garrulous down home affection. "You OK?"

"Actually, no," Andrea confessed. "I'm struggling here and so are the kids. But I have some money. I just need to get back on my feet. I think if I had a few days away…"

"You can have all the days you want," said Erin. "That's what Lupen would have wanted for you and certainly for your children. You just get yourself up here, OK? Do you have a car?"

Andrea's ancient Mazda for years had gotten her to the Monterrey wharf every day. Now it would carry her and her babies into the northern woods.

Erin gave Andrea directions: Highway 101 to Highway 121 west at Cloverdale and after forty-two miles a turn onto a dirt road near Gowan's farm. She couldn't miss it though Andrea wondered how could she not.

"Saturday OK?" asked Andrea.

"Any day is OK," said Erin.

It was a homecoming to a home Andrea had never known. Dry summer winds blew through the trees as she drove across undulating ridges to fall at last into a valley of towering redwoods.

She found Erin waiting at the gate to a long dirt road that climbed again into the woods sprouting from a deepening ravine.

"A good trip, darlin'?" asked Erin as she leaned into the driver's window. Her entire face was a smile.

"How are the kids?"

Chase was asleep in his car seat while the baby slept in a carrier also fastened tight by an embracing seat belt.

"You worried?" asked Erin. "You sounded worried when…"

"Not now," said Andrea. "I have some money. I have a car. I have my children. And they are my children. That's the good news.

That woman has no claim on my kids. On the other hand, I can't collect child support. That's the bad news."

"Not so bad," said Erin. "You have family. That is, if you want it. I know that's what Lupen would have wanted for her child…and for you."

Andrea tried at first to resist the stirring of her instinct to survive. Erin was more than a new friend. She was a link to her love for Lupen and a source for its renewal. A school of love might have taught Andrea how relationships invariably strive to become families and either succeed or don't depending on the verity of love's allegiance and the strength of its tenderness. Lovers can search every shore for intruders and yet miss the jeopardy under their own skins.

"Winery in Philo has an opening in their tasting room," said Erin. "Jasper has the details. But let's get you and the kids settled in the cottage. Nothin' but time now. We don't hurry much up here."

It surprised Andrea to think that Lupen, her lost, addicted and rambling first love, was now the maker of her essential deliverance. Andrea felt enfolded in one of time's lucky and beneficial furrows. She had arrived safely and without fear. She had Lupen's baby and now she had Lupen's family. She was a multitude and no longer alone.

NINE DAYS,
NINE MONTHS,
NINE YEARS

nine days

Charles stood in a long line. He had stopped at a market in Petaluma to buy groceries before driving to the coast. One check-out lane was open and the cashier was helplessly engaged with a customer who disputed his bill. The long line grew longer and Charles, waiting at the end, shouted "we're drowning back here, call the Coast Guard."

The woman in front of him turned and smiled.

It was how Charles met Regina.

"I'm glad someone has a sense of humor," said Regina.

"Happy to oblige," said Charles. "It's my experience that a lot of the things that frustrate and upset people are often very funny."

"Oooh…very true," said Regina. "How do you come by your optimism. Are you a therapist?"

"Oh no," said Charles. "I know a few therapists and only one is an optimist."

Regina laughed.

"That's pretty scary," she responded.

"You're telling me?" Charles answered. "You can't imagine what it has cost me to find that out."

Regina laughed again.

"Are you serious?" she asked.

"Not really," said Charles. "I just enjoy finding the fun in things. Even this stupid line that is making us all late for something, but not anything important. Yet see how grumpy everyone is. Everyone but us."

The grocery line solidarity of Charles and Regina grew after their purchases into a further conversation outside the store followed by a short walk to an adjacent coffee bar. Two hours later Regina remembered that friends were coming to her house for dinner.

"Can I see you again?" Charles asked.

"Yes, of course," said Regina. "This has been fun."

"I'll phone you tomorrow," said Charles. "Maybe you'd come out to the coast for a walk on the beach."

"I'd love that," said Regina.

The two new friends then parted, Regina to return to her large family home on D Street and Charles to his one bedroom cabin in Salmon Creek. The two new friends were surprised to learn they were born in the same month of the same year. They were the same age and so there was no need for either to announce what that was. Regina engaged Charles with her insouciance and candor while Charles spoke crisply and elegantly about his life as a journalist and writer. Regina learned that Charles was a bachelor in the same moment Charles learned Regina was a widow. It was a delicious opening for both and a stunning coincidence that a suspicious person might have thought star-crossed.

Charles was a bachelor but had twice been a husband, a fact he did not hide from Regina, thinking her simply a new and compatible friend. Regina had been married to the same husband, a wealthy physician from an established local family, for nearly forty years until he contracted pancreatic cancer and died within three months of his diagnosis.

"Poor Gunther…he knew more about the disease than the doctors that took care of him," Regina told Charles in an unguarded moment. "And then he was gone."

"It must have been a big blow," said Charles.

"Not really," said Regina, surprisingly comfortable with her newly engaged stranger. "He left me everything. The house, the investments, the children…"

Charles heard the children and wondered if he were meant to laugh. Instead, he nodded knowingly,

"Do you have children?" Regina asked.

"One," said Charles. "A son. That's all. One is enough."

"I have three," said Regina. "And often that feels like too many."

"Mine is grown and gone," said Charles.

"Mine are gone," said Regina. "But two are anything but grown."

Were either Regina or Charles to recall their first meeting, it would always be with a fondness attached to the pleasure of an unexpected thrill. As each thought later, it was thrilling indeed to meet a stranger that within minutes spoke with an appealing candor and that after an hour penetrated deeply to the core experience of each. And the wit. Neither Charles nor Regina had ever before met anyone so cleverly engaging as the other, someone who could in moments plumb the depths of another life's experience while their own was also plumbed.

Charles waited for Regina's arrival. It was three days after their first meeting and Charles wondered nervously if she would actually arrive. Regina had sent Charles an e-mail to confirm and also to accept his invitation to drive out to Salmon Creek for a walk on the beach and afterward to enjoy a dinner that Charles would prepare. She was to arrive on the second Saturday of a crisp, windy March.

Just after his wind-up grandfather clock chimed twice Charles heard a car's engine rumble across a small rocky hill above the Bodega Dunes and slowly slide into his shallow, sandy driveway. He looked outside to see a dark green Mercedes. He descended a short flight of stairs to meet Regina as she climbed out of her car. She wore a bulky blue ski jacket over a grey flannel jumpsuit and had tucked her long hair under a wool stocking cap. Was she cold, wondered Charles, or was she just hiding her hair's smoky white highlights? Charles also had a hat but did not put it on. He was grateful to have enough hair to comb, even if it was as grey as the fog that still had not lifted and that shrouded the shore with its cool, moist gossamer.

"Not exactly spring!" Regina shouted.

"It's not spring!" Charles responded ."Two more weeks until spring."

"But this is California," Regina countered. "It's always spring here."

"This is Northern California," Charles announced as he walked across the driveway to meet his guest. "You may get spring in Peta-luma but here at the coast it's never assured."

"I won't argue," Regina answered. "I'm prepared."

And she was, booted and capped against a prevailing twenty-five knot wind that stirred the sand raised by each of her footsteps to-ward Charles. As she arrived he took her hand and pointed toward the stairs.

"I have coffee brewing," he said. "and a fire in the stove. Come in out of the wind."

"You have a charming home," Regina told Charles after climb-ing the stairs to enter his cabin, a three-room flat built cleverly over a garage and workspace.

"And what a view…"

"Well, it's home…" said Charles.

"How long?" asked Regina.

"I played here when I was a kid," answered Charles. "My father built it. He died just after my last divorce. Thank God my ex and I had already settled. It became mine free and clear. And just in time."

"In time for what?" asked Regina.

"In time to get out of an apartment lease in Windsor that was going to break me," he answered. "The second ex was merciless. Fortunately some of my stories did pretty well and the royalties were enough to cover the groceries."

"You write stories?" Regina asked.

"Yes..a sideline…short mysteries that feature a bungling private detective who appears inept and dangerously clumsy until he solves the crime, the bad guys go to jail and everyone, and most impor-tantly the readers, dig how clever he really is. It's an old shtick… remember Columbo on TV? Remember the Sixties?"

Regina did not.

"Similar *modus operandi*…play dumb and get people to talk…it was an old enough plot device that I could bring it back but with some twists. Anyway, the second ex took a chunk out of my income but, thankfully, she had a pretty good job of her own as a junior high vice-principal. And then my dad died and I got this cabin…"

"I've never been divorced," said Regina, interested in Charles' writing but drawn more deeply into his life.

"Was it hard to break-up?"

"No harder the second time than it was the first. Easier, in fact. I had a son with my first wife. He never liked the second and when we split up he helped me move."

"The paintings," Regina said suddenly as her eyes roamed around the living room. "Where did…are they yours?"

"I didn't paint them," said Charles. "They're by an artist I know. A dear friend. He used to go backpacking with me. Do you like art?"

Yes, said Regina, she loved art.

"They are…" Regina sought words she couldn't find and, instead, blushed.

"They just are," Charles responded. "Let's leave them for awhile and take a walk. They'll be here when we come back."

Charles led Regina across a sandy strand and through a high dune that bordered the protracted and mile-long beach of Salmon Creek. The wind pushed and caught them both, nearly blowing Regina to the ground.

"Where are we going?" she shouted.

"South…" answered Charles. "I know a place out of the wind."

Their hike continued in silence as a fierce gale pushed them hard down the beach. After twenty minutes, Charles reached to pull Regina along a path that climbed a still larger dune. At its apex, Charles shouted.

"Here…come here!"

Regina arrived to see a structure built from driftwood that offered both shelter from the wind and a wide view of the ocean. Charles led her inside and to a makeshift bench. The wind made her eyes water but did not bite and Regina relaxed enough to lean into Charles for a share of his warmth.

"You OK?" Charles asked.

"I'm fine," said Regina. "This is just so weirdly wonderful and beautiful."

A deepening rapport seemed to be forming and, after a half-hour of sitting and gently cuddling, Regina and Charles returned to the beach house under a different spell.

"And this is really your home?" Regina asked as she sat at the kitchen table and watched her host juggle pots, plates and bowls in a kitchen that was the entire east wall of his living room.

"For now," said Charles. "For now and probably forever. I could do worse. I'm free and clear. No mortgage. As long as I pay the property taxes…well, I could die here. It's about time I had a little luck."

"You haven't been lucky?" asked Regina.

Charles stopped talking. It was a moment he needed, which was a moment he sometimes skipped in his urgency to be an entertaining host. He now could think of nothing funny or sarcastic to say about not being lucky.

"It's not just about luck," Charles answered. "It's what we do with living. There are choices we make that before we know it become entanglements and that wind us into relationship with subjects and forces of all kinds. We can become trapped in our own trappings. Do you know what I mean?"

"I was trapped," Regina answered after a pause. "It was a somewhat happy trap. But a trap all the same. I didn't know it until Gunther died. Now I do…"

In what seemed the act of a magician, Charles waved his arms wildly over the cabin's small corner stove before serving up both a generous chef salad and a plate of thick pasta noodles smothered in a fragrant white sauce. He poured them each a glass of white wine and sat down.

"And what was your trap?" Charles asked.

Regina took a sip of wine and took some time to swallow.

"That I thought I was free," she answered. "Gunther made us rich with his medical career but it meant that I would have to give up teaching. The only thing I could make for myself was our babies. Three children…I love them but they came at a great price to me. I did not know that until Gunther died. I don't blame him for what he wanted. I blame myself for not demanding what I needed."

"And what was that?" asked Charles.

"My own share of our life together. My own life within our family life. It might have been grand and I might have loved Gunther more, might have given more to my children if I had taken more for myself."

Charles nodded.

"That's something you seem to understand now. How does it make you feel?"

"Regretful," said Regina. "Sorry. And the children know. Edward, he's the oldest. He'll be 40 this year and he's just another Gunther. A successful doctor. Wants me to sell the house and move into a condo or assisted living. Wants to get me out to pasture where he can see me but not worry about me. The other two…well Jasmine is two years younger than Edward and can't seem to hold anything together. She just left after another months-long visit. She says I 'owe' her so much though she's often homeless and I know drugs play a big part in her instability. She was married once to a musician. It lasted a couple of months. She tried college and dropped out. She works in hospitality, which means that wherever she lands, she works as a waitress for awhile before it wears her out or the drugs kick in. Not good. And there's the baby—Jacob—the surprise child we weren't expecting. Damn, I was 43 when he was born and barely got through the pregnancy. Raising him took everything I had left as a parent."

Regina's honesty surprised her. Charles made her comfortable and asked her questions that touched her deepest experiences.

"It sounds as if you have a lot on your plate and that you're feeling alone," said Charles. "I think I understand how that feels."

"Yes…you're kind to ask," Regina interrupted, eager to regain control of her feelings, if not the conversation.

"Tell me about your son…"

"Marcus is smart, precocious and 38 years old," said Charles. "He was born to my first wife Melanie. His childhood was filled with a certain kind of wildness I still can't grasp. Easily distracted and easily seduced. He lived mostly with his mom after the divorce. Visits with me were adventures, to say the least. He'd get lost regularly: at parks, at movies, on vacations. One year we were on the Boardwalk in Santa Cruz and he just took off. It was midnight before the cops found him playing pinball games at the arcade. I called it his stray dog complex, as if he'd catch a scent of something and just follow it wherever it took him. When he was a teen his mother pushed him at me to the point I had to threaten to renegotiate her child support payments. He was twenty before I caught on to his problems with alcohol. A bad car accident and, gratefully, he wasn't driving. But it opened the can of worms that has become his life with me: a few arrests for public drunkenness and one DUI…he works in retail and moves around a lot, as if he needs to run from his record in order to keep a job and stay ahead of himself…"

"And his mom?" asked Regina.

"She's no help," answered Charles. "She's…she's just no help."

"We sound like twins of a sort," said Regina. "I have more kids than you, sure. But they all have problems, don't they? And some of those problems—in fact most of them—are still ours."

"Must be our birthday month," said Charles. "Though you're the Cancer and I'm the Leo."

"But we're both 65," responded Regina. "Maybe this is some kind of fiendish senior-style adolescence. It was only fifty years ago we were both fifteen. What do we know? Fifty years feels like nothing."

"And we love them," said Charles. "After all this, and no matter what they say or do to us…we…love…them."

Charles said the last three words slowly and with emphasis as if it were more than a thought and really the uttering of a pledge.

Dessert was oatmeal cookies and coffee that Charles served on the cabin's high back porch and under the deeply black and star-pocked sky of one of winter's last long nights. The ocean roared its windy slaps against the sand. Charles slipped his arm over Regina's shoulders which were wrapped in a heavy blanket provided by her host and that held them both together. Charles thought to ask…but didn't. He had served his guest only one glass of wine so she could drive safely home. Though for a moment it seemed to make perfect sense that he ask Regina to stay the night and for him to make friendly and clever love to her and with the same friendliness and cleverness that each found in the other. But Charles knew that his wit and joviality were offered to everyone and in a way that both linked him to others and also protected his most vulnerable instincts.

It was Wednesday. Charles drove to Petaluma to have dinner with Regina in her home. On the drive Charles listened again to the radio news of a Malaysian airliner that had vanished from the sky and could not be found. The entire Indian ocean was being searched by the air forces of several nations and after a week, still nothing. *It's 2014,* thought Charles. *How does a plane carrying more than 200 passengers just disappear?* More curious was the lack of any transmission from the plane. No Mayday. No anxious pilot crying out for help. A hijack? Perhaps. It had happened before. But not without a trace. And there was no trace. The plane's disappearance was a disquieting mystery.

Charles parked his car on D Street. He wandered up the sidewalk past the mansions originally held by the city's early founders and many now the exclusive properties of the town's young and restless *nouveau riche*. Regina's home stood out and, at three stories, was nearly the block's largest.

"Well, hello….!!!" Regina announced as she opened the front door. A crowd of chattering women stood behind her, all talking as they grabbed their coats from two hall closets and then pushed inelegantly past their hostess.

"Night, hon," a woman shouted as she squeezed between Regina and Charles. "It was grand…"

"Grand…" Charles said to Regina. "Have I missed the party?"

Regina laughed, but barely.

"Women…the women who…well, it's a club of sorts…" Regina spoke haltingly. She was embarrassed.

"They were supposed to be gone by now…"

"And they're leaving," said Charles quickly. "Perfect timing."

Regina laughed again but with an enthusiasm that seemed to convey her relief.

"Come in," she said at last to Charles.

"Where would you like to put me?" he asked.

It was the wrong question. He thought it an attempt at disarming humor but, in the crush of the crowd, not disarming enough to amuse Regina.

"Wait in the kitchen," she said cooly and at last.

"Where's the kitchen?" asked Charles.

"There…" Regina pointed vaguely down the hall, obviously distracted and maybe also irritated.

Charles worked his way through the hall's slender passage and past women who stared at him as if he were the only and unwelcome male at a sorority slumber party.

"They raise money for the library," Regina told Charles after sending her last afternoon guest out the door before rushing back to the kitchen to find her new and only evening guest talking with her maid.

"That's really nice," said Charles. "Millie says she's fixed our dinner. Right Millie?"

The maid, an older and matronly woman, looked back at Regina. She appeared embarrassed.

"You can go now, Millie," said Regina. "We're fine. Thanks."

"Bye, Millie," said Charles, who seemed to be milking the chaos of his arrival for any shred of humor.

In a few minutes all but Regina and Charles were gone from the home, which for a moment created a stilted distance between them.

"I'm sorry to be so late," said Regina. "The women…well, it's important…"

"I'm sorry to be so early," said Charles. "I couldn't wait to see you."

For a moment Regina felt intimidated by Charles and his soft sarcasm until his last words broke through to express the meaning of his presence before her.

I couldn't wait to see you.

These were unfamiliar words to Regina who for a moment tried to recall if she ever before had heard them.

"Let me give you a tour," Regina announced as she reached for Charles' hand and led him back down the hall and into the home's large living room plush with furnishings, paintings and treasures, its shelves and surfaces cluttered with vases, small plates, and numerous mounted photos. Regina handed Charles a small sculpture of Pan that rested on the mantle.

"From Italy," said Regina. "At least the 15th century…"

Charles promptly dropped the sculpture that, luckily, missed the hardwood floor and skipped off a nearby chair and onto the carpet.

"No harm," Regina said hurriedly as she recovered the piece.

"Be careful," said Charles. "I'm a bull in a china shop."

The tour continued, Regina running ahead as if in a hurry to share with Charles the trappings that were emblems of her life. Charles followed her upstairs, passing a room that stopped him, a room filled with books and photos and that featured a wide, large oak desk.

"It's Gunther's study," said Regina as Charles stood tentatively at the doorway and stared in at a nearly wall-sized color photograph of an older man wearing a three-piece suit, his expression strong and firm. Arranged around the photo were various certificates and awards. The room appeared to be a sanctuary to Regina's deceased husband. It is his study, Charles heard Regina say, as if her ex might still be alive somewhere and at any moment need to return.

"Impressive," Charles said, slightly flummoxed by the room's display of Gunther's long, seemingly impactful and well-recorded life.

"The children…" Regina said hesitantly as she sensed her guest's unease. "They wanted this. Here…there's more…follow me…"

The tour continued as Regina pointed out paintings, furnishings and more rooms brimming with art and furniture. She ran ahead once again to close what Charles knew to be the door to her bedroom.

It was a tour Regina might have hoped would open her life to Charles, though its many elegant trappings seemed to leave Charles even farther behind.

Money cares for Regina, thought Charles, *while I care for money and in amounts so tight and small that Regina might not even itemize them.*

Wealth cared for Regina and because she was rich she did not need to care about money. And because Charles was not rich he would always care about money. These were words he could barely say even to himself though they left a feeling that rippled between them and in a way that momentarily distanced him from Regina until she laughed and, again, ran ahead of him into the kitchen.

"Come on!" she shouted. "Thanks to Millie, there is a genuinely artisan meal waiting for us. Let's eat."

Her spontaneity returned to Charles the common playfulness of a new and goofy friend. It was a feeling both immediate and irresistible. Charles knew Regina also felt it.

Dinner was a rash of smells and flavors: a tower of greens and cheeses Regina said was a salad and that was followed by a pasta entree presented as a chicken carbonara that paired reasonably well with the bottle of Zinfandel brought by Charles. A dish of roasted Brussels sprouts was smothered in a wine sauce and a dessert of chocolate mousse was served in tall glass dishes likely kept for this one provision. The food was what Charles later recalled, food so delicious it left him uncharacteristically speechless. Though this didn't seem to matter. Regina, fueled by the wine and aroused by the presence of her chosen guest, had so very much to say that all Charles really needed to do was to chew and to listen.

"How long?" she asked in response to Charles who himself asked how long she had lived in Petaluma.

"I can't recall when we arrived. At least twenty years…yes, twenty. Jacob was born just before we moved here and he's 21 now. Still here, though. I wish he'd finish school or at least finish something."

"He's the student?" Charles asked as he tried to recall the order and names of Regina's children.

"Only when he feels like it," answered Regina. "He's a surfer. I often think surfing is his life. He's out at the coast more than he is anywhere else. He's probably out there now. When they finish riding waves he and some friends hang out at a small bar in Bodega. He'll walk in here around eight. And he'll be famished. You'll see."

"So he still lives at home," said Charles.

"On and off," said Regina. "He's working now. Has a job as a server at the Italian restaurant downtown. Works the long weekend, Thursday through Sunday. Pay isn't great but the tips are good. He's saving up to move in with his friends. They have an apartment near the JC in Santa Rosa. They're students and I keep hoping they can pull him back into some classes. He's a good kid but sometimes I think children are just pets with thumbs."

Later in the kitchen Charles offered to rinse dishes while Regina slipped them into the washer. Regina handed him an apron and as he leaned over the sink he stood aligned with Regina who took a dish from his hands and placed it on a washer shelf. They bumped often until Regina pushed hard against Charles who caught her mischievous smile and pushed hard back. In a moment they were face to face and eagerly wrestling and giggling themselves into an embrace that lasted longer than their giggles, long enough to express a pleasing, momentary and wordless consensus. A flow of feelings followed that brought back words.

"This is sweet," Regina said as Charles slowly released her. They both laughed as if both understood a joke that still had no punchline. But their mutual irreverence might be the first step toward a loving and arousing conspiracy to enjoy what was left of living, for each of them and possibly together.

Who's he?

Driving back to Salmon Creek Charles recalled the words that ended abruptly his embrace of Regina. Her younger son had walked into the kitchen to see his mother holding close a strange and unknown man. And it was not an unreasonable question. Though, as he reviewed the evening, it occurred to Charles that the boy named Jacob who had asked it had no regard for his mother and even less for Charles. Introduced awkwardly, Jacob turned away from Charles to look directly at his mother and to ask his question.

What's going on?, Jacob asked.

"Nothing's going on," Regina had responded, surprising Charles with her defensive tone.

Well, that's good, answered Jacob as if the house were his and his mother and Charles were simply its naughty guests.

I'm home now, Jacob said to his mother without looking again at Charles. *What's for dinner?*

Regina told her son she had a guest and that dinner was over and that Jacob was on his own.

Really? Jacob snorted. But I'm starving.

Charles excused himself and left the kitchen. It was several minutes before he heard Jacob's raised voice and the slam of a door. Regina then emerged from the kitchen and approached Charles.

My son is hungry and I need to feed him dinner, Regina told Charles.

Charles heard himself say it was time to leave. Regina did not object.

*It's complicated…*Regina tried to speak but Charles embraced and quieted her.

He said it was OK and invited Regina to come out to Salmon Creek to spend Saturday with him.

Oh yes. Of course. Yes. she said quickly.

Driving home Charles addressed both his affection and his concern. They would walk the beach. He would take her on a drive north. They could have lunch at the lodge in Timber Cove and drift back for an evening snack at the cabin. What would happen? Charles tried to suppress any expectation.

Charles awoke Saturday morning to find his life in retreat. He was retired, or so he said. Retirement was another word for a survival built only from what remained of his unanchored existence. Were it not for his beach cabin, Charles might not even have a place to live.

He had his social security but no pension. He had a home but no income to derive from it. He wrote his four mystery stories each year but what they earned barely paid his property taxes. The wealth created with two previous partners dissolved with the dissolution of the marriages that, managed by expensive attorneys and fed by unfettered hostilities, cost a bundle. The second ex was Marcus' mother. Yes, he described himself as retired, which was another way to say he could no longer find work.

"It's a beautiful day!" Regina shouted from the bottom of the creaky wooden stairs that led to the cabin's upper floor.

"The sun is out…is that what you mean?" asked Charles.

"The sun is out…and I'm out here…seeing you."

Regina's words were quieter as she climbed to meet Charles who dropped down to take her hand in a way that produced an inelegant but firm embrace.

"I have you for the day…the whole day?" asked Charles.

"The whole day and into the night," answered Regina.

Was her comment meant to be whimsically ribald or just a loose description of a time frame?

"Good," said Charles. "I'm fixing you dinner. Hell, I'm taking you to lunch."

"I brought some things," said Regina. She entered the cabin and dropped a burgundy burlap tote onto a chair in the upstairs kitchenette.

"Some snacks and other stuff for later," she said.

There would be a later though how late later would be was not discussed.

"Just hit a hundred thousand miles," said Charles. "It's a great little car."

Regina offered to drive her Mercedes but Charles said no.

"I know the way," he said firmly.

"Well, I could probably figure it out…" Regina countered. "I mean, its one road and one direction…"

"This way you get the views. I've already seen them a hundred times," said Charles.

So they sat together in Charles' 2009 Honda Civic while he backed out of the driveway. Regina listened for a moment as the engine screamed over the sound of wheels crunching gravel. In a moment they were at the shoreline, tracing the slender river of asphalt that drew them north.

"That's where Jacob surfs," Regina said as they climbed the gradual grade aligned with Salmon Creek Beach.

"That's where everyone surfs," said Charles.

His comment quieted Regina who could not tell if her driver was being informative or sarcastic. Charles felt the chill.

"I mean…it's been a surfing mecca for decades…quite a history. And it can be challenging. We get a lot of champion surfers out here, especially when storms in the north Pacific stir things up."

"I didn't know that."

It was all Regina said.

"Sometimes I photograph the surfers," said Charles, trying again to support a flow of feelings as well as words.

"I should show you some of my photos."

"That would be nice," answered Regina. "This is a beautiful day and we seem to be the only ones out at the coast."

"Still winter," said Charles. "Might get to sixty degrees today, though. A clear day despite the wind."

The sky and hills blew by as Charles drove north and as he swept into turns that opened to the ocean's wind-driven white caps, all splashing violently and across a blue and green vastness that reached beyond every western horizon. North of the historic site of an old Russian fort, Charles pulled over at a small gulch.

"My favorite," he said. "No one comes here."

Regina followed as Charles hiked out to a point that commanded limitless coastal views north and south.

"It's beautiful," said Regina. "It's beautiful and so empty."

"It's beautiful because it is so empty," said Charles. "No sign of man's hand on the land."

"It is men, isn't it?" said Regina. "It is men who put their hands on the land."

Charles heard her and for a moment Regina wished he hadn't.

"Yeah…" answered Charles after a pensive pause. "I don't know what to do about that. It's a reason I like this little spot. It's free, open and untouched."

His response was vague but accepting and Regina accepted his acceptance.

When they sat down in the Timber Cove dining room to order lunch, she took a moment to thank him for hearing her at the beach.

"I'm interested in anything you have to say," said Charles. "I enjoy you, Regina. I like you."

Lunch moved them back to a conversation that raised questions and engendered intimacies. They took particular care with the ways they were alike and offered each other a deepening curiosity about the ways they were different. So many words were spoken and all of them heard.

Driving back, Charles took a road that led through the coastal hills and to a winery in Seaview where they roused the owner who gave them tastes of his new releases. Driving back to the coast Charles felt Regina's hand on his shoulder.

"A lovely afternoon, Charles," she said warmly.

It was enough and also not nearly enough. There would be more. Returning to the cabin, Regina entered the bathroom to freshen up while Charles started dinner.

Wine was poured and words, many more words were spoken until there were no more words.

"Dinner in ten minutes," Charles said as he approached Regina who stood at the window and watched the sun set.

"Beautiful," she said as she turned to face Charles.

And then there were no more words. Charles turned off the stove and together with Regina walked away from the kitchen. Both knew that unless one was searching, there was nothing to find.

It was so quickly the morning of their ninth day. They awoke together laughing and naked…and hungry. It was a pleasant surprise for Charles that Regina had packed in her burgundy tote a nightgown and a bottle of silky lube. And now what? As Charles turned what was left of their dinner into a breakfast, Regina showered and dressed. At the table they shared a wordless understanding that going forward there would be words and more words for days, for months and perhaps for years in a conversation that had only just begun.

nine months

Charles kept his camera close. In this first year with Regina he had become her lover and now her husband. Charles documented the moments that shaped and grew the love of their marriage and that were now the anchors of his new life. Digital technology allowed him to use a camera to make hundreds of photographs at no real cost. Now he could afford to print his images at any time and in any way. Those photos he made into larger images he loved, some of which now hung on the wood walls of his beach cabin. One was a photo that caught Regina running toward him up a dune, her face wild with exuberance. He loved his photo art, both the making and the showing of it.

Another image featured his new stepson Jacob twisting on a surfboard as he plowed through the threatening tunnel formed from a breaking wave. Jacob had not liked Charles until, unknown to Jacob, Charles spent two weeks surreptitiously photographing Jacob and his friends surfing at Salmon Creek. At a Sunday dinner Charles gifted Jacob with several large photographs made during a particularly stormy day of driven and vicious surf. One photo caught Jacob standing defiantly on his board while a towering wave pushed him hard into its violent and crushing curl. Jacob remembered his wipe out. But the photograph caught only the last moment when, a vigorous strength and fearlessness evident in his eyes, Jacob forced his board forward through the wave's violent collapse.

"That is so fucking cool!" Jacob shouted as he held up the mounted image.

"I have more," said Charles calmly. "I'll share them with you. Would you like that?"

Jacob's quick affirmation, his head bobbing up and down in a kind of violent assent, sealed a deal. From that day forward, Jacob was a friend to Charles who made a point of appearing regularly at the Salmon Creek beach, his camera obvious and in hand.

Charles also knew that Gunther never liked Jacob's surfing life, never liked Jacob's friends and never approved of Jacob's path that diverged so far from his own. And what kind of father lets his son wander away from the true path, the secret of living learned over decades that allowed Gunther to become and to stay rich. There was no other way and yet there was.

"A child's birth is a new bookmark in the story of passing time," Charles once told Regina when she complained about Jacob's rudeness. "Neither a father nor a son can always understand that, especially in their embittering time together."

"One chapter ends. Another begins," Charles said. "Gunther was one installment in life's drama. Jacob is another."

"And how do you know this?" Regina asked.

"I've been both a rebellious son and a frightened father," he answered. Charles understood well that one generation's presumably sacred past was merely another's problematic prologue.

It was a welcome year for Charles. He both lived his art and made it. Photography grew further as the center of all creation. Photos of his windy coast, photos of Regina, photos of the new people in his life and of his few older friends flowed lovingly. They were objects that made him the subject of conversation and also the subject of interest. At no time before had Regina or her family had such dedicated visual attention. Gunther never took pictures and no one else in the family knew how. Jacob, in particular, reveled in the documentation of his hobbies and celebrations. Regina, at first frightened by her lover's visual passions, tried to hide from view. But his photos of her were stunning, even in the shy and undeveloped understanding she had of herself as a woman, and as one old enough not to welcome any mirror of her aging. Within a few months Charles was posing Regina at her bedroom window, her nearly naked body wrapped lightly in a burgundy colored bed sheet as she turned on loving command to bend into a forest of sharp shadows formed from the afternoon's fading sunlight.

"You are such a beautiful woman," Charles would say…and then repeat it again and again, while the photos he shared with her—and only her—gave Regina her first reflected views of herself as a kind of goddess, a woman of innate and magical beauty in full command of her desires. And at the end of such a photo session, Charles was invariably a suppliant and beneficiary.

Regina was attractive. It was what others might have thought about her at anytime in her six plus decades of living.

"But this is the first time I've ever thought this about myself," she said to Charles after a particularly rewarding photo shoot.

Charles at first did not understand how Regina's feeling of herself as beautiful was not a habit but an awakening.

"Others tell me I'm looking better, that I must be getting past my mourning for a dead husband. But I've never mourned Gunther. I am beginning to feel joyous and open in ways that exist only because Gunther is finally and gratefully gone."

Charles knew loss. And now he wondered how to bring his enduring losses to a feast with a woman now celebrating so large and brimming a gain.

On a Wednesday afternoon Charles made his way down a path above Shell Beach and to the site of an informally and roughly erected labyrinth, its spiraling trail dug and cleared from the hard, dark mud of a coastal bluff. Walking the labyrinth, Charles came upon clutches of photos, colored rocks, small statues of saints or gods, placards painted and colored, small pieces of memorabilia from buttons to postcards, most all piled and inscribed with words to inspire remembrance. *We love you Ted* read the fading ink on the back of a windblown photograph. Charles reached to turn it over. He met the grin of a boy proudly holding up a large fish, blurred in the image by its still wiggling body. Charles recognized the photo as a Polaroid image likely made sometime in the early Fifties, though only recently placed here. The labyrinth was filled with such artifacts, left by the living to commemorate the recently dead. There were stories in all the arrangements of these objects, images and relics. There were losses, some expected and others incomprehensible.

Charles picked up a notebook and opened it to read the last page of a diary, it's lightly applied but handsome script likely the handwriting of a young woman. *I will love you always. I don't understand why you left. It doesn't matter now. Love is all that matters. It was the best…*In a small pile at the labyrinth's center Charles found the photos of two children not older than five. He recognized them from a news story a month before that reported their drownings in a horrible accident that sent the mother's truck spinning out of control and into the mouth of the Russian River. Charles lifted his camera and framed the images in his viewfinder.

He could not remember when he first found the labyrinth. But he had visited weekly for more than a year. He thought himself a journalist, one who tracked ends rather than beginnings including the grief of losses by those still able to commemorate them. These were for him sacred images that dwelled on death and some kind of crossing over, which Charles knew he found way too interesting. Though he had promised himself he would not cross over without a push. He would not leave without being shown the door.

"You are a photographer?" asked Edward.

"Yes," said Charles. "Among other things…"

"And what are those…other things…" Edward asked again.

Charles struggled with his quiet resentment of this man so many years younger than himself who, more than asking an ingenuous question, seemed to be conducting an interview.

"I write mysteries," Charles answered. "Several have been published."

"That must be exciting," Edward said obligingly. "Do they pay well?"

"They pay," answered Charles who was beginning to resent Edward's line of questioning.

The dinner with Regina's oldest son and his seemingly voiceless wife Rene was not going well.

"Charles is retired," Regina had said to interrupt Edward's first interrogation of her lover.

"He lives at the coast in a home he owns."

Edward nodded.

"What do you think Rene?" Edward turned toward his silent wife. "A home at the coast? Retired? A good prospect?"

"A prospect for what?" Regina interrupted.

"What you do with your life is my concern," Edward said firmly as he looked directly at his mother. "I need to look after you."

"What I do with my life now is none of your concern," answered Regina.

Charles pushed his chair away from the table as if to move out of the line of fire.

"Your mother is a dear friend," he said. "I hold her in high regard."

"Do you want to marry her?" Edward asked impetuously.

"Honey…" Edward's wife Rene finally spoke. "It's not important."

"It certainly is," said Edward. "Mother has significant wealth and…"

"What in hell are you saying?" Regina nearly shouted at Edward. "Do you think you could ever speak for me?"

"I'm just concerned…"

Edward answered, clearly unable to explain his concern. As a dinner guest he wasn't in the position to label his mother's good friend a gold digger. But it was what Edward thought and Regina knew it.

"You have no reason to be concerned," Regina responded. "This man is a kind and generous friend and you owe him a deep apology for even suggesting he might be any threat to you."

In a moment Edward recognized he was not yet the heir to his father's fortune. His mother was. He had no say and, were he not respectful, he might lose whatever say he ever could have.

The evening passed into an awkward silence as Edward and his wife remained cool and contained. Charles introduced the coast as a topic but Edward met every one of Charles' openings with a closing comment. It was another way to say farewell before anyone could even say hello.

Rene looked on and said nothing else until Edward said they would be leaving.

"Let's go," she said. And that was all.

"Need to leave the land of sunshine," Jasmine told her mother. She was calling from Phoenix where she had gone six months before to take a managing job in retail.

"And where are you going?" asked Regina.

"Not sure. Coming home first…you know…need to sort some things out and that's where I do it."

Regina's house was still Jasmine's home and Regina wondered if it would be always. She worried her daughter was preparing for another fall. It was discouraging for Regina to think of herself as the eternal watcher standing alone in a field and waiting always to catch her daughter on the rebound, to catch her before she was seized and swallowed by wolves.

Charles offered to do a barbecue at the cabin when he heard of Jasmine's imminent arrival. "I'll invite my son. Marcus is her age…just a year off. They might have a lot to talk about."

"Anything would be better than that dreary dinner with Edward," said Regina.

"Not so bad," said Charles. "He'll come around…"

"Come around when?"asked Regina.

"When there's no other choice," answered Charles. "When you marry me."

Regina, standing on the slender porch of the cabin, turned quickly.

"Did I just hear…?"

"Is it a surprise?" asked Charles.

So many questions and all pleaded for answers.

"No…" said Regina. "I mean Yes…"

"Yes, it's surprise?" asked Charles.

"No," answered Regina. "Yes, I will marry you."

And what would this look like? There were few words either could say to create a picture of anything or anywhere beyond what they were now. Charles and Regina were in love with each other. And that was enough for a current moment.

Regina invited her children to a beach cabin barbecue and included Edward's wife Rene. Charles invited his son Marcus, who had spent the last year living in Eureka.

"I'm studying film at the JC," Marcus told his father. "I could become an actor."

It was another of his son's dreams of the future built on the loamy sand of all the vanished trails that had gone before.

"I'm pretty busy right now," Marcus added. "Don't know if I can…"

"It's important," said Charles firmly.

"OK" answered Marcus. "When…?"

Among the surprises as Regina's children clamored up the stairs to the small rooms and porch of the cabin was the warm manner of Marcus who welcomed everyone to the barbecue and especially Jasmine who connected with him immediately. Both knew well their generation's aggregate lore and lexicon. Later after dinner Marcus would take Jasmine for a walk in the dunes and not return with her until the stars were out.

Jacob recited a history of the Bay's local surf culture while Edward and Rene were quiet and seemingly respectful until Edward, slightly drunk from three glasses of wine, made a barely intelligible dinner toast to his mother and her new "friend." The cabin dinner set a tone that swept away all other tones. It seemed nearly a relief to Regina that Edward had nothing bad to say anymore and that both Jacob and Jasmine appeared comfortable and perhaps even happy that their mother had found in Charles a respectful and even adoring "friend" while all avoided the use of the word "partner" that now more accurately described Regina's link with Charles.

All their guests left together, Marcus offering Jasmine a night cap at The Tides and a ride home.

"It went well," Regina said as Charles washed dishes and she dried them.

"It went better than well," Charles responded. "My son and your daughter…they hit it off, didn't they?"

Regina did not respond. She was busy enough with a larger embrace of her own new life. She never before had chosen a person to love. Always she had been the one chosen.

They were in their time of love and clear about what this meant to each. It was not clear what this would mean to their families. Charles had the impression, if not the knowledge, that Regina's older son would never abide a new husband for his mother. What would he do about it? Charles could not say but understood a son's leverage might, in both proximity and time, be more influential than a lover's.

But Charles had asked and Regina had accepted and as they stood in the jeweler's cramped retail shop to pick the shape and stone for an engagement ring paid for by Charles, he asked again.

"Are you sure?" he said as she modeled briefly a gold band inset with a sparkling emerald.

"Never more sure," she answered. "This proves it."

"And how shall we tell them?" Charles asked as they drove away. The ring would be fitted and ready in a week.

"A dinner…the holidays are coming. Thanksgiving? We have a lot to be thankful for."

Charles thought it should be sooner and not on a day devoted to family traditions.

"We're breaking new ground," he said. "Let's pick our own day and make it a special one."

They agreed to a dinner in Regina's home on September 21st. It was a Sunday and also the first day of fall.

"Easy to remember," said Charles.

"And sooner than later," said Regina. "I can wait."

What could not wait was the essential transubstantiation of their unvarnished love into a way of life. What would they be? What relationship would they have together while also bound by all the tendrils of their families? How would they function as a couple—always lovingly and fully engaged with each other or returned slowly but ultimately after months or years to their separate occupations and interests?

A common trust grew delicately from the days and nights they now spent together, though most of their nights were spent at the beach cabin, conveniently out of sight of Regina's family. When Jacob was absent, Charles occasionally arrived at Regina's home to stay the night. But when Jasmine returned to live with her mother, the cabin in the dunes became their only go-to home when Regina and Charles were not traveling. Frequent trips away allowed them to share hotel rooms, a holiday rental, and even a tent, where they could sleep together without controversy. That their love was controversial, much of its sting cultivated by Edward's acute disapproval, seemed itself a preposterous situation that reduced two older adults to the kind of conniving more typical of two sneaky, delimited teenagers.

"He's afraid you'd take all my wealth," said Regina. "That's because he thinks it is his."

"It might be," responded Charles. "He is the oldest. Some children—boys in particular—seem to think that's a privileged perch."

"That's for me to decide," said Regina. "And I haven't decided. I'm still living my life. And it is mine now. Maybe I'd leave it all to you."

"Oh no," Charles answered firmly. "Don't put it that way. That won't happen. I won't let it. You have a family. You've had this family for a long time. They are your children. No…a thousand times no. I love you and you are all I will ever want or need."

Regina's thought was meant to be a feisty toss-off but she was taken with how deeply Charles heard it. And how firm he was in a conviction he would want no part of a legacy.

"But if you're sick I'll take care of you," declared Regina. "There would be no expense I would not…"

"And I will care for you," Charles said, interrupting her. "That's enough. I have enough."

Charles spoke from the heart, even as he knew that if he were alone nothing he had for himself ever would be enough to care for him. But he would not marry Regina to become a wealthy heir. And that others might think this was nearly enough for him to make marriage a deal breaker.

"I hear you," said Regina after a long pause. "I think I understand. But if I die first I must know for my own loving peace of mind that you are cared for. And I can care for you. There will be enough for everyone and I can still care for you."

Eventually Charles consented to a marriage agreement that assured Regina's children would receive their inheritance, while leaving room for her stated intention that, if Charles survived her, a portion of the estate would provide him essential and comfortable medical care for the rest of his life.

"And that's all," said Charles. "Thank you, but that's all. Not the home, not any of your property or your treasures, nothing but enough until I die. And without you it is hard for me to imagine how much longer I even might wish to live."

They would announce their engagement quickly. The fall equinox fell on a Sunday and though Regina thought this news might surprise her family and friends, no one was surprised. Anyone looking at a list of those invited would have suspected immediately the creation of a broad family audience for what might be important family news. Regina's children, including as always Edward's wife, were obvious. And it might not have been a tip that Charles' son Marcus had been invited since he had attended other dinners and during recent months had stopped by to visit with Jasmine and to take her out for dinner or drinks. Enmeshment was telegraphed instantly by the invitation extended to Regina's cousin and her husband who lived in Santa Barbara and rarely visited. And the attendance of one of Regina's closest college friends who had traveled to Petaluma from Seattle.

"Big news," Edward said to his wife. "But what? Is she going to marry that fuck?"

"What if she does," Rene said. "It's her life."

"She's my mother," said Edward. "Even if I don't have a say, I can have an opinion."

"Maybe so," Rene responded. "But your mom has the last word."

Edward was quiet and left the room. A week later he asked his mother if there were a pre-nuptial agreement and if he could read it. Regina answered "yes" followed by a firm "no."

The dinner went quickly as everyone in attendance held back their anxious expectations. Dessert was served by the caterers as Regina stood to tap her wine glass with a fork.

The announcement was quick, Regina and Charles both standing as Regina described how they met, how they found their way together, how close they were now and why—time and their arrival at the delta of each of their life's flowing rivers—made it important for both that they join together now.

"I am very happy," Regina said.

" I am very lucky," Charles said.

No doubt, Edward whispered under his breath, though he stood first to offer a toast to his mother and her betrothed.

"My mother was deeply saddened by the loss of our father," Edward said. "I know that a search for new happiness is not an easy one and I sincerely hope that her search is over."

Regina was quiet, aware she was never saddened by Gunther's death.

Edward was followed by Jasmine who, now dating Charles' son, suggested her hope a "new family" might form around this "wonderful marriage." Marcus followed Jasmine to say how much he loved his dad and that Regina was an extraordinary woman.

"It's what mom wants," said young Jacob. "It's cool."

There followed a sprinkle of applause and then everyone was quiet as they sat to finish dessert and drink their coffees.

Later, Edward wandered into his father's study and picked up the 15th century sculpture once held by Charles the first evening he visited Regina. Charles had dropped the sculpture and it would have broken had it not hit a chair arm and bounced onto the carpet. Edward also dropped it, but it hit the hardwood floor and shattered into small, countless pieces.

Charles and Regina were married on the winter solstice. It was a cold December Saturday but there was no rain. The wedding was held in Regina's larger of two living rooms and was attended by some 40 guests. More than 30 were friends and relations of Regina. Besides his son, Charles invited two fellow writers he met with regularly at a local cafe. A distant cousin lived in rural Oregon and sent his and his family's regrets. It was thoroughly Regina's wedding, though Charles' son—ever more and now deeply connected with Jasmine—took a surprisingly active role in the ceremony's planning. The wedding was officiated by a local Unitarian minister and the reception also held in Regina's home. In so many ways it was Regina's big show though all eyes were on Charles and his son Marcus. They were the family Regina was now joining though some quipped irreverently they were the people Regina was now adopting.

Before nightfall the newlyweds, suitcases packed and stored in the backseat of Charles' Honda Civic, were given a send-off for a two-week honeymoon at a coast-side home in the north county's Sea Ranch owned by one of Regina's club friends. When they arrived in the night's chilly darkness they found the home's kitchen well-stocked with foods and beverages so that they might never need to leave. And they did not. Not for days.

January's quiet epiphany arrived on a Tuesday just as the newly-weds returned to Petaluma. Charles parked his Civic in the D Street home's broad driveway just behind Regina's Mercedes.

"We're home," said Regina.

"I guess we are," answered Charles. "It will take some time to get used to."

"I'll make it easy," answered Regina as she reached to give her new husband a fleshy, wet kiss.

Charles opened the Civic's trunk and pulled out their luggage. He saw Marcus run toward him from the house's broad back porch.

"Been here long?" Charles asked.

"Couple of days," said Marcus. "I'm Jasmine's guest."

Charles had questions but did not ask them.

"We have dinner for you," said Marcus. "Jasmine's preparing a roast and potatoes. I've made an apple pie."

"Thank you," said Regina. "While you're at it, open a wine."

Marcus nodded and ran back into the house.

"Did they know we were on our way?" Charles asked Regina.

Regina had circled the honeymoon's return date on a kitchen calendar.

"Where are your brothers?" Regina asked Jasmine as she entered the kitchen, a travel bag over each of her slumping shoulders.

"Edward was here last weekend by himself and left this morning," answered Jasmine. "He said he was looking for something."

Regina wondered immediately what Edward might be looking for.

Jacob was with his friend Andy and, even though it was a school night, he was spending it at Andy's house.

Jasmine approached Charles and swung her short arms around his neck in an awkward hug Charles did not expect.

"Welcome home, stepdad," Jasmine said quietly, smelling slightly of a sweet wine and pressing hard against him. It was not exactly the welcome of a daughter but it was, even as an unexpected surprise, a gesture of regard.

Dinner brought news that held little interest for Charles or Regina. Not much occurred over the holidays though a conversational lacuna developed around the time Jasmine had spent with Marcus.

"Hanging out, mostly," said Jasmine. "Marcus comes over after work. I fix him some dinner. Then he goes back home to the beach cabin."

"Work?" Charles asked Marcus.

"Have an assistant manager's job at a downtown department store," said Marcus. "I'm enrolling in classes at the college in Cotati."

"Theater?" asked Charles.

"Business," answered Marcus.

Yet another major thought Charles. *Maybe it will stick. But will he?*

In any event Marcus was now in Charles' permanent midst.

"And the cabin?" asked Charles. "You're…there?"

"Yeah," said Jasmine quickly before Marcus could speak. "I visit him when I can…" immediately concerned she had said too much.

"Are they an item?" Charles asked Regina as they climbed the big home's creaky stairs to the master bedroom.

"We'll know soon enough," answered Regina.

"I'm surprised," Charles said.

"I'm not," responded Regina.

Charles had slept before in this large and intimidating bedroom with Regina. But now he would live in it. He entered after his wife, who was now the previous wife of the bedroom's previous male occupant and within the moment—this moment—previous to all the new and unexperienced moments yet to occur.

"Well, here we are," said Regina as she turned to face the approach of Charles who then embraced her at the foot of the bed and fell with her upon it.

nine years

Charles walked again the length of the beach. Seven times in any day. He just kept walking. After several nights alone in the beach cabin, Charles had nowhere else to go. And no one else to go with. No way to spend a wedding anniversary, Charles thought as he rambled recklessly back across a dune. It was cold and made colder by a harsh and driving winter wind. And it was night. A pitch black moonless night, though the darkness did not bother him. He could not go to sleep even after not sleeping for days.

"Too many questions," Charles said to himself. "How did I end up with so many questions?"

"It was an accident," he stammered. He could not count the number of times he had said this, though he long ago stopped saying it to Regina. And then, as he always did, Charles concluded inconclusively there was nothing to be done that had not already happened.

He crossed the dunes and hurried shivering up the cabin's fog-drenched stairs. He opened the door and entered, struggling to push the door shut against a furious wind that now whistled through the cabin's rafters and shook moving shadows from the glow of a flickering porch light. The night was a timeless haunting though Charles now counted every moment of passing time. In two weeks Charles would turn 76. In another two weeks so would Regina. They were both too old to address the deaths of others, though their own was now much more than a passing thought.

"I should phone her," Charles said to himself, knowing he would not. He and Regina had not spoken in weeks, not since Charles told her he needed a few days at the cabin to gather up his son's belongings. Regina did not object. She had Jasmine's life to reassemble among the treasures and artifacts still stored at the D Street home, which was also Jasmine's home until she moved with Marcus to the beach cabin. It was where they lived together until the week in November when also together they died.

"It was an accident," Charles said again to no one. "It wasn't their fault."

The few days he was to spend at the cabin had turned into a month. And surprisingly, or not surprisingly, Regina had not phoned. Had not tried to reach him, though they were both now the parents of dead children and shared at the core of their experience the same shattering loss. But they were out of words. After weeks of sudden and inarticulable horror and two funerals the day before Thanksgiving, it was more than either could manage.

"We need a rest," Charles had said, not realizing Regina might think he was asking, not for a rest from their grief, but for a rest from her. It might have seemed reasonable. They were having trouble. In their ninth year of marriage Regina and Charles grappled with the management of accrued but also tiring intimacies that ranged from particular and irritating tones of voice to the expression of difficult feelings that both assumed would never be difficult until, of course, they were.

Their marriage became an experience so lovingly greedy and plebeian in a way Regina had never known with Gunther. And she loved the fun with Charles, the risk, the silly and sudden spontaneity that in its goofy meretriciousness was so different from the cultivated and structured existence she lived with Gunther. She had accepted her first husband's coolness and his need for full control as part of a bargain that gave her comforting wealth and three new people who were all darling as long as they remained children.

In the fifth and happiest year of a second marriage, Regina told Charles she wanted to abandon the D Street house and move with him to the cabin at Salmon Creek.

"We could travel anywhere," she said. "We could have any amount of fun."

Regina had never felt so free and her warm and seemingly limitless love for Charles made it possible for her to imagine anything.

Though when she expressed her wish to sell her home, Charles held her back. And for her sake and not his.

"I've been a dollar short and day late all my life," he said to her. "When you throw something away you often can't get it back. And you still have your children to think about."

And Regina did think about her children. Gratefully, Edward had backed off his assumed role as his father's conscience and the child who must perpetually remind his mother that, since his father was dead, his mother must live as if she also were dead.

Though now Regina faced living with the real and abiding death of her only daughter. And it was a loss so different from the loss of her husband, a man whose blood she did not share but that together with hers formed the surging and ever circulating blood cells of all her children. It was the blood spilled when a drunk driver crashed his Porsche into Marcus' ten-year-old Fitt and drove it and Marcus and Jasmine over the last embanked turn on the Panoramic Highway.

It was night and the two lovers were taking the scenic route home to Bodega Bay though it was dark and there was nothing to see. The Porsche driver's car stalled at the edge of the bank, held back from falling by the inertia acquired from its collision with the Fitt. The driver, a Marin county assistant district attorney with a serious drinking problem, waited frantic and inebriated at the side of the road until a curious driver stopped, discovered the accident and took command. A phone call brought police quickly who questioned and then arrested the DA whose last quoted comment was something to the effect of *"Why me?"* And it was truly all about him and not his victims. A headline in the next day's newspaper blasted the story that a county DA was the apparent drunk driver responsible for the death of two young residents of Sonoma County who had the misfortune of making a turn on Panoramic just as the DA pushed his Porsche into the highway's opposite lane.

Well, this is how it looks, thought Charles, not yet ready to grasp how it would feel. It was the very worst any parent ever might imagine and he and Regina both were burdened now with the excruciating intimacy of their children's deaths. *It was not their fault,* Charles thought, as if such a truth would offer any solace. *They did nothing wrong.*

Only one person did something wrong and he—as Charles and Regina saw in their many court appearances—would pay for it. Though his punishment meant nothing to Regina or Charles. The perpetrator of this loss could not choose his punishment. It would be chosen for him, though Regina and Charles did have a choice. And it was in front of them now. But why choose to be punished? What did they do that was wrong?

Time was spent going to the arraignment and, always, the pre-trial appearances of the hapless and former assistant DA: arrested and held without bail for several months, divorced by his wife and now broke and broken. But he was sober now, sober forever which appeared to be the most excruciating aspect of his punishment. The former assistant DA had no escape and for a very brief moment Charles felt a pang of empathy for the poor loser. Was he born to lose? And for a moment Charles could stand high above his feelings and their circumstances and see only the absurd conjunction of this man's painful, wanton life with the hopeful glow and good will of his son and Regina's daughter. It was a strangely symmetrical converging of a twain, much like the Titanic and its fateful iceberg.

Really? thought Charles. *Is that it?*

And then again Charles would try to imagine his son and Jasmine laughing, in love, and delighted as their lives came to a crashing and sudden end. Or were they fighting, maybe lost in a lover's quarrel that, as much as the expressed affection of their warm, self-less love, was still a painful and also distracting feature of all deeply connected humans.

"They loved each other," Charles said to Regina in the darkness. "They did nothing wrong."

"But did we?" Regina asked. "If they had never met…"

"Then we never would have met," Charles answered.

They were otherwise speechless that first night when the officer arrived a little after ten o'clock to give them the news. A son and a daughter were dead and in circumstances that made no sense in any purposeful or meaningful way.

"It was an accident," said the officer. "It wasn't their fault."

He was experienced in delivering bad news and did not think his comments would be helpful. But he made them anyway. He made them with the hope they might relieve, even for a brief second or two, the guilt survivors always felt after the loss of dearly loved children. It was the worst kind of loss. And the officer knew it. He knew how the wheels would turn. And in this case the mother would wonder if the joy of a new marriage might have planted for her daughter the seeds of a tragedy.

"They were perfect," Charles said as he held Regina, her first tentative sobs now a roaring storm against his chest. "They had so much…"

And Charles stopped speaking, knowing that Marcus and Jasmine no longer had anything and that he and his wife no longer had Marcus or Jasmine.

"I can't!" Regina shouted. "I can't do this. I can't."

"We have to do something," said Charles, his arms tight around his wife. "We have no choice."

But there were choices…many more and many kinds of choices and as time swept them through the maelstrom of an at first shared grief, they each began to feel the tugs of a deepening regret.

Claiming the bodies broke both of them. An inquest was required because the deaths of Marcus and Jasmine were likely the result of a crime and the county coroner needed to fully assess the circumstances of their deaths which required autopsies that left both bodies opened and then resealed by rough, ugly stitching. Marcus and Jasmine were involved with nothing other than themselves. No drugs. No alcohol. Though Jasmine was found to be several weeks pregnant but not long enough to leave a fetus with any recognizable features and no chance for a life outside the womb. It was news that crushed Regina to the core.

Meanwhile news reports confirmed the assistant DA named Andrew Merkle had twice before been stopped and admonished for driving while intoxicated though in both instances he was given a courtesy ride home by a friendly sheriff's deputy and not arrested. It was a scandalous fact that implicated the sheriff and angered the judge assigned to the case. Merkle was put on administrative leave and eventually resigned. Later, he was charged with second degree manslaughter in a case that revealed a kind of good-old-boy corruption in county law enforcement and infuriated Charles and Regina. And the trial dragged on for months. There would be no closure for Regina or Charles, or Jacob who was shattered by the death of his big sister, or Edward, who felt only the revival of a certainty his mother never should have married Charles.

"You are the host now. You will never again be a guest."

As Charles sat alone in the beach cabin he recalled how Regina's words, spoken to him on their honeymoon, affirmed the cultivated growth of a love that was as much returned as it was given. And the surprise was the way Marcus entered into his relationship with Regina and found therein her daughter, Jasmine.

"They certainly seem to like each other," Charles said to Regina one afternoon.

"More than that," responded Regina. "They see each other."

"They certainly don't see anyone else," said Charles jokingly.

And they didn't. After dating for a year, they had moved into the beach cabin together. Jasmine had taken an assistant manager's job in the dining room of an upscale Petaluma restaurant while Marcus enrolled in the nearby state college to finish a degree in social services. By the summer after their parents' wedding Marcus was working as an assistant director for a local non-profit serving immigrant families while Jasmine had been promoted to restaurant general manager and given a bonus for buying the restaurant's locally regarded wines.

Their first weeks in the cabin became months and the months

turned into years.

"It is their time now," Regina said to Charles during that pivotal fifth year of their marriage when Regina had suggested they move to the coast and spend the rest of their lives traveling.

"We could give them the house…" Regina said. "They would take care of it. And Jacob…well…he'll be in college and…"

Plans began to form as Regina relaxed into the release of all her trappings to the children she so dearly loved and respected. And in her heart and mind she counted Marcus among them. He was, so much more than Edward, an unconditional lover of all life's possibilities.

Until Marcus and Jasmine were no longer alive and no longer unconditional. Conditions suddenly grew back like winter weeds and Regina, along with Charles, faced the curse of a road either taken or not taken. It did not matter. The road they walked together brought Jasmine and Marcus to a dark steep highway and into a collision with a drunk driver that drove the two young lovers over an embankment and to their deaths. In a moment Regina concluded she did not deserve happiness while Charles concluded he was an un-indicted co-conspirator in the death of his son. Jacob was crushed by the death of his loving sister and aroused to vengeance against the accident's feckless perpetrator. Only Edward found something in the bad news to honor and regard. And as he watched his mother and Charles grieve, quarrel and then separate, Edward waited expectantly. If any vulnerable territory opened between Regina and Charles, Edward would stake his claim and try to own it.

"They are good for each other…as we are.."

These were Regina's words a week before the accident. They were words spoken over the years as Marcus and Jasmine made with their lives a mirror of their parents' love. In these years of loving and living Charles had found his writer's voice, publishing a novel a year and earning respectful reviews in a New York literary magazine.

"As we are…"

Regina later remembered these words long after a past of hope and kindness had become a present unrelieved of grief and guilt. She had thought for a moment that Edward might have been right about her marriage to Charles, right and for all the wrong reasons. How else to explain how a loving new marriage could bring about the death of her dear daughter? Charles, too, was driven into a lonely and obsessive shame. *I should never have done this* he said repeatedly to himself as he wandered alone through the cold and windy dunes of Salmon Creek. How could their marriage bring about the deaths of the people Regina and Charles loved most?

"But our marriage had nothing to do with it…"

Charles might say this to himself, but never to Regina. Though he could not know that Regina said the same words to herself and nearly as often.

On the second Sunday after the accident, Marcus' mother arrived. She was not expected. Charles had not seen her since the second year of his son's life when she left and never returned. In his later adolescence Marcus began a search for his lost mom and found her at a halfway house in Cincinnati. Mandy was nearly fifty years old and without resources but Marcus used the proceeds of a summer job to fly out to see her. In his voluble departure he told everyone how much it meant for him to see his "real" mom. Two weeks later he returned in silence.

"Are you OK?" asked Charles.

"Yeah…" Marcus at last answered. More silence followed and then Marcus' last words ever spoken about his biological mother.

"She's a drunk."

Mandy phoned the big house and spoke with Regina who was at first shocked to hear Marcus had a still living mother.

"Yeah, that's me," said Mandy.

"Where are you?" asked Regina.

"Downtown," said Mandy. "Just got in. When's the service?"

"It's already happened," said Regina.

"Damn. So there won't be a reception?" asked Mandy.

"It's already happened," Regina said again. "What do you want?"

"Let me speak to Charles," Mandy demanded.

Regina gave Mandy the cellphone number of Charles.

An hour later Charles phoned Regina.

"She's a loon," he said to Regina. "She was looking for a payout. Still thinks in some way that being a mother entitles her to an inheritance. She's crazy. But no worries. I called a cab and sent her back to the bus station. She gets it. She took a chance. And like so many she has taken it just did not work out."

"How did you meet her?" asked Regina, concealing her real question which was *Why did you fuck her?*

"One of my life's low points," said Charles. "But one that gave me the best son a father ever could have. So I guess one never knows."

Charles accepted an invitation from Regina to come home to the Petaluma house for a dinner with her. Jacob was away and they would be alone. Charles heard the word home arrive through the phone and tried to stifle a sob structured for him by the irresistible grip of a still unbearable grief.

Regina asked Charles what it was like to live in the little beach house so fully occupied by Marcus and Jasmine .

"Not easy," he answered. He had found his voice only to lose it again in the pool of despair he knew might eventually shrink and yet never disappear.

"But I'm closer to them here," he said. "And it's the reason I haven't touched or moved anything."

"I can help you…with that," Regina answered, her own voice quavering as she tried to form a sentence.

Regina watched Charles climb the steps before opening the front door to greet him with a fond and lasting hug, which Charles returned with all the strength he could gather. Both held tight as each sobbed uncontrollably, as much for the recovery of their touch as for the shared loss of their children.

"We need to meet at the beach house," said Regina as they ate the seafood pasta prepared for them by Millie.

"We need to look through their stuff and decide…"

Regina could not finish her sentence.

"What we keep and…?" asked Charles, careful not to suggest the disposal of anything owned and touched by Marcus or Jasmine.

"What we can bear to keep," answered Regina. "What we can't or won't want to see…or what they owned and even loved but that now has little value to anyone else."

"I see," said Charles. "It could get complicated. But we'll be together, sweetheart. We will."

The endearing term, not heard for weeks by Regina, brought her heart farther into their discussion.

"We can bear any pain together," said Regina.

Charles knew something of what was in the cabin but had left most belongings untouched, most drawers and cabinets closed, and had slept on the living room couch so he would never have to enter the bedroom.

They agreed to meet together the next Sunday at the cabin, but as Charles prepared to leave Regina took his hand and pulled him away from the door.

"Stay with me tonight," she said to Charles as he stood quiet and vulnerable before her. And it was not difficult to slip together into the house's big and familiar bed and to do so in such a comfortingly familiar way. Within moments their arms were around each other in yet another familiarity that, while it would not yet evoke their passion, would leave them both touching and held as the dearest of friends and at last, and even if just momentarily, above ceaseless tides of loss and sorrow.

It was important that Regina and Charles at last decided to go together to the coast. They did not say it, but the thought of going alone to the cabin, or anywhere alone, no longer made sense. They needed each other and needed for each to need the other.

The first difficult moment for Regina arose when she found the couple's sex toys in a drawer of the small table next to what was obviously Jasmine's side of the bed. A half-used bottle of lube rested next to a vibrator sheathed in a bright red velvet bag. For a brief moment Regina indulged a prurient and nearly arousing curiosity until loss fell like a sinking shadow into her heart and she sat on the floor to moan all manner of grief suggested by the end of her daughter's incipiently lovely life. Charles found Regina and sat to hold her until her composure brought up the fact that sexual pleasure was central to her daughter's happiness and that, before her untimely death, she had fully and willfully sought it and enjoyed it.

Night fell before they could finish what they thought a first phase of the work needed to clear, organize and retrieve the remaining trappings of their children's life together. And it was on the drive back to Petaluma that Charles suggested they move out to the cabin.

"We could finish this work," he said. "We could take our time."

He did not say that after a month of living there alone, he was nolonger afraid of ghosts, his or the children's. In fact, he had found some comfort in sharing the space they had so fully made their home.

Regina, who years before had suggested such a move, at first said nothing until, in a quiet moment she pushed herself against Charles, reached around his neck and kissed him hard on the cheek.

"Yes," she said. "Yes, yes. We will. Yes."

In the days and weeks and months that followed them out to the coast, Regina and Charles determined to pick up all the pieces of their losses, to search for what were becoming sanctified memories of Marcus and Jasmine first by an inventory of their belongings and writings that modeled the qualities of a very true love. Joy was reflected in photographs, art, silly notes scribbled and left on table tops and in drawers. And as they gathered up the trappings of their deceased children, they replaced them with trappings of their own lives: photographs, gifts, talismans and belongings that amplified the memory of their children as well as their own grown and fully transcendent affection. It was at times too much for Regina and Charles to feel fully the stark and thorny pain of their irretrievable loss. Though they grasped within weeks that their children had at the end shared a good life filled with good love.

And Regina and Charles had created for themselves a love that would extend well beyond them and into the pores and souls of their children and all who might follow. Though no one had any reason to think what it might mean for the dream to end, not with the death of the founders' love but instead with the death of their children. And now it was clear to both Regina and Charles that the beach house was a kind of holy ground where they both could live together with a loss only the other could grasp and understand.

"We didn't create a love together to protect us from tragedy," Regina said one morning as she made breakfast. "But tragedy has arrived and here it is…and here we are…We would never, either of us, choose to be here. But we are here together and, thankfully, so is our love."

Later, on a walk across the beach Regina saw a dead seal, its eyes wide open until Regina approached to see the seal no longer had eyes, just empty sockets. And the seal was motionless as the wind pushed sand over its body. In whatever way all organic mechanisms generate and sustain a living creature, they also participate in bringing about its dissolving end. At one time Regina and Charles could not imagine so dear and deep a loss or how they ever would survive it. Now Regina felt herself forced to consider how brief was the embodiment of any experience, especially within the limitless vacuum of a dark and burning universe. Life came slowly. Life left quickly. But life was still a precious miracle and still as incomprehensible as it was crucially and everywhere evident.

Acknowledgements

For nearly two decades I worked as a family counselor assigned to assist parents experiencing high conflict divorce. Everyone's story was different, and yet where their children were concerned, always the same. I wondered myself, after my own two divorces, why people marry the wrong person. But it never mattered to the children, left too often to process by themselves the pain and trouble of a failed family.

I understand much more now and I can see how the terms of any attraction can also seed the eventual failure of love. Abiding love requires attention, vigilance and ongoing truth. The pains of intimate conflict are impossible to avoid but that is what lovers often do: run from and ignore difficult feelings or blame the other for their pain. Love is wonderful but love is never perfect. Daily work is required to sustain it.

I am grateful to my life's most difficult relationships and for the lessons learned in my work helping angry, divorcing parents find a way to parent their children together. I am deeply grateful for my dear wife and partner, Claire Marie Beery, whose truthful friendship is the foundation of a love stronger than I've ever known.

These stories also benefit from my editor, A. Cort Sinnes, whose insight and truthfulness help me always to say more clearly what I hope and try to say. There are many reasons someone marries the wrong person. And sometimes being the wrong person is one of them.